INTO THE UPPER COUNTRY

Nick Meints

Author's Note

This is a work of fiction that contains real people and real events. The historical notes at the end of the book will explain what is fact and what is not.

Throughout history, humans have shown themselves capable of committing horrendous acts of violence against one another. Today we call those acts atrocities. The Europeans who encroached upon the Great Lakes during the 18th century and the area's Native American inhabitants weren't exceptions. Both groups committed what we would consider atrocious acts in the conflicts that arose from such disparate cultures and beliefs colliding.

In this work, I use terminology that Europeans or American Colonists would have used during the 18th century in their dealings with Native Americans, much of which is offensive to modern ears. Where applicable, I have tried wholeheartedly to use the correct terms and names the tribal members themselves would use, though this is sometimes difficult because usage and spelling of terms and names differs from nation to nation, tribe to tribe, and band to band. For example, the Ottawa (Odawa) and Chippewa (Ojibwe) Indians are culturally related peoples that refer to themselves as Anishinaabe or Anishinaabek in their language, Anishinaabemowin (Ojibwe), of which there are numerous dialects. The Iroquois Confederacy (Haudenosaunee) included the Seneca (Onodowaga) tribe in its ranks.

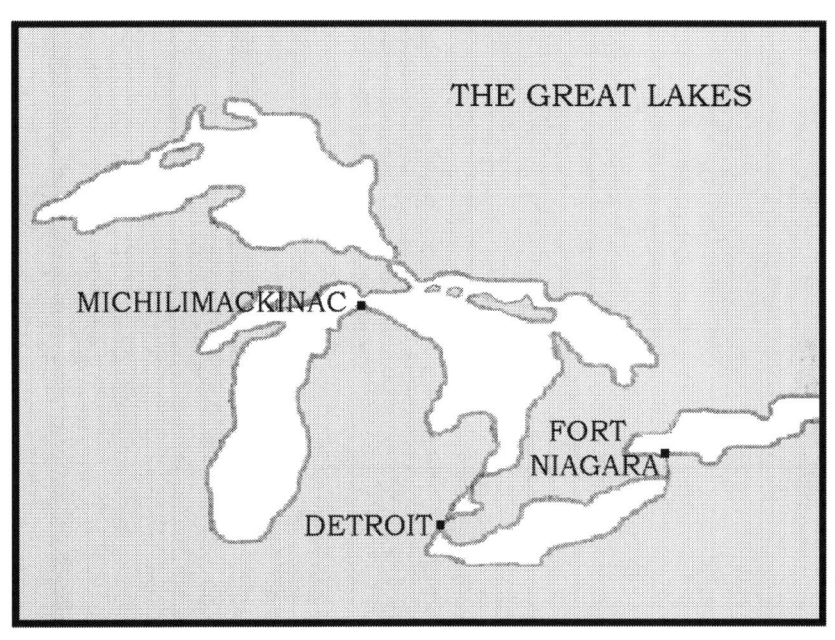

CONTENTS

Prologue   Quebec. 1759.

Ch. 1   Lancaster, PA. January 1762.   1

Ch. 2   Lancaster Barracks. February 1762.   14

Ch. 3   Lancaster Barracks. May 1762.   25

Ch. 4   Philadelphia, PA. July 1762.   39

Ch. 5   The North Atlantic. August 1762.   53

Ch. 6   Detroit. October 1762.   77

Ch. 7   Michilimackinac. November 1762.   101

Ch. 8   Michilimackinac. December 1762.   117

Ch. 9   Michilimackinac. March 1763.   134

Ch. 10   Lake Michigan. April 1763.   162

Ch. 11   L'Arbre Croche. May 1763.   173

Ch. 12   Michilimackinac. May 1763.   178

Ch. 13   L'Arbre Croche. June 1763.   219

Epilogue   222

Historical Notes   225

Prologue

Quebec. July 31, 1759

The *Centurion's* 24-pounder guns thundered across the water as the men of the 60th Regiment of Foot, the Royal Americans, scampered over the sides of their transports. The soldiers' red coats shone brightly against the dark wood of the hulls as they struggled down cargo nets and into the flat-bottomed bateaux bobbing next to their mother ships.

"Move it, ye damned lubbers!" a crusty boatswain cursed.

The Royal Navy sailors manning the small boats sweated and swore at the cannonade while pleading with the infantrymen to hurry aboard. The swabs, their discomfort written on each line of worry creasing their faces, were eager to be done with the day's business, and ready to put some open water between them and the enemy. With the infantry filling the last of the benches, the sailors used their oars to push off from the wooden hulls towering over them.

Samuel Avery, one of those red-clad infantrymen of King George II, clung to the gunwale of his bateau as it left the relative safety of the transport's hull and made for the beach. A scene Mars would envy spread before him. Three hundred yards to his right, the fourth rate *Centurion* belched smoke and lead from its gun decks, subjecting the beach and bluffs to a rhythmic bombardment. Not to be outdone by the Navy, the Army flung cannonballs from its supporting batteries beyond the Montmorency Falls to the east. The stone citadel of Quebec loomed over it all from its cliff-top perch three miles upriver, a massive blue flag covered in King Louis' *fleurs-de-lis* flying from its battlements as a taunt to the British fleet.

Shot shrieked over the dozens of small boats as they strained toward the shore a thousand yards ahead, their cargoes of infantry and grenadiers making the pace painfully slow. A geyser of white water erupted only yards from the oar-tip of the diminutive sailor in front of Samuel. It seemed the covering fire pouring from the *Centurion* and the British land batteries was doing little to vex the French on the bluffs, and their answering cannon shots began falling among the flotilla in earnest. Pillars of water sprouted amongst the boats like great mushrooms.

"I wouldn't want to be you lot," the sailor cackled in Samuel's face, the stench of rotting teeth and old grog pouring from the man's mouth.

Samuel swallowed his breakfast a second time, then cast his gaze over the tiny oarsman's straining shoulders to the approaching shoreline. He saw a rocky strip of flat ground pocked with shallow pools of water from the recent high tide. The ground ran for only fifty yards or so before ending in towering, grass-covered bluffs. If the splashing shot weren't enough, white smoke issuing from the bluff confirmed it was occupied and fortified.

"Looks like a beach fit only for corpses," Samuel remarked, cringing from the cold spray of the St. Lawrence River that ran under his wool coat and down his back. "What fine gentleman thought of this bold maneuver?"

Corporal Fritz Meyer, only a few years removed from the King's possessions in Hanover, grunted on the bench next to Samuel. "Stick close to me," he said in thickly accented English. "*Die Franzosen* will be waiting for us."

Pops of musketry joined the deeper booms of cannon, telling Samuel their bateau had breached the range of musket fire. Angry whines of flying shot streaked by his ears. Suddenly, the sailor in front of him let out what sounded like a grunt of annoyance, as if he'd only just stubbed his big toe. A confused look passed over the man's face, then he slumped into Samuel and his oar dropped. The boatswain cursed, and Samuel handed his musket to Fritz and wrangled the dying man from his bench. He picked up the oar and dipped it, falling into rhythm with the others.

"You'd make a fine sailor," Fritz said, and his red face broke into a smile.

"Ye damned lubber," Samuel managed as he pulled.

Craning his neck, Samuel could see the approaching beach. The objectives assigned to the first wave of the assault – French redoubts under the bluff – sharpened in view as a gust blew away the powder smoke. Another cannonball splashed close, and Samuel could only hope that Fritz shielded the pan of his Brown Bess from the spray. The sailors redoubled their efforts to reach shore, anxious to disgorge their cargo and return to the safety of the deep river. Samuel answered their strong pulls with his own.

Casting his eyes along the heights above the beach, Samuel spotted the unmistakable white coats of French Regulars rising from their entrenchments along the bluff, firing and ducking down in the clouds of smoke that followed. The brilliant coats flashing in the gunpowder mist made it look as if specters defended the cliffs.

Turning to Fritz, Samuel huffed, "I thought we were going to face militia."

"*Jeneral* Wolfe started this dance too early," Fritz grumbled, referencing the bombardment deemed necessary by the brass. "Gave the *schwein* time to move *die infanterie*."

A well-placed cannon shot ripped through a bateau thirty yards away. Its occupants screamed and died from the splinters of the boat tearing through them. The St. Lawrence turned red as the boat sank beneath the waves. The living struggled in the water while their comrades rowed past with no intention of rendering assistance.

Samuel put his head down and bent his back for lack of anything else to do. He didn't need to see the ball that might kill him. "For the love of God, just let us get to the beach," he pleaded. "Only swabbers should die on the water."

Just as the whine of balls seemed to crescendo, the boat's bottom scraped across sand and rock, lurching the men forward. Samuel looked up in disbelief at having made it. Fritz wasted no time, spilling over the side and screaming, "Advance!"

Samuel dropped his oar and flung himself over the gunwale. He struggled through the shallow water, gaining the beach only to lose his footing and tumble into a tepid puddle. His tricorn landed beside him, and he reached out for it with no more urgency than if it had fallen off from a gust of wind while he worked in his garden. But a musket ball snatched it away before his fingers could close on the fabric, bringing him back to the task at hand. He struggled to his feet and ran.

The broken rock of the beach slowed his progress, and he sensed men falling around him from twisted ankles and piercing shot. "*Kommen sie!*" he heard Fritz's voice, and he steered for it.

The grenadiers had landed first, and were already in the process of scaling the sand embankment of the first redoubt. Canadian militia manning the sand fortification ripped off panicky musket shots, felling a few of the grenadiers. But, unwilling to cross bayonets with professional soldiers, most of the farmers and tradesmen soon abandoned their positions and tried to hightail it up the bluff to their compatriots' entrenchments. Some made it. Many more fell from shots through the back.

Samuel dove to the cover of the just-taken redoubt's sand walls, squatting next to a winded Fritz, who handed over his musket. They listened as the grenadiers inside the redoubt finished off the few surviving militia. English curses and laughter answered the pleas for life in French, then the tip of a bayonet or the crack of an officer's pistol finished them. The grenadiers' losses on the beach had boiled their blood.

Samuel couldn't blame them. Looking back over the corpse-strewn ground and the detritus-filled river, he marveled that any of the grenadiers still drew breath. With the sounds of dying Canadians filling his ears, he mumbled to himself, "Might live through this after all."

As if in answer to his audacity, French muskets opened up from the bluff. Several fellow infantrymen were struck dead instantly or collapsed with grievous wounds, their screams adding to the din. The urge to fight back and make some impact on the day's course spurred Samuel from the cover of the redoubt. He took aim at a white coat high above him. Smoke erupted from his musket's muzzle and pan, obscuring any effect his shot might have had. He ducked back down and reloaded from a crouch.

Captain Sanders, the company commander, stood gallantly in the open with wig askew and sword in hand for all his men to see, as was his duty as an officer and a gentleman. "We shall wait for the supporting attack from the east, then advance!" he called out, before several balls punctured his bright red officer's coat. Dropping to his knees, Sanders moved his mouth as if to issue more orders, but a spout of blood was all that came forth.

One of the company's sergeants managed to pull the dying gentleman under cover before he expired.

The grenadiers, their thirst for action not satiated by their defeat of mere militia, bayed for a crack at the French Regulars. Picked for their size and bravery, they weren't ones to wait prudently while under a murderous fire. First one, then another charged from the redoubt, with the intent of summiting the bluff. It wasn't long before the entire Grenadier Company was on the move. The French Regulars saluted the grenadiers' bravery with witheringly accurate fire, causing tremendous losses.

Samuel fired off several more shots from his musket in a futile effort to cover the grenadiers. He watched in horror as red-coated men rolled lifelessly down the bluff, one by one. Something had to be done to relieve the pressure on them.

The second redoubt! Samuel thought. A hundred and fifty yards up the beach, the yet-to-be-taken position was enfilading the climbing grenadiers. Perhaps if it could be won, another route up the bluff could be found and the grenadiers could be supported.

"Lieutenant Peyton!" Samuel yelled.

The young man looked up, wide-eyed, from the sand hole he was digging with his sword.

"We must support the grenadiers, sir! We must move on the second redoubt!" Samuel shouted.

Samuel's platoon commander seemed thankful for some direction in the madness. He regained his senses and straightened himself up to not quite full height under the barrage. "My platoon!" he croaked. "We shall take the second redoubt!"

A cheer rose from the sheltering men. Anything was better than waiting to be picked off by the frogs overhead. They formed up quickly under what cover the redoubt provided, then stepped off, pushing along the base of the bluff while under deadly fire, using small trees and sandbanks for cover as they advanced. Miraculously, none fell as they closed to within striking distance of the second redoubt. Peyton halted them behind a fold of ground that provided some protection from their objective. They tightened ranks, coming into a line three deep and ten wide, with Samuel and Fritz side-by-side at the front.

"Ready, Fritz?" Samuel asked.

"*Ja,*" Fritz answered coolly.

"We shall give them the steel after a volley! Fix bayonets!" Peyton ordered, waiting for the metal pokers to be affixed to the men's musket barrels. When the platoon was ready, Peyton bellowed, "Forward march!"

The men stepped off calmly, rising over the fold and coming face-to-face with the sand embankment of the second redoubt.

"Halt!" Peyton ordered. "Make ready!"

Samuel dropped to his knee along with the rest of the front rank.

Canadian militia, wild-eyed, popped up from the embankment and fired, many of their rounds flying high. But at least one hit. Samuel heard a grunt down the line and the sound of a man collapsing.

"Present!" Peyton called.

Samuel leveled his musket along with the rest of the platoon.

"Fire!"

The last syllable was lost in the discharge of thirty muskets. A cloud of smoke obscured the redoubt, but Peyton already had his sword raised and was moving forward. "Advance!" he called.

The platoon stood and surged forward. Samuel was one of the first to scramble over the bank. Without thought, he plunged the point of his bayonet into the bowel of a stupefied Canadian. His fellows swarmed past and added to the carnage as he watched the impaled Canadian's eyes look down in horror at what Samuel had wrought. Not intending to wait the many minutes it would take the man to die, Samuel yanked to withdraw his poker, but it stuck fast.

"Christ!" Samuel gasped, raising his boot to kick the dying man off his blade as he pulled a second time.

The Canadian barely whimpered as the steel finally withdrew, along with an eruption of blood and shit.

Pivoting side to side to meet an enemy thrust that didn't come, Samuel soon realized the second redoubt had fallen. His fellows had cleared the few Canadians with the fortitude to stand their ground without much of a fight. The survivors had taken flight and were headed up the bluff.

"Pursue!" Peyton ordered.

Samuel joined the other soldiers in scaling the far embankment and making after the retreating militia.

A piercing cry, one that could freeze the blood of even the hardest veteran, issued from the grass to the platoon's right.

"*Indianer!*" Fritz screamed.

Samuel turned in time to see a huge Ottawa warrior with a shaved pate emerge from beyond musket smoke. The vision of death buried his hatchet in the tricorn of a British soldier, then screamed into his victim's eyes in triumph as blood spattered across his own painted face.

"Adjust right!" Peyton cried as he brought up his sword to block a heavy war club.

Order amongst the platoon broke down as the Ottawa got in between them. It was every man for himself as the warriors picked their targets and went to work in hand-to-hand combat. The redcoats fended them off with their bayonets as best they could.

A bare-chested warrior, his face black with paint, came for Samuel with a hatchet in one hand and a knife in the other. Samuel gave ground slowly as he held the point of his bayonet forward. Each stared into the other's eyes, aware that only one of them would draw breath after this encounter.

The warrior struck first, lunging low as Samuel thrust in defense. Ducking under the sharp tip of the bayonet, the warrior knocked the musket up with his hatchet and slashed with his knife. Samuel felt his side open as he brought the butt of his musket down onto the back of the extended warrior. The walnut stock struck a kidney, stunning the warrior to his knee. Samuel recovered from the slash before his foe could regain his feet, and stuck the dazed man through the back, puncturing a lung. Straining with effort, he withdrew the bayonet from the sucking wound and rammed it in again and again while the warrior's eyes rolled into the back of his head and he collapsed in the sand.

"Retreat!" Peyton shrieked from somewhere in the melee.

A shoulder slammed into Samuel as he withdrew his bayonet for the last time. Sprawling in the sand, he looked up to see a native with a stolen officer's gorget raising a ball-headed club for a killing blow. His own musket was in the sand, feet away. He was defenseless.

A bayonet pierced the warrior's armpit, and Samuel saw shock in the Ottawa's eyes as Fritz withdrew his blade and knocked the dying man down.

"*Kommen sie!*" Fritz barked, reaching for Samuel.

Samuel struggled to his feet and reached for his musket, just barely grasping it before Fritz pulled him away. Fritz led him back down the beach as they retreated in disorder with the surviving members of the platoon.

Samuel didn't hear the shot that hit him. It was as if his foot just suddenly gave away. He tumbled in the sand, not knowing what had happened. Fritz tried to pick him up and pull him, while Samuel tried to regain his feet. That was when the pain hit, dropping him to the ground. Samuel screamed in agony as he saw that a ball had shattered his ankle. Fritz could only stare at the wound in horror.

Ottawa warriors yelped and cried for blood down the beach. Fritz reached down and made to drag Samuel to safety.

"No!" Samuel cried in pain. "Leave me!"

"*Nein,*" Fritz gasped, redoubling his efforts to drag him.

Samuel punched Fritz in the face, sending the corporal sprawling. Fritz shot up, indignant.

"Get your thick Teuton skull out of here," Samuel gasped.

The little Hanoverian ignored him, turning to the advancing warriors and pulling the small double-barrelled pistol tucked in his belt. He prepared to defend his friend to the last breath.

"Fritz!" Samuel said, drawing the man's eye. "Go!"

Stricken, Fritz shook his head, aimed the pistol back down the beach, and cocked both hammers. Samuel reached up and grasped the wrist of Fritz's pistol hand. Fritz looked down into his friend's face.

"My boys, Fritz," Samuel said. He smiled as he fumbled for the pistol. "You have to take care of my boys."

Tears streaming down his face, Fritz released the pistol and nodded. "*Ja,*" he said.

Samuel grasped the necklace hanging from his neck and yanked. The cord gave way, and he thrust the small silver medal into Fritz's fist. "Now go!" Samuel yelled, pushing Fritz away with what strength he had left.

Fritz stumbled and ran, sprinting through the sand and beachgrass. He heard the first barrel of the pistol fire. The grunt of a warrior followed. He was a dozen paces further when the last barrel discharged.

Ch. 1

Lancaster, PA. January 1762

A cold wind howled through the graveyard, blowing snow and ice from moldering headstones that poked from the frozen ground. Young Sam Avery pulled the old blanket wrapped over his threadbare clothing tighter against the tempest, squinting in the weak daylight of the new year. When the wind dropped and the silence of the dead fell again, he examined the inscription on the wooden headstone to his left.

> Here Lyeth Samuel Avery
> Pvt. 60th Regiment of Foot
> Quebec. 1759

The carpenter had done a fine job, a testament to the pay he'd received. The headstone was the last thing the King's Army had provided the Avery family, besides broken promises. The script was legible and true, the furrows made by the chisel deep and uniform. Kneeling on the hard ground, Sam wiped away a layer of snow, revealing more wood that had faded to a ghostly gray. He wondered how long his father's name would stand against the elements that battered it day after day, season after season, the carpenter's work be damned. Would the name still be there years from now? Decades? *Surely not,* Sam thought sadly.

To his right, a newly-hewed headstone rose over of a mound of freshly turned earth.

> Here Lyeth Shannon Avery
> Wife. Mother
> Lancaster. 1761

The shallow depths of the chisel marks in the green wood betrayed a hastened hand, one that had worked for charity rather than pay. The differences in the headstones laid bare the story of a family fallen from some semblance of prosperity to destitution in only two short years. The sprigs of evergreens still adorning the grave from the internment couldn't hide that a woman little better than a pauper lay there.

Sam ran his fingers over the mound of earth. The unforgiving winter had already frozen the ground hard. "You left us with nothing," he said softly.

His mother gave no defense.

Footsteps crunched through snow over the quiet. Sam stood and turned and saw a red coat bobbing between headstones. A King's soldier, not an uncommon sight in the garrison town of Lancaster, approached. He was a short, stocky soldier, his regimental coat buttoned and his collar turned up against the cold. The blue breeches he wore under brown marching gaiters betrayed him as a member of a royal regiment.

Squinting, Sam smiled and murmured, "It can't be."

Full, rosy cheeks betrayed the approaching stranger.

"Uncle Fritz!" Sam called, striding toward him.

"Sammy!" Fritz boomed in a voice Sam had not heard in years, a voice that had filled the Avery home during happier times. The soldier covered the ground between them and wrapped Sam in a bear hug of surprising strength for one a head shorter than most.

Sam broke away smiling, a few tears falling unbidden. "We didn't have word of your coming. When did you arrive?" he asked.

"The First Battalion marched in this morning."

A simple epaulet on Fritz's coat drew Sam's eye. "By Jove," Sam said, fingering the cloth, "they've made you a sergeant. The King must have lost his marbles."

Fritz beamed. "I am a fly on the King's *arsch*, but he has been good to me."

"I'm glad one of his subjects feels as such. You must quarter with us!" Sam thought not only of the company of their father's dear friend but also the resources the sergeant could provide them. "William will be so happy to see you."

Fritz's face turned serious. "I heard of your poor *mutter*."

Sam turned and looked back at the fresh grave. "Don't be sorry for her, Fritz," he said, his voice catching. "She took the easiest path after father died."

"Don't be angry with her, Sammy." Fritz put an arm around him. "She couldn't bear this life without him."

"Leaving us with nothing more than a small mountain of debt and a pack of baying creditors. She spent most of the last year in her cups."

"Her heart was broken."

Sam frowned at Fritz. "And what of her sons' hearts?" he asked.

The sorrow of having no answer played across Fritz's face and softened Sam's. He rapped the small bear of a man on the back and forced himself to smile.

"Well," Sam said, and wiped away a tear, "now that the First is here, we might just make it through the winter."

Fritz stepped back and looked Sam over. He saw a lad of nineteen who had missed more than a few meals since he'd last seen him, during a brief sojourn for the battalion before Wolfe's assault on Quebec, when Samuel had said goodbye to his sons and wife for what none of them realized was the last time. Sam's normally full face was sunken. His stout frame was missing much of the muscle it had carried the last time they were together. The lad's skin had only a touch of its normal coloring, adding to a general appearance of ill-health. But Sam's dark hair and kind green eyes still rendered him handsome, even in his depleted state.

Feeling a pang of guilt at Sam's plight, Fritz said, "Let me say hello to your *vater*."

Sam smiled mirthlessly. "You know better than any that he's not there, Fritz. The Army didn't even bother to bury an empty pine box for him. His skull's probably being used as a cup by some northern sachem," Sam said.

Fritz wrapped his arm around Sam and led him back toward the graves. "Don't speak of the dead in such a way. It is *verboten*."

The pair stood and looked over the headstones for a long moment, a fresh wind and a few stray flakes of snow their only companions.

"How did it happen, Fritz?" Sam asked. "These corpses that surround us might be more forthcoming than the Army has ever been, or you have been."

"I told you," Fritz said, shrugging. "It was in my letter."

Sam tilted his head back and laughed. "Writing has never been your strong suit, especially when it's in the King's English. It took poor William a month to decipher those glyphs you sent."

Fritz huffed. "As I said, he was killed by *Indianer* outside Quebec. Ottawa."

"And the circumstances?" Sam pressed.

After a long silence, Fritz said, "He was wounded. I had to leave him where he lay because of a promise he'd sworn me to some time before. That's all I will speak of it."

Sam saw the little sergeant's eyes well with tears as he looked down at the grave. "The promise?"

Fritz straightened and met Sam's gaze, the tears disappearing. "I promised your *vater* years ago that I would take care of you and *Wilhelm* if anything should befall him. Now that your *mutter* has left us, and I see the state of you..." He looked Sam over, shaking his head. "It's time I fulfill that promise."

"Your quartering with us and providing some rations will surely help," Sam said. "And with the rest of the First quartered for the winter, I think we shall make it through till spring. Soldiers' boots always need mending."

"Crawling into the spring by cobbling shoes is not the life your dear *vater* wanted for you."

Sam shrugged. "It's the only life we have."

"The regiment still owes your *vater* fifty acres."

Sam scoffed. "And will until the second coming. And we know as much of farming as you of cobbling."

"*Ja,*" Fritz nodded. "*Ich bin nur ein soldat.* But I know one hundred and fifty acres is much more than fifty. It would fetch a fine price, especially now that *die Franzosen* are close to defeat."

It took only a moment for Fritz's words to land. "You want us to join the regiment," Sam said, and smiled.

Fritz looked into Sam's eyes. "*Ja.*"

Sam thought for a few moments, and then said, "The King still hasn't compensated us our fifty acres for the blood father spilled. What makes you think he'll do so for William and I. We are on the very edge of his realm. He doesn't care if a couple of poor cobblers get what's owed them."

"*Der krieg* is almost over, Sammy," Fritz explained. "Old debts will be settled when everything calms. The King will not forget his most loyal subjects. Mark my words." Fritz held up his hand in an oath.

Sam looked back to his father's grave. "William is only seventeen, and now that mother and father are gone, I'm responsible for him. And here you are asking me to lead him into the Army, the very path that that took our father from us."

Fritz sighed. "I made a promise, Sam. The promise of a *soldat* and a friend. I promised your *vater* that I would watch out for the both of you. If I had wages saved, or plunder buried in some deep wood, I would hand them over gladly. Every farthing."

"I know you would," Sam said.

Fritz held a hand to his chest. "I can think of only one way to make good on my promise to your *vater*: by offering the stability of His Majesty's Army. And now with *der krieg* coming to an end, the Sixtieth will be a safe a place as any for you and your brother."

"This war might be ending," Sam acknowledged, "but these days there's always another just over the horizon. We have no desire to fight the King's enemies across the seas. This country is not much, but it's our home."

"The Sixtieth will never leave *Amerika*," Fritz responded. "You will serve three years, then you and *Wilhelm* will receive your land, along with that of your *vater's*. If not, I shall march into the King's chambers in Whitehall myself."

Sam looked off to the west, trying to see the mountains and forests beyond the high hills. "One hundred and fifty acres in some Indian-infested backcountry."

Fritz smiled. "The land of opportunity."

Hating himself for even mulling the idea, Sam sighed, and said, "William can be many things, but I fear that being a soldier is not one of them." He and Fritz locked eyes. "He's soft."

Fritz's smile grew. "A good sergeant's trade is sharpening soft lads. In one season, your brother can be formed into a soldier, Sammy.

Your *vater* was, and thrived. So will *Wilhelm*. He's got a good head on his shoulders."

Sam smiled. "That he does. His mind is much too big for this small place."

"Then give the boy a chance," Fritz practically begged. "Let him see some of this great continent. It's that or he cobbles shoes for the rest of his life, waiting for starvation or sickness to carry him to his grave."

Sam gave no answer. He thought long and hard about the proposition.

Fritz dug in some deep pocket. "Your father wanted you to have this." Fritz held up the medal that Samuel had given him just before his death. "I never would trust it to a post rider."

Sam reached for it and held it up. The little silver medal spun on the new cord Fritz had attached it to. The familiar, well-worn image of a man bearing a child on his shoulders could be seen in the silver. Sam had seen this medal dangling from his father's neck countless times as a child, and though he did not know its meaning, he knew that it had been passed from Avery man to Avery man since well before his grandfather had crossed the ocean.

"You are head of the family now," Fritz said. "You must do what's right for you and your brother."

Sam gave the medal one last long look, then stuffed it into his pocket.

Fritz stepped closer and put his hands on Sam's shoulders. He looked into his eyes and said, "Take the King's shilling, Sammy. Do it for *Wilhelm*."

***

Walking down the frozen, muddy streets of Lancaster, Sam's mind churned over Fritz's offer. *How could we have come to this?* he thought to himself.

The Avery family's fortunes had been on a downhill march ever since Samuel moved his family to Lancaster from Philadelphia, when Sam was only eight and William six. Samuel, a cobbler by trade, had sought out a more fruitful and less competitive business environment in the interior of Penn's colony. He didn't count on war with the French breaking out only a few years later. Pennsylvania's interior colonists became more worried about Indian raids and where their next meal would come from than having the latest trends in footwear. Samuel got by for a few years by mending soldiers' boots and the heels of the very rich, but it was never enough to provide anything close to comfort for his family.

One evening, his growing boys begging for food and his wife threatening to turn herself out to the soldiers at the barracks, Samuel marched down to the Conestaga Inn and took the King's shilling for a promise of fifty acres upon his discharge. The 60th Regiment was happy to have him. They had just lost dozens of men to the massacre that occurred after the loss of Fort William Henry.

Young Sam, aged only fourteen, took over what meager business his father still held. The family survived with his earnings and what Samuel could send home from his soldier's wages and plunder. They managed to step back from the precipice of starvation for the next two years.

That changed with word of Samuel's death at Quebec. The Army showed little inclination to honor the payment of his death pension, telling Sam to wait until the end of the war, when the frontier had settled, or get a lawyer. He might as well have been told to petition the King himself. They had no money for a Philadelphia lawyer.

Shannon Avery fell into a deep depression at the loss of her love. Rum-induced inebriation became the only place she could find solace. This increased the family's debts and reduced the efficiency of the business that Sam – now with the help of young William – tried to keep afloat.

As the year of our Lord 1761 wound to a close, the boys were starving, the business was practically shuttered, and creditors hounded them every step of their day. Shannon had died the night of the first freeze, her body discovered where she had fallen during her nocturnal wanderings between the grog shop and home. Samuel had tried to console his brother by telling him that she'd gone peacefully, slipping away from the cold. Hers was a much better end than what they now faced. Starvation was a horrible way to die.

After his graveside reunion with Fritz, Sam returned to the general store Mr. Thompson kept. A faded sign bearing an old shoe stood over a small side door. Sam pushed the side door open for the last time in his life, finding the two dark rooms that had been his home for ten years just as he'd left them. William sat at the shop counter, his long frame hunched and compressed, with his face buried as it always was in a tattered old edition of Mr. Franklin's *Poor Richard's Almanac*. The boy dropped the volume and gave a sad smile.

With the light of the sole window, Sam took in his brother. William's cheeks were sallow and hollow, resembling those of an old man. His skin had an unhealthy grayish tinge. The threadbare clothing he wore clung to what Sam knew to be more bone than muscle. One harsh sickness this coming winter would surely see William give up the ghost.

Letting out a long sigh at the state of his brother, it was then that Sam knew he had to do something to save them both.

***

"Are you sure about this, Sam?" William asked. They strode over the frozen mud of Lancaster's King Street, passing dark houses and a few storefronts. The only other souls they saw were newly arrived soldiers meandering under the moonlight, and a few Christian Indians huddled in front of a church, their sleeping forms wrapped in blankets.

"We're out of coin, William," Sam said simply.

"But with the First arrived, we'll have plenty business mending boots."

Sam stopped and turned to his thin, tall brother, who looked about to topple over from the weight of the old blanket wrapped about his shoulders. William's hair was fair while Sam's was dark. His features were finer than Sam's, lending him a gentler look. His eyes were still full of the childlike innocence he had yet to outgrow, a striking feature for one that was at least a head taller than most every person he stood beside. Those innocent eyes looked down at Sam with a sheen of anxiety.

With a calming smile, Sam said, "Mr. Thompson has threatened to turn us out of the shop over our debt. We could mend a thousand pairs of boots and still not have enough to pay him and the other creditors mother borrowed from."

"But Uncle Fritz–" William tried to say.

"Uncle Fritz," Sam said, stopping him, "has provided us with a way forward. We shall take it, or we'll be reduced to eating the leather of the shoes we're supposed to be mending."

William's lip quivered and his big Adam's apple bobbed as he swallowed. "I don't think the soldier's life is for me, Sam. The French and the Indians will eat me for their breakfast."

Sam smiled and put a hand around his brother's shoulder. "The French have lost Canada and are not long for defeat, William." He peered into William's eyes. "It's three years, then we are the masters of our own destinies. I promise I will not let anything happen to you."

William looked unconvinced, but managed to nod weakly. Sam turned and strode on, his brother following.

They rounded a storehouse and heard sounds of life for the first time in the frozen town. What could only be raucous merrymaking carried over the cold air, and Sam directed them towards it.

The stone building of the Conestaga Inn sat before them. Several of the King's Regulars lazed about outside, smoking from clay pipes and talking animatedly amongst themselves. Sam offered his pardons and brushed by them, opening the heavy wooden door to a scene that couldn't stand in greater contrast to the winter's depths outside.

A fire roared in a large hearth, filling the crowded room with warmth and dancing light. Hanging pots near the flames emanated the smells of rich stews, and the tables were covered with plates of meat and winter vegetables that set Sam's mouth to salivating. Regulars and townsfolk sat at the long tables, drinking and laughing away the cold, dark night. Sam stood for several moments, letting the feeling of being truly warm – a feeling he'd not felt in days, even weeks – soak through his bones.

"I'm hungry, Sam," William groaned, looking over his brother's shoulder at the hanging stews.

"Soon, William," Sam assured him, searching the room. In the back corner, he spied Fritz. He dragged William along as he made for their old friend, the lanky boy having to hunch in fear of his hat being knocked off by the beams crossing overhead.

The pair arrived in time to see a young lad no more than William's age draining the remnants of a tankard to the cheers of Regulars. With a final effort, the boy finished the ale and dropped the mug, revealing a shilling clenched in his teeth. Fritz and two corporals roared there approval as the Regulars throughout the inn raised their own tankards in support, shouting praises and drenching their throats with ale.

"Get something to eat and drink!" Fritz yelled over the noise, sending the lad off as one of the corporals diligently recorded his name on a piece of parchment.

Fritz turned and saw the Avery boys standing before him. A smile of relief spread across his face as he opened his arms and strode towards William. Fritz wrapped the boy's wispy frame in a hug and boomed, "*Wilhelm!*"

The sight of the little corporal hugging the giant set several Regulars to hooting and pointing at the sight.

William managed to smile as he struggled to breathe. "Uncle Fritz," he said.

Fritz pulled back, a drunken gleam in his eye as he looked from one Avery to the other. "*Mein junge!* You have come to take the King's shilling?"

William looked to Sam, then to the hearth and its adornments of sustenance. "Yes," he managed.

Fritz turned to Sam.

"Yes, Fritz," Sam said evenly.

"*Korporal* Kane," Fritz ordered.

A thick Irishman produced two tankards of ale and thudded them onto the wooden table. "We'll have to get this one a bucket," he said, and gestured to William, appreciating the youth's height.

Fritz theatrically produced two shillings, then plopped one, then the other, into the foaming ales.

Sam didn't hesitate. He picked up the pewter tankard and drained it in only a few gulps. He caught the shilling in his teeth as it rattled forward, then slammed the empty tankard onto the table. A riotous cheer went up from the Regulars. Sam took the shilling from his teeth and looked at the corporal with his quill. "Sam Avery," he stated.

The noise died and every eye in the inn turned to William, the expectation being that the ale would prove no match for the towering youth. Sam watched the color drain from William's face as Fritz motioned for him to pick up the tankard. With one last pleading look at his brother, William tilted the tankard skyward. He only managed half the ale before he sputtered and coughed it over himself.

The regulars erupted in hisses. William seemed to shrink into himself as the chorus of disdain continued.

"Tha be Samuel Avery's lad?" Corporal Kane asked in his thick Ulster brogue.

Quick as a cat, Fritz snatched William's tankard and swallowed the remnants in one go, gripping the shilling in his teeth. He took William's hand and spit the shilling into his palm as the hisses turned to triumphant cheers. "We will make a soldier of you, *mein junge!*" Fritz called, to further acclamation.

Fritz turned to the regulars and held up his tankard. "Celer et audax!"

"Swift and bold!" they thundered back the regiment's motto.

William stared at the coin for a long moment, then turned to the corporal. "William Avery," he said softly. He watched as his name was scratched onto the rolls of the 60th Regiment, the Royal Americans.

***

Sam and William took the oath in front of the magistrate the next day, then stood in front of the regiment's quartermaster not long after. Sam's head throbbed from the ale he'd drank the night before, and William looked sickly, but Sam knew it wasn't from drink. After he'd had his fill of stew, William regretted the price he'd paid for it.

At least our bellies are full, and will be from here on, Sam thought.

The quartermaster put a pile of coins in front of each of them and said, "Your enlistment bounty."

Sam's eyes widened. He'd never seen such an amount. They'd be able to pay off their debts much sooner than he ever could have hoped. He reached greedily toward the pile.

The quartermaster swatted his hand. "We have to fit you out with kit," he hissed.

Seeing red, Sam bit his lip so he wouldn't do something foolish. He was in the Army now, and subject to Army discipline.

A private brought forward two pairs of boots and plonked them down. They were identical, so Sam knew they'd probably fit him and be too small for his brother. The quartermaster reached for their coins.

"Hold on, sir," Sam said, stopping the man. "We're cobblers, and each have a fine pair of boots we made ourselves." Sam gestured down to the only thing of value he still owned.

A ruthless smile fell on the Quartermaster's face. "Sorry," he said, scooping up coins. "You're issued boots, so you'll pay for them. And if you don't want them..." The quartermaster reached for the issued boots with his other hand. "I'll just–"

Sam snatched both pairs, wiping away the quartermaster's smirk. Maybe they could get a few pennies for them out on the street, but nowhere near the amount the King had deducted for them.

With a snarl, the quartermaster ordered his minion to carry on. Blue breeches, white dress gaiters, brown marching gaiters, white stocks and shirts, black tricorns with white edges, canteens, and two haversacks and knapsacks were produced. Several more coins were pared away from both piles.

Two Long Land Pattern muskets were then brought forward. Sam hefted the eleven-pound musket comfortably, having shot and hunted with his father hundreds of times. William, never one to seek out any circumstance that required shooting, held his as if it were a club, much to the quartermaster's annoyance and the amusement of the private assisting him. An ammunition pouch and a bayonet in a cross belt were also produced for both.

"The King provides the arms," the quartermaster droned.

"Mighty fine of His Majesty to provide the arms we'll need to kill his enemies," Sam said, smiling.

The quartermaster gave him a long look, but chose to ignore the comment.

Finally, the garments that sent shivers through Britannia's enemies across the globe were brought forth. Two red waistcoats and red regimental coats were plopped in front of them. Sam picked up his new uniform and felt the hair raise on the back of his neck. Even his disdain for the Army could not keep him from admiring the crimson cloth as he draped it over his shoulders. It had no ostentatious regimental lace around its blue lapels and cuffs, and simple brass buttons were its only adornment. It was heavy enough to provide some protection from winter's bite, but it would be a sweat box under the summer sun. The coats, as with everything else, were issued with very little thought to the size of the wearers. Sam's was a little tight in the chest. William's was much too short at the cuffs. The quartermaster's smile returned as he scooped up the majority of their coin piles, leaving only a couple shillings in each.

Looking at the depleted piles, Sam said, "There's hardly anything left."

"Welcome to His Majesty's Army," the quartermaster barbed with relish.

Ch. 2

Lancaster Barracks. February 1762

"Poise your firelocks!" Lieutenant Leslie called to the platoon standing in the thin morning light.

Sam moved his musket from his shoulder to in front of his face, steadying his left hand above the lock, just as he'd done for thirty-odd mornings.

He wasn't sure the exact count. The monotony of the past days had caused them to all blend into one long mass of toils and threats.

"Too far, lad," Corporal Kane rebuked William, who was standing next to Sam. Sam heard his brother grunt as the corporal shoved the musket closer to his face.

The corrections had gotten rougher with every new day. William's lack of progress with drill, the foundation of soldiering, had begun to crack the patience of even the most tolerant NCOs in the regiment.

"Cock your firelocks!" Leslie called.

The line rang with clicks as the men pulled back their hammers.

"Present!" ordered the lieutenant.

Each man on the line stepped back with their right foot in a fluid motion and dropped the barrel of his musket so it pointed across the drill yard.

"Too far!" Kane hissed from behind, kicking William's leg in. "Up!" He swatted William's musket barrel with a ramrod so it raised level with the rest of the line.

"Aye, Sam. Good!" Kane whispered, taking in Sam's form.

The lieutenant called out, "Fire!"

The line of muskets exploded, belching smoke towards the hay bales fifty yards away. Sam immediately brought the butt down from his shoulder.

"Half cock your firelocks!" Leslie commanded.

"Quicker!" Kane ordered William.

Sam could tell his brother was getting flustered, and he could see the barrel of his musket quiver from the shaking of his body.

"Handle your cartridge!" Leslie called out in sing-song cadence.

Sam removed a cartridge from his pouch and tore it open with his teeth.

"Prime!" called Leslie.

Sam dumped a small bit of powder into his pan, priming his musket.

"By God, lad, get the powder into the pan!" Kane now yelled at the struggling William.

"Shut your pans!" shouted Leslie.

"Shut it, lad!" Kane roared.

"Charge your cartridge!"

The line shook their remaining powder into their barrels and dropped paper and ball in behind.

"Draw your rammers!" said Leslie.

Ramrods were withdrawn from the undersides of the muskets.

William dropped his and had to scamper to pick it up. The sound of a swat reverberated over the line as Kane brought his ramrod down on William's backside. Sam tensed in anger as his brother yelped in pain, but concentrated his fury on ramming down his shot as Leslie called, "Ram down your cartridge."

Sam slid his ramrod in and out as William struggled to ram down his shot.

"Return your rammers!" Leslie ordered. "Make ready!"

The line raised their muskets in one motion and brought them to full cock.

"Present!"

The muskets fell as one to point toward the target.

"Fire!"

Another eruption of smoke enveloped the drill yard. After the ringing in his ears faded, Sam heard William murmur, "Oh, no." A gust of wind revealed the cause of William's consternation. Twenty yards away, William's ramrod stood up from where it had embedded in the ground. He'd forgotten to withdraw it before firing.

"By my sweet Virgin Mary!" Kane bellowed.

Leslie sighed in bored dismay. "Sergeant," he drawled.

"Sir!" Fritz, standing next to him, acknowledged. "*Korporal* Kane, teach the private that to lose his rammer is to lose his ability to reload."

"Aye, Sergeant!" Kane answered. "Private, retrieve your rammer!"

William's fear-filled eyes shot to Sam. Sam made a pleading gesture toward the ramrod, hoping his brother would get moving.

The crack of Kane's ramrod against William's backside sent him scurrying forward.

"Move, lad!" Kane yelled.

William lurched forward and nearly dropped his musket, sending Kane into another torrent of abuse. The lanky lad scampered on while Kane's ramrod swatted repeatedly at his backside.

"Move along!" Kane ordered as he drove William. "At the double!"

William reached the ramrod and fumbled his musket, dropping it into the mud. Kane choked with rage as William scrambled to withdraw the rod from the ground while shielding himself from blows and attempting to pick up his musket, achieving neither. Kane raised his ramrod to deliver a harsh blow as William gave up and curled into a ball.

A firm hand checked Kane's strike. Enraged, Kane turned and saw Sam gripping his wrist. The corporal's eyes registered disbelief as he took in this private holding him back. Sam was spared having to decide his next course of action by the wind suddenly being knocked from him.

Sprawling across the frozen mud of the drill yard, Sam sucked in cold air greedily, feeling pain in his ribs with each breath. Standing over him, Fritz held his sergeant's pike ready for another strike, his red face contorted into what could only be disappointment.

"Sergeant," Leslie said as he came up beside Fritz, "we must teach these backcountry colonials that they do not lay their hands on the King's NCOs and officers."

"*Ja*, Lieutenant," Fritz affirmed.

"Fifty lashes should do," Leslie ordered casually, then stepped off.

"*Ja*, Lieutenant," Fritz acknowledged, his eyes turning from disappointment to pity.

***

The leather straps bit into the flesh of Sam's wrists, the burning pain made even worse by the icy wind that licked at his skin. His bare torso shivered uncontrollably against the cold wood as Corporal Kane checked the knots holding him to the rack. Sam's discomfort was only matched by his humiliation. Fifteen hundred eyeballs were there to bear witness to his punishment. The men of the 1st Battalion would take heed of what awaited troublemakers.

Corporal Kane finished checking the straps and looked Sam full in the face. The Irishman's brown eyes held no malice. No sympathy either. Just a steady gaze. Kane reached quickly into his pocket and produced a small flask. "Have a nip, lad. It will help with the pain to come," he said.

Sam gulped greedily from the flask, tasting rum that he knew would help dull his senses. Kane withdrew the flask and shoved a wooden dowel wrapped in leather into Sam's mouth. "Bite down," he whispered.

Sam gripped the object in his teeth and gave an almost imperceptible nod of thanks.

Kane stepped away as the 60th Regiment's sergeant-major called, "Battalion, tenshun!"

Sam didn't see the men snap to rigidity behind him, but he heard their feet stomp against the frozen parade ground in unison.

In front of Sam, a door opened in the headquarters building that made up the north end of the parade ground. Out stepped a short Lieutenant Colonel with a rather round face, the commander of the 1st battalion, Henry Bouquet.

Bouquet didn't even deign to look at Sam as he strolled passed in his immaculate officer's uniform. Sam heard the portly lieutenant colonel take up position behind him and clear his throat. Lieutenant Leslie and Fritz came forward and conversed quietly with their superior. Sam gleaned nothing from their mumbled words before the pow-wow finally broke up.

Waiting and Shivering, Sam began to hope his ordeal would just begin so it could finally end.

After a drawn-out silence, Bouquet finally spoke. "Men of His Majesty's Sixtieth Regiment," he said, his Swiss-French accent audible, "this private has struck one of the King's non-commissioned officers."

Shaking his head, Sam could only laugh. He'd merely grabbed Kane's wrist, and they were saying he'd struck him. *Am I too violent for the King's Army?* he thought.

"God created His universe with the intention that it be one of order," Bouquet resumed. "Order out of the chaos. We must strive to fulfill God's will and fulfill our destinies within His designs. When one upsets the natural order, when one steps out of their place, as this man before you has, it is the duty of his betters to show him the error of his ways. It is our duty to make him submit, and by God," Bouquet's voice rose, "we shall do that here today!"

Bouquet seemed to take a moment to get his emotions under control. Sam heard the man's feet scrunch through the frozen mud of the parade ground as he paced.

"Many of you are not long for postings in the interior," he started again softly. "This great continent teems with the agents of disorder. With the French no longer able to hold the bit in the mouth of the savage, there are now over a million Indians residing over the mountains that have no guidance from civilized minds. It is your charge," he now yelled, "to bring order to the chaos! You will deliver the light of His Majesty's civilization into the dark reaches of this land!"

Bouquet calmed again by pacing, and said, "If we do not uphold the Godly virtue of order among our own selves, are we any better than them? If we do not obey our betters, how are we to expect them to obey their new father, His Majesty King George? If we cannot be civilized, how can the savages ever be?"

Another long pause as the pacing continued. "Sergeant-major," Bouquet said softly. "Administer the private fifty lashes."

"Sir!" the sergeant-major barked.

Bouquet strode into Sam's view, walking as if he'd just issued the most mundane order he'd ever given. The lieutenant colonel calmly mounted the porch of the headquarters and went inside without another look, or another thought.

The drummer for Sam's company, a young lad of thirteen, popped into his view. The boy smiled cheerfully. "Don't worry, Sam," he chirped, holding up his instrument for inspection. A drumstick with six leather straps attached to its top danced in front of Sam's eyes. "I cut the straps fresh." The boy grinned. "Fifty lashes with a fresh Cat won't draw too much blood."

Sam tried to mumble a thanks, but the dowel in his mouth prevented him from being understood. The drummer boy disappeared to take up his station. Another cold blast of wind shrieked across the parade ground. Sam convulsed involuntarily from fear and cold as he waited for the first blow to fall. He thought he could hear William sobbing from somewhere in the ranks.

The battalion's drummers rolled their sticks across their drumheads.

"Commence!" rang out the sergeant-major's voice.

The sound of the Cat cutting through the air beat out the wind and drums in his ears as Sam dug his teeth into the dowel.

Searing pain, like the pain he'd felt when he'd grabbed a hot pot as a babe, sliced across the skin of his back, then spread throughout his body.

"*Eins!*" Fritz called out.

The Cat sang again. Another sear crossed Sam's back as tears sprang from his eyes.

"*Zwei!*"

Another *whoosh*. Sam's knees buckled from the pain, but the straps on his wrists and ankles held him in place.

"*Drei!*"

Sam didn't even hear it coming the fourth time. He just felt the bite.

"*Vier!*"

Sam's mind began to detach itself from this cruel place.

"*Funf!*"

The feeling of being cold slowly drifted away.

"*Sechs!*"

The pain in Sam's wrists had become inconsequential.

"*Sieben!*"

All that was left besides Fritz's voice was the lightning streaks of the Cat on Sam's flesh.

"*Acht! Nuen! Zehn!*"

Then even the pain began to dull.

"*Elf! Zwolf! Driezehn!*"

Until finally there was only silence and nothingness.

***

The smell of rum brought Sam back. Pain shot through him as he regained his senses. Wiping tears from his eyes, he saw that he lay on his stomach on a pallet in a dark room with a low ceiling, the only light coming from tallow candles. The pewter mug under his nose was withdrawn and the smell of sickness almost overwhelmed him. He was in the regimental surgery, surrounded by the myriad of illnesses that came with army life.

"Drink it," said the surgeon, a skeletal fellow who looked the part of the harbinger of death. He thrust the mug into Sam's hand.

Sam took the mug and drank greedily, realizing his thirst. He drank the rum down in only a few scorching gulps. "Water?" he begged the surgeon, holding up the empty mug.

"Are you daft?" the surgeon chided, not wanting to give his patient anything as dangerous as water. "I'll bring you some small beer."

The surgeon disappeared as Sam looked about. Several fellows on pallets moaned with fever, their sweating skin having erupted in pustules of pox. Sam knew they'd be lucky to make it out of the surgery alive, and if they did, their faces would carry the scars for life. Stinking buckets of sewage and rags surrounded a lad who looked as if he was already a corpse. Sam seemed to be the liveliest of the lot. Wishing to remain so, he took a somewhat cleaner strip of linen and covered his face in an effort to shield himself from the bad air and vile humors surrounding him. He'd have to carry himself from this place of sickness sooner rather than later, otherwise he'd join these wretches in their misery.

Black boots filled his vision. He looked up, expecting to see the surgeon returned with his ale. Instead, Fritz's round, red face stared down at him. "Fritz," Sam greeted through the linen.

"Sergeant Meyer," Fritz corrected, though not unkindly.

"I'd stand at attention," Sam groaned, "but I'm afraid I'm a little under the weather at the moment."

Fritz surveyed Sam's back, showing a twinge of sorrow.

"How bad is it?" Sam asked.

Blowing air through his teeth, Fritz pulled up a small stool and sat. "You'll have the scars for life, but it looks like they've been dressed well. Hopefully your wounds won't mortify," Fritz said.

"What doesn't kill you, eh?"

"Many good soldiers have felt the Cat, Sammy. I'd reckon half the regiment has been striped by her. Just don't be one of the poor devils who has to feel her twice. Most don't survive the second meeting."

"I was protecting William."

"*Nein!* You were not protecting him."

Sam chuckled. "I think Corporal Kane would have beaten him half to death if I hadn't intervened."

"*Ja,* you stopped him taking a beating today, but at what cost?"

"The cost of my bloody back," Sam said, and smiled.

"That, and much more. *Korporal* Kane was getting the boy used to what he'll have to face on the field," Fritz explained.

"A drunken Irishman with a rammer coming for his backside on the battlefield? I don't think that's a tactic even the French would stoop to."

"Fear, Sammy." Fritz leaned in. "That's what he'll face. The fear a man feels when he stares across open ground at the thousand empty black eyeballs of the enemy's muskets. Today, with that rammer, that was only a taste of fear. What is the boy to do when there's nowhere for him to hide? What is the boy to do when you can't save him because you're standing next to him in the line?"

"I told you he's no soldier."

Fritz shrugged, and said, "No man is born a *soldat,* but a *soldat* can be forged just like any implement. All one needs to do is apply the proper force and pressure. You need to allow that to happen, for *Wilhelm's* sake."

After taking the rag from his mouth and using it to wipe his brow, Sam tossed the linen to the floor. He looked up at Fritz with nothing more to say.

Fritz leaned back and crossed his arms, a contemplative look coming to his face. After a long pause he said, "On the Plains of Abraham, after your papa was gone, we formed up in front of *die Franzosen* to finally take Quebec. We held no advantage in numbers, nor any advantage in ground or artillery. We were exhausted from scaling the cliffs during the night. They had their backs to the city gates, *their* city gates. They had every reason to fight like devils. The Canadians were defending their homes. The Regulars were defending the empire of their king, and we were invaders.

"Montcalm, in his powdered wig, stepped across the field with forty-five hundred fresh frogs formed up in line." Fritz's eyes gleamed. "And all we could do was wait and let them come."

Sam, unable to hide his intrigue, propped himself up on his elbows, wincing in pain as he did. "What happened?" he asked.

"They came." Fritz beamed. "The first hundred paces, they maintained their formation. The Regulars swept forward in row upon row of bright white uniforms that seemed to shine under the sunlight. They were a magnificent sight. We waited, wordless, still as statues, watching their progress with a mix of admiration and respect.

"But soon the braver ones among the enemy started edging past their meeker *kameraden.* Then some of their militia started firing from a great range." Fritz waved a hand, as if brushing away an annoying fly. "Stupid and wasteful. Ineffective. We stood and waited, weathering what few balls landed among us. As they closed with our line, their formation started to break. Their lines started to bow and bend. What we thought were disciplined soldiers fast become a mob, every man acting on his own accord. Only the flats of their officer's swords kept them driving toward us. Some, their fear making them like animals, ran at us in fury." Fritz pounded his chest. "We stood as one. Our respect became disdain for their unsoldierly manner."

"When they reached fifty paces," Fritz continued, smiling with pride, "we finally deigned to move, leveling our muskets and letting fly the first volley." The smile slowly disappeared from the sergeant's face. "Those men became chaffs of wheat beneath a scythe." The look in Fritz's eye turned to one of pity. "They fell in scores, as if their lives were snatched from them by the wind. Most of their militia broke and ran at the first sign of their friends' blood. It took us only fifteen seconds to reload and give them a second volley. Those that made it to our lines still standing were met by a wall of steel. They were quickly cut down with the bayonet or shot at close range. Then we loaded ... fired ... loaded … fired … loaded … fired … until there was nothing left in front of us but a field of dead frogs."

Sam imagined the scene. A green field filled with the white uniforms of the French. Some bodies still as stones. Some wreathing under the sun like worms caught out after a rain. "All because the fear had been beaten out of you by some corporal?" Sam asked, and sighed.

Fritz gently slapped his hand. "*Nein*! You cannot beat the fear out of a man. That is not what *Korporal* Kane was trying to do. An infantryman's oldest friend and companion is fear. He carries it with him to every battlefield. *Korporal* Kane was merely making the first introduction for *Wilhelm*."

Fritz held up a finger to make a point. "A King's soldier must learn to wear a face of granite as he stands in front of a foe greater than he," he said. "*Wilhelm* must learn to be as firm as rock while his heart thunders in his chest and his bowels empty from the terror before him. He must use his fear to hone his senses to the sharpness of a bayonet point, then he must drive that point into the enemy's chest. That is the only way he will survive in the face of the foe. That is why we drill. That is why Kane barks at the lads. That is why we win!"

Sam could say nothing to that. He understood what Fritz was trying to say, but he also knew that he could never sit back and watch someone hurt his brother. *Three years*, he told himself. *Three years, then one hundred and fifty acres*.

"*Wilhelm* will be fine," Fritz said, and stood. "He's got his *vater's* blood running through his veins."

"I hope so," Sam said.

Fritz looked down the surgery, taking in the filth and pestilence. "Can you walk?"

"If it's out of here."

"Come," Fritz ordered, helping Sam up off the pallet.

Sam groaned in pain as he stood, feeling as if every wound on his back had just ripped open anew.

"Better to die in the barracks than in this hell," Fritz spat.

"I'll take your word for it," Sam said, his eyes streaming as they hobbled out of the surgery.

***

Fritz eased Sam into the company's barracks. The squat log building was packed with the sleeping forms of privates, NCOs, and even a few whores and children. The stove in the middle supplemented the body heat of the sleeping forms, making the atmosphere comfortably warm but thick with the smells of unwashed bodies.

Fritz gently laid Sam down on the pallet he shared with William. "Goodnight, *mein junge*," Fritz whispered.

"G'night, Fritz," Sam said to the retreating form of the sergeant.

Fritz made his way to the stove, where the NCOs had taken the warmest spots. Sam tried to get comfortable on the pallet next to William's sleeping form. A difficult task with the aches of pain from his back.

Just when he got settled, a whisper came from the darkness. "Sam?"

Sam reached out and grasped his brother's ankle, his feet being next to Sam's head. "I'm alright, William," he said.

William whimpered. He was crying. "I want to go home," the boy pleaded.

Sam lay still for several silent moments. He finally sighed and said, "The regiment is our home now, William."

William let out a low wail.

Sam closed his eyes and listened to his brother sob in the darkness.

Ch. 3

Lancaster Barracks. May 1762

The spring sun shined down on young men who were beginning to look the part of His Majesty's soldiers rather than imposters in ill-fitting uniforms. Basking in the sun's warmth, a bored countenance that even a jaded veteran could respect plastered across his face, Sam winced in something approaching disgust as he thought for the hundredth time about how easily he'd fallen into the soldier's life. He excelled at the mindless drill the officers put them through hour upon hour each day. He could follow orders quickly and without further explanation, and he bitched and moaned the appropriate amount for an enlisted man. Never more, never less. The lashes on his back had mostly healed, and his standing in the eyes of the company's NCOs had risen, along with the puckered skin of his scars, much to his annoyance.

Sam looked to his left. William stood there with the four other new soldiers of the company, his elbow crooked over the barrel of his musket, looking every part the soldier in his regimental coat and tricorn. He'd pulled his fair hair back and pleated it in the tight queue that all the men wore by regulation. The ruddiness of his cheeks spoke of the hours he'd spent drilling in blustering winds under low winter suns.

Sam had let the corporals and sergeants of the company do the work that needed being done on William after the discussion he'd had with Fritz in the surgery. Rebukes and corrections, sometimes quite painful ones, had finally turned William into a passable soldier. Even Fritz eventually declared himself pleased with William's transformation. Sam was relieved that he no longer had to bite his tongue and restrain himself from stepping in for William. The NCOs had no more cause to go after the lad.

But the eyes still betrayed William's unease with soldiering. Even then, with the men at rest, William's eyes darted right and left over the parade ground, constantly on the lookout for a drunk private looking to fight, or an angry NCO who might find some infraction in him, or some other unknown danger that would most certainly befall him if he ever rested his gaze. Sam plainly saw the discomfort in his brother, no matter how well he hid it.

Sergeant Meyer cleared his throat, and the new men of the company gave him their attention. "You can now stand in the firing line with the battalion, and I trust you can at least fool the enemy into believing you are *soldaten*, and perhaps worth a musket ball meant for a veteran. But that is not the only way my company will fight. Through the long years of struggle, in which many better men than you have died, we've learned the backcountry calls for a … *special* kind of warfare."

Four armed Indian warriors strode to Fritz's side from behind the gathered men. A sense of unease settled over the young soldiers. Only moments earlier, they had been doing so well at playing cocky. Now they shrunk at the painted faces staring hard at them.

Sam stole a few glances before turning his eyes away. The warriors wore the light moccasins that many of the soldiers had traded for to wear while off duty. Buckskin leggings covered their lithe legs up to the loin cloths tied at their waists. Two were bare-chested, their torsos' only adornments the cartridge pouches draped across them. One wore an old linen shirt. The final, who'd walked with the long, confident stride that marked him as the leader, wore the red waistcoat of a King's Soldier. Sam wondered how the man had come upon it. All four had their hair shorn in the warlike style of the Iroquois, their domes mostly shaved except for long, greased tufts sprouting from the back-middle of their heads. Several turkey feathers were entwined in the leader's black strands.

These men were nothing like the pitiful remnants of the Susquehannock tribe Sam was used to seeing in Lancaster. None of them wore the cross around their neck. None bowed their head in deference or fear at the presence of white men. The look in their eyes belied indifference to the soldiers around them, if not outright disdain.

Sam saw his brother staring at the warriors with his mouth agape. A sharp elbow in the ribs and a look of admonishment got William to at least shut his maw.

"For too long," Fritz said, and raised his chin, "we tried to fight like gentlemen against the French and their savage allies, meeting them in line on the field of battle. For that, we were subjected to the ambuscade and the *coup de main*. A civilized man can only take so much before he is driven to uncivilized necessities. One of those necessities is learning to fight the backcountry way." A smile spread over Fritz's rosy cheeks. "You will learn to fight like *die wilden,* the savages.

"Otayonih," Fritz said, and gestured to the Indian in the waistcoat, "of the Seneca tribe of the Iroquois, an old friend from our New York campaigns, will take you into the forest for the next fortnight. When you emerge..." Fritz paused to check himself. "*If* you emerge, you will be given your hatchets and take your place as rightful soldiers in the Royal Americans."

Sam turned back to William, expecting to find his brother's face a mask of fear. He was surprised when he saw something like eagerness.

"Otayonih," Fritz invited.

The four warriors stepped toward the six young soldiers.

Sam almost recoiled before he heard Fritz order, "Do as they say!"

The warrior in the old shirt reached Sam and immediately took the haversack from his back. The Indian tossed down Sam's rations as if they were only rubbish. He gestured for Sam to remove his boots as he rifled through his pack, taking out the moccasins Sam had traded for a month ago and tossing them to him. The other warriors moved through the group of privates doing the same, discarding packs and stripping regimental coats from the lads. Soon the privates stood clad in moccasins and waistcoats, their packs discarded.

Their paring done, Otayonih and his warriors turned without a word and broke for the treeline at a trot. The privates stood and watched the retreating Indians, then looked to Fritz.

With a smile on his face, the Hanoverian barked, "*Schnell!*"

William hefted his musket and broke into a run, following the Indians. Sam and the others spared one last longing look at their discarded gear and rations, then broke to catch up.

***

The first days passed in a blur of constant movement. The lads suffered mightily from the strain. Garrison life was sedentary by nature, and none of the young soldiers had experienced a campaign.

Few among them had ever traveled more than ten miles in a day, and never at the blistering pace set by their Indian guides. Those who lagged behind – and most had at one point or another – had been informed by Otayonih that they were welcome to stop and rest at any moment. But if that was their choice, they'd have to find their own way home. The threat of being left in the dark woods pushed even the most exhausted and downtrodden of them to keep their feet in motion.

Sam was pleased that he and William had not been among the stragglers. Much to Sam's surprise, his brother's long legs seemed to consume the rough leagues with something approaching ease. Before sleep each night, the brothers whispered guesses of how many miles they'd traveled over the previous days. A hundred? Maybe more. Always headed west, and all through the thick wood of the backcountry, their feet never falling on anything more expansive than a deer path or a warriors' trail. They avoided the few roads that marked civilization. Homesteads were given wide berths. And all the while, the Avery brothers maintained their pace towards the front of the pack.

Wolf. That is what Otayonih meant in the Iroquoian tongue. That is surely what the man was, and what they were all becoming. They carried only their weapons and ammunition. Food was scavenged or hunted from what game they could find in the hills. Water was drunk straight from streams, cold with the runoff of snow. Nights were spent under the stars around low fires, or no fires at all if they had nothing to cook. The men would huddle together for warmth during the cold darkness, just like a pack of wolves.

Whenever they took a minute's rest, the Seneca would teach them how to move through the trees without disturbing the world around them. They taught them how to read the signs of the woods, how to sniff out a stream on the breeze, and where an easy meal could be found under a log. They showed them how to start a fire with nothing but some dry tinder and a bow. They taught the young lads how to dress a wound with moss from the trunks of the great trees that grew along their marches. They spent their evenings looking at the stars, familiarizing themselves with the constellations that could help guide them through the woods.

Their march halted on the eighth day. The band had come upon a ridge that overlooked a thin ribbon of roadway. Sam did not know that this was the road Brigadier General John Forbes had hacked through the great wilderness some years earlier, during the height of the war with the French. The road pointed toward Fort Duquesne, the flash-point of the conflagration that eventually enveloped the whole world. Forbes had succeeded where Braddock had failed years earlier, taking the fort from the French. Fort Duquesne had been renamed Fort Pitt, and was now held by the British. But the King's grasp was weak.

The roadway was the only line of communication to the companies stationed at Fort Pitt. Regular columns of supply wagons trundled down the road to keep the garrison fed and armed. One of those columns crossed in plain view of Sam. Sam didn't know if they'd dropped on the column by chance or by Otayonih's skill. But Otayonih always seemed to know everything that occurred within a day's travel of their little band, so Sam guessed it was no roll of the dice that had brought them to this meeting.

Under Otayonih's direction, the men pulled back from the road and stripped their waistcoats. The Indians found a small stream and went about smearing mud on the pasty white skin of the privates, the entire time laughing to themselves and asking how the soldiers' ancestors ever survived the old wilds with their blazing skin. The privates' faces were already black from the soot of a cooking fire the day before. When the warriors were satisfied their charges would not immediately give them away, they moved back to the road.

The ten men spread themselves in the trees ten paces from the roadway. Sam sheltered behind a thick oak, his back propped against the trunk. William crouched ten paces to his right, hardly visible through the undergrowth. One of the Seneca hunkered down ten paces to Sam's left. All that was left to do was wait for the column in silence.

Sam looked to William. The boy had truly thrived since leaving Lancaster. His fears and timidity had fallen away as soon as they'd left the strict routines of the garrison. The fluid rhythm of the Indians' day seemed to suit William much more than the rigidity of the drill yard, and everyone was shocked at how hearty he showed himself to be on their long marches. Sam had even heard William talking with Otayonih deep into the night as the rest of the band slept. The younger Avery seemed to be fascinated with the Seneca's way of life, and he wanted to devour Otayonih's tales and knowledge. Sam didn't much care why his brother was suddenly thriving. He was just glad that William smiled again from time to time.

William's eyes lacked his garrison-wrought paranoia as he scanned the road in front of him. His fair, wispy growth of beard contrasted greatly with his soot-blackened skin. He held the musket steady in front of him, never wavering.

The sound of a horse neighing carried through the young leaves on the trees. It wasn't long before the squeak of a wagon axle followed. Sam slowly turned his head to take in the road. A lieutenant with a bored, vacant look rode by on a mare. Red-coated infantry surrounding the four ox-drawn wagons at the center of the column marched along in the grips of drudgery-induced torpor. Only a corporal looked to the woods on his left.

Sam froze as his eyes met the corporal's. He thought he'd given up the band before the sallow man's gaze wandered on. The corporal had been unable, or unwilling, to see the eyes that stared back at him out of the dark forest.

One of the Seneca warriors silently slithered behind Sam, moving parallel to the roadway. After a few moments, one of the privates skulked past, making much more noise than the Seneca but still not enough to alert the column.

The rear of the column marched by, and it was finally Sam's turn. He slowly rose and moved off at a trot. Sam returned his brother's wide smile as he passed him. It was as if the two were just wrapped up in some child's game that encompassed the whole world. He avoided the dried leaves and sticks littering the forest floor, keeping his footfalls light, just as Otayonih had taught them. Without alerting the column, he passed the rest of the band in their hiding places and took up a good spot further down the road.

With a care that he hadn't possessed only a week ago, Sam pushed his musket through the undergrowth until his barrel was pointed at the road. The bored lieutenant cantered into view. With a feeling of exhilaration laced with stomach-turning revulsion, he brought the point of the barrel up so that it covered the officer's chest. The gentleman had no idea that his life was only a trigger's pull away from being snuffed out.

Not enjoying the power he felt, or perhaps enjoying it too much, Sam let the barrel fall slowly away as he looked over the column. How easy it would be for his little band of six young men – nary a veteran among them – and four warriors to make this column disappear. They would never be heard from again. The officers at Fort Pitt would only be able to shake their heads and rattle off dispatches to Lancaster. The column would soon be forgotten, replaced by another. It would take longer for memories of the men to fade, but not too much longer. Just more victims swallowed whole by a hungry continent. Sam wouldn't be surprised to learn that his brother had many of the same thoughts.

In William's bookish mind, the redcoats resembled the Roman legionnaires of Varus marching through the Teutoburg Forest. These men in front of him, just like Varus's legionnaires, were lethal when given the opportunity to fight the style of war for which they'd spent their lives training. But the Germanic tribesmen of the northern forests never had any intention of meeting the Romans on the open field. Instead, they cut the Romans' extended column to pieces as they marched over dark woodland trails. It was a defeat that had been repeated by Braddock's disastrous march on Fort Duquesne, centuries later.

The Averys didn't know that Braddock's transformation into the modern-day Varus led to the formation of units like the 60th Regiment. The Indians had proven time and again that they would not oblige their enemies anything close to the European way of fighting, and it had only taken a couple more years of horrible losses to forest ambushes and lightning attacks for the powers that be to recognize that their soldiers needed to start fighting like the natives of this vast, forested warzone. That was why Fritz had his men stalking through the woods with Otayonih. The men of the 60th would not be lost to some dark forest.

For over a league, the band stalked the column. With every mile, the privates ventured closer to the road, testing themselves and the skills they'd gleaned from the warriors. William had gotten within a couple feet of the road at one point. He could have easily stuck his bayonet in the ear of a fat sergeant riding one of the wagons, if he'd chosen to do so. They never gave away their position, and the soldiers never knew that they were prey, much less that their predators were only paces away.

The band broke off the stalk in the late afternoon. They retreated to a high saddle, where they made their camp. Otayonih told the boys that he was proud of them for their stealth, and he broke out his pipe to smoke with the lads. Sam and William smiled as the pipe was passed around the circle. They went to sleep feeling as if they were kings of the great wilderness.

***

The fire's orange glow lit the faces of the ten men, its crackling flames licking at venison sizzling on skewers suspended over the coals. Bright embers drifted through the warm spring air and up into the night sky, joining the vastness of stars spread overhead.

William had felled the deer that afternoon with one well-aimed shot from forty paces. He'd stalked it with Otayonih for half an afternoon. The Seneca had taken his brightest pupil on the final hunt of the trek. The privates looked longingly at the popping meat, eager to partake in the feast that would close their time in the woods. Every white face wore a look of relief that he had survived the fortnight with this wolf pack. Only William's face showed more than that. Only his held a tinge of sorrow, and only Sam saw it.

"Why do you fight with the English, Otayonih?" William asked.

The Seneca warrior took a long draw from his tomahawk pipe, letting the smoke billow about his head while he contemplated his answer. "Our English father, King George, called on the Haudenosaunee. The Onodowaga, the people of the great hill, who you call the Seneca, answered his call with the rest of the fires of the confederacy. In exchange, King George gave us gifts of steel," he said, and held up his tomahawk, "muskets, powder, and rum. His great warriors told us that they would keep his white children to their side of the mountains if we joined him in battle against the French. They told us he respects the old wampum belts we exchanged with the Dutch. Two lines of beads moving down the belt show our two peoples. The two lines show two ways of life. Never shall the two touch. Always will they remain separate."

"Then why are you helping us?" Sam asked. "Two ways of life." He gestured around the fire. "Why teach us your ways?"

Otayonih bared his white teeth and laughed loudly, his warriors joining him. "We have shown you nothing, Englishman, except how to live in the woods for a few moons. You are but a babe still at the breast of his mother."

The warriors howled louder, and the privates laughed along. Sam smiled and nodded, understanding that to be true.

William remained serious. "Don't you find it appalling fighting against your Indian brothers?" he asked.

Otayonih spat into the fire. "Are the French your brothers? The Spanish? You all come from the same land across the sea. You all have the faces of ghosts. Does that mean you are bound by blood?" he asked.

William cocked his head. "No."

"The Algonquin, Huron, Ottawa: they are no more our brothers than the French are to you. We have fought them since before your ships crossed the water. We would be fighting them if you never set foot in these lands. King George's war is only another chance for us to collect the scalps of our enemies. We thank him for this."

William took that in as he stared at the fire.

Otayonih kept his penetrating gaze on the young lad, finally asking, "Why do you fight for your father, King George, when so many of your brothers along the sea do not?"

"Because we were hungry," Sam interjected.

Many of the privates around the fire nodded at that. Empty bellies, not any sense of duty, had driven them into King George's Army.

Otayonih's eyes fell on Sam. The warrior nodded in understanding. "It is a father's duty to provide for his children. It is a son's duty to obey his father," he said.

"What is it like in the west, Otayonih?" William asked. "We've heard that we're to move up the lakes, that we will be taking over French forts to keep the local Indians in check."

The smoke from Otayonih's pipe glowed from the light of the fire, briefly obscuring him. "You will be among the enemies of the Haudenosaunee. The Ottawa, Huron, Chippewa, Abenaki, Sauk, French–"

"The Frogs are beat," a private interrupted. "They're suing for peace as we sit around this fire."

Several of the lads laughed and nodded at that.

"But you did not defeat the Indians of the lakes," Otayonih silenced them. "Those peoples spilled much blood for their French father, lost many young warriors for their French father, but King George has no more defeated them than a warrior who stands at dawn has defeated the night. He forgets that dusk will soon come again."

"But they lost Canada," the same private added.

"Did it fall into the sea!" Otayonih boomed, causing the private to flinch. "Did the birds pluck it away and carry it into the sky! No! It is still there, where the sun sets and the sky dances during winter nights! The Indians are still there, on the land their ancestors have lit their fires on for generations! The French father cannot give it over at the stroke of a quill! Was it ever his to begin with?"

The private chose not to answer. Instead, the young man tried to shrink away from the light of the fire, desperate to escape Otayonih's gaze.

"You said dusk is not far away," William said. "What does that mean?"

Otayonih took another long pull from his pipe as the privates sat and thought about the peoples to the west. "A prophet!" he finally boomed, causing several lads to recoil. "A prophet of the Delaware has had a vision. His words have traveled along the hunting trails and rivers. Many wampum belts have been exchanged between the tribes."

The privates looked to one another as Otayonih went silent and smoked.

Sam finally cleared his throat and asked, "What was the vision, Otayonih?"

The warrior's teeth appeared again in a smile. "The Indian has lost his way. Our white fathers have brought us nothing but lean times. They have brought us a god who only loves his children if they forsake their ancestors' way of life and the spirits of their woods. Our women and children die from the pox and the bloody flux. Our warriors spend too much time under the spell of the white man's rum. The steel you give us rusts. The muskets you provide break. Our powder rots and we run out of shot. Our young men have forgotten how to draw the bow and find the right stone for tomahawks, so we must hunt our lands until they're empty to trade for more of your goods, because we cannot make them ourselves.

"The prophet says this is not our way. He says that we must forsake your goods and your bleeding god. We must return to the old ways of the forest." Otayonih took a long look at each of them. "He says that we need to rid the land of our ancestors of all white men."

Several of the lads' eyes went to the tomahawks on the warriors' laps. Sam had the uncomfortable realization that his musket was stacked, along with the rest of the privates', a dozen paces away. Every one of them could be dispatched in only a few breaths with one word from Otayonih.

Otayonih laughed loudly when he saw the looks on his young charges' faces. He passed his pipe to William, making it clear that he had no intention of harming them. The privates' nervous looks melted away with the realization that they were safe, for now.

"How do you feel about this prophet, Otayonih?" William asked, grimacing from the harsh tobacco.

The smile on Otayonih's face slowly turned from one of mirth to one of sadness. "The steel of my tomahawk cuts better than stone," he said. "My musket shoots farther than my old bow. When our women and children die from the pox, we take the women and children of our enemies. And our father, King George, respects our hunting grounds and the old treaties."

The Seneca warriors nodded along somberly.

But the smile on Otayonih's face grew again as he said, "And your priests leave me alone when I show them my scalps and my many wives," which brought the lads to laughter. "And rum keeps me warm on cold winter nights."

This drew calls of "hear, hear" from the privates.

Otayonih waited for the laughter to die, then continued, "The old ways are too far gone to go back. The Haudenosaunee must find their place in this new world."

Sam took the proffered pipe and inhaled the rich smoke. "I hope the Indians of the lakes come to that same understanding without too much trouble," he said, and exhaled.

Otayonih looked at him with a pitying smile. "For your sake, I hope the same."

***

The morning cadences of song-birds woke Sam. He rubbed the sleep from his eyes as he rolled from his spot in the dirt. Sleeping privates lay sprawled around the smoldering remnants of the fire. The Seneca were nowhere to be seen. The remains of the deer carcass had disappeared with them.

Sam woke the other privates, and they went about gathering their meager things. They then went down to the stream near camp to wash away the grime and soot covering their bodies and faces. They took turns pleating each other's hair, none of them pleased to be taming the wild locks that had flown free for the past fortnight. One private took a razor from his mud-splattered waistcoat and they hacked at each other's facial growth, drawing blood that washed down the cool stream.

When the lads were somewhat passable as the King's soldiers, Sam led them down the hillside. They broke out of the woods, and the valley that Lancaster resided in took shape. The sounds of civilization carried up to them.

Most of the lads stepped off with a spring in their step, eager to return to the barracks and its promise of regular chow and less strenuous garrison living. William was the only one to hold back.

Sam turned and looked at his hesitant brother. He knew William had no desire to return, but Sam also knew that there was nothing for him in the woods. Otayonih and his warriors would be half a day's journey away by then, and desertion would see the skin of William's back stripped down to the bone before a sure death.

Sam went to his brother and put an arm around his shoulder. "Swift and bold, William," he said.

After a few long breaths, William repeated, "Swift and bold," and let his brother lead him back down the valley to a life that neither really wanted.

It was a life that would soon lead them west, into the interior of the great continent.

***

"*Kompanieee*! Tenchun!" Fritz bellowed.

The men snapped to under the glorious sun of a spring morning. Captain Etherington, a short fellow with a jovial face, moved forward with Lieutenant Leslie and several privates. The privates held the reason for this gathering of the men in their hands.

The six recently returned privates stood in line at attention in front of the company. Sam had to squint as Captain Etherington appeared in front of him.

"Private Avery, is it?" the Captain asked.

"Sir," Sam answered, saluting with an arm across his musket.

"Did you learn anything from our noble Indian allies?"

"Yes, sir," Sam answered, knowing the captain did not want him to expound any further than that.

"There's a good lad." The captain beamed.

Etherington motioned to one of the privates, who produced a hatchet that was much like the tomahawks Otayonih and his warriors had never let far from their grasps.

"Take care of her," Etherington commanded, running the hatchet through a loop in Sam's cross guard.

"Sir!" Sam acknowledged.

Etherington had already moved on to present William his hatchet and was making the same small talk with the lad. Sam looked down at the deadly weapon. A small silver plate with the words "CELER ET AUDUX" etched upon it rested just above where one's hand would grip the hickory haft. He used his free hand to run a finger over the inscription, and he felt something he hadn't imagined he'd ever feel in the Army. A sense of pride washed over him. He looked up to see Fritz beaming at him from his position in front of the company. Sam returned the smile.

Ch. 4

Philadelphia. July 1762

Dust from the Germantown road filled Sam's nostrils as the 1st Battalion plodded through clouds kicked up by their own marching feet. Etherington's Company – its paper strength close to a hundred men – marched with sixty-two Regulars, with Etherington and Lieutenant Leslie leading on horseback. Amongst the enlisted were two sergeants, five corporals, and the young drummer that had striped Sam. The lad beat rhythmically on the skin of his drum, much like he'd done on the skin of Sam's back. Twenty-two men were laid up in the battalion surgery back in Lancaster. Half of them would probably not survive their ailments. Ten men were absent without leave and considered deserters.

  The dust-choked road was only the first stretch in a journey that would span almost three thousand miles. In Philadelphia, the Regulars would board transport ships and make their way up the coast, past New York and Boston, sailing by the Fortress of Louisbourg, where 14,000 redcoats had planted the Union Jack after much bloodshed four years earlier, and enter the St. Lawrence to reach Quebec. They would work their way upriver until reaching the first of the great inland lakes, Lake Ontario. From there, they would head for the cascading falls at Niagara, which they'd portage around to reach Lake Eerie. It would then be an easier journey by sloop to the fortified town of Detroit. After that there was one more great lake to conquer, Huron, before they reached their final destination: a place called Michilimackinac. Sam thought they might as well march to Jerusalem and back while they were at it. That journey might prove less arduous.

  "I can't wait to see the city," William said from beside him.

  Sam looked south, seeing church steeples and the tower of the newly constructed State House soaring over the city. Since the Averys had left for Lancaster, Philadelphia had grown into the largest city in the colonies, bypassing Boston as it burgeoned to a staggering 20,000 souls. Of course, Sam would have been shocked to learn that Lieutenant Leslie, a native of London, looked upon the metropolis of Philadelphia as little more than a mud-filled provincial village.

As they marched through the city's northern suburbs, Sam was surprised by the lack of enthusiasm that greeted the King's soldiers. Traffic on the road gave the soldiers the courtesy of the right of way, but that was probably more to avoid the flat of an angry officer's sword or the swat of a burly sergeant's pike than out of respect. Some of the folks along the roadside even looked at them with downright hostility.

One rough-looking fellow even spat and hissed, "Damned lobsters," as they strode by.

"Not the friendliest of lots," Sam said to no one.

Corporal Kane, marching in his file, overheard and said, "The Frogs are beaten, Sam. The Indians are tamed or pushed over the mountains. The colonials can now lie safe in their warm beds, thanks to us. What use are we to them now? We've outstayed our purpose. They'd just as soon see the backs of us."

Not very thankful, Sam thought. But he guessed that life was different along the seaboard. The dangers of the frontier were a long way away, and the Indians hadn't been a threat to Philadelphia for generations. And now, with the French out of Canada, these city dwellers must have thought they were safe as anyone could be in the King's empire.

The companies reached the massive barracks newly built on the Northern Liberties. The enlisted stowed their belongings and, after a passionate description of the pain and death that awaited any deserters, were given leave for the rest of the day. Fritz found William and Sam loitering around the parade ground, unsure of what to do with their new freedom.

"Let me buy you an ale, *meine jungs*," Fritz said.

William looked to Sam. The younger Avery had avoided Fritz ever since Sam's back had seen the lash.

Sam gave William a reassuring nod, then smiled at Fritz. "If you're buying, *Sergeant Meyer,*" Sam emphasized with mock gravity, "better make it two ales a piece. The march has made us quite thirsty."

William cringed and waited for his NCO to explode.

Fritz's face grew redder, but his lips soon curled into a smile, and he let out a howl of laughter as he slapped Sam on the back and shouted, "*Rotzloffel!*"

Sam laughed along with Fritz as the sergeant pushed the two boys toward the road leading into the heart of the city. William could only shake his head, unable to understand army life in the least.

Fritz acting much more like the dear family friend than the stiff sergeant soon put William at ease. The little Hanoverian told old stories of their departed father with a twinkle in his eye, choking up and hiding a tear more than once. Sam and William could relate. Their father's passing still cast a pall over them, even after almost three years. Fritz was telling a particularly hilarious story – when the duo had stolen a pair of army mules and rode some distance to a tavern – when the peel of the city's fire bell cut through the dusk.

"Look," William said, and pointed south. The sky over a row of houses was starting to glow with the beginnings of a fire.

"Come!" Sam barked automatically.

The red-coated trio rounded a corner to see a stately home succumbing to flames. Dozens of men were running bucket lines from a pump to the adjoining dwellings, apparently having already given up on saving the structure where the fire had originated. The soldiers watched as the flames slowly worked their way up from the basement kitchen to the first floor.

A sorrowful wail of fright carried through the flames. Sam realized there was someone still inside. Without thinking, he ripped off his regimental coat, dropped his tricorn, and stripped his waistcoat. Fritz saw this and began doing the same. William started to mimic them. Sam reached out and stopped his brother. "Stay here, William," he ordered.

"But–" William tried to say.

"Stay!" Sam called as he made his way toward the flames, Fritz following.

The men manning the buckets called out warnings and cursed the pair's stupidity, but Sam and Fritz did not listen.

The heat pouring from the front door hit Sam as if he'd opened an oven and stuck his face inside. There was no way they could possibly get through it. He was contemplating retreating when something wet fell over his shoulder. Turning, Sam saw that William had taken his and Fritz's coats and soaked them with pump water. The younger brother gave them a prideful smile and motioned for them to get going. Sam gave him a quick nod and threw the coat over himself.

Smoke burned their throats as they plunged into the flames and began making their way through the first floor. Their coats steamed as the water boiled away, and the only thing pushing them deeper into the blaze was a soft whimper that led them to the dining room. They found a maid cowering under the table, her singed bonnet covering her scorched face. Sam and Fritz knelt down and spread their coats out for protection.

"Is there anyone else!" Sam yelled as the fire began to really roar.

"Abigail's upstairs," the maid pleaded.

"Bloody hell," Sam cursed. He looked to Fritz. "Can you get her out of here?"

"*Ja!*" Fritz said.

"Then go!" Sam pushed them toward the front of the house. He covered himself again and made his way to the back staircase, climbing the steps as they creaked and buckled. The entire structure seemed close to giving way.

Reaching the landing, Sam dropped to his knees and inched his way through the impenetrable gloom of dark smoke. An ungodly shriek sounded from down the hall, forcing him to keep his wits as the smoke threatened to overwhelm him. Practically swimming through the blackness, Sam's hands fell upon a closed door. "Is anyone there!" he called.

Another howl rose over the sound of the flames.

The poor girl must be burning alive, Sam cringed. He pushed his shoulder into the door and fell into a room that had yet to be touched by the fire, quickly shutting the door behind him. Turning, he found what looked to be a nursery. Frilly curtains covered the window and lacy doilies rested on every surface. A moan of fear came from a small iron-framed bed in the corner. Sam got down on his elbows and crawled under the smoke, pushing little wooden toys out of his way as he came upon the bed.

"No worries, little miss," Sam soothed as he rose over the pile of blankets.

The blankets shot back and revealed a horrifying sight. A creature with sharp fangs and more hair than skin reached for him. Sam gasped and recoiled across the floor, his back slamming against the now hot door. The creature, grotesquely clad in the pink dress of a little girl, leaped from the bed and shot forward, trying to wrap its arms around him. Sam screamed in terror and braced himself, but no fangs sank into his neck. Only a thankful cooing issued from the hairy attacker.

Looking down with one open eye, Sam saw pleading brown eyes looking up at him. A memory from his childhood came. A troupe of performers had come to Philadelphia from England when he was a young lad. He remembered a smartly dressed chimp amongst their company. The little hairy beast had been trained to go around the crowd with his tiny hat held out for coins. Young Sam had even dropped a halfpenny into the hat at his father's urging.

Abigail was a chimp. Knowing he could never disentangle himself from her strong grasp, Sam wrapped the beast in his coat and opened the doorway a crack. A wall of flame seemed to jump for him, and he slammed the door shut. The floor beneath his feet began to warp and buckle from the heat. Frantically, he looked for some escape before they were roasted where they stood.

There was only one way out.

After one last breath of choking air, Sam charged forward and shouldered through the frilly curtains and thin panes of the second-floor window. He landed on the sloped roof of the porch, slowly rolling with the shrieking Abigail until he felt himself falling. He instinctively turned so as to land on his back, which struck the cobbles with a thud. The wind rushed from him and stars blazed to life in his vision. Indignant, Abigail now saw fit to sink her teeth into him, nipping Sam's arm in payment for his troubles before she shot off.

A pair of hands hooked under Sam's armpits and began dragging him across the uneven stones, causing more distress to his poor back. He cursed and swatted William away, flipping onto his belly and crawling from the intense heat until he felt his skin no longer singeing, where he collapsed.

A pair of exquisite, buckled shoes suddenly filled his vision. Sam, even in his state of pain and exhaustion, admired the craftsmanship of such fine footwear. Intrigued to see the owner of such a pair of shoes, he managed to look up. A merry face with a mirthful smile looked down at him.

"My compliments, good sir," the man said, and nodded.

Again, hands intruded under Sam's armpits, lifting him from the cobbles. He turned to see Fritz, his face covered in soot but otherwise uninjured, and William holding him up. William barely paid him any mind. He could only stare at the gentleman in front of them.

"Mr. Coates's home is a loss, I fear," the man said. He stared past Sam, taking in the inferno. "But he'll be much pleased that you rescued his dear Abigail." The stranger nodded to a pair across the street.

Sam looked to see a man clad in a fine suit holding the chimp as if it were a child. The dandy soothed and comforted the beast, offering not even a glance to the conflagration that had been his home.

"Allow me," the stranger said, "to buy the three of you an ale once this blaze is under control." With that, the man stepped off to organize the men battling the fire.

"By Jove," William exhaled.

"What?" Sam practically coughed, still dazed from the smoke and flames.

William smiled. "That was Benjamin Franklin."

Gulping air, Sam gazed at the man extolling those fighting the fire to put their backs into it. "That geezer?"

***

Ale shot from Mr. Franklin's nose as he convulsed with laughter. Sitting in the Tun Tavern off Front Street, Sam had regaled the group for the second time about his reaction to pulling back the blankets and finding dear Abigail. Sam shook his head and grinned ear to ear as the gentleman slowly composed himself and wiped the ale from his face.

"Mr. Coates," Mr. Franklin finally managed, "brought that chimp back from the Guinea Coast some years back. When she made her debut in society, she was the talk of the city for months. No one could blame the old fool, though. He said the chimp reminded him of his dearly departed wife, though I'd daresay the chimp is easier on the eyes." Mr. Franklin howled again, almost falling from his chair.

Sam, William, and Fritz joined in the laughter, imagining the chimp dressed in fine silks during a lavish society ball.

"That Mr. Coates is an odd fellow," Mr. Franklin said, and caught his breath, "but a thankful fellow." A twinkle lit the graying gentleman's eye as he dropped a purse that rattled with coin on the table in front of Sam. "With Mr. Coates' compliments."

Sam scooped up the bag, feeling its weight as he disappeared it into a deep pocket.

Watching the purse vanish, Fritz asked, "And for the fine sergeant who saved the gentleman's kitchen wench?"

Mr. Franklin smiled and said, "I'm afraid there's no great shortage of kitchen wenches in Philadelphia."

"I'll buy your ale tonight, Fritz," Sam offered.

The Hanoverian perked up and smiled at that.

"You certainly wouldn't have to travel to the Guinea Coast for a scullery maid," William chimed in, his tongue loosened by ale.

Mr. Franklin looked at the young soldier with intrigue. "Ever been to Guinea?" he asked.

"Lord, no!" William beamed. "But I've read much about it. I used to mend the shoes of the wife of our deputy governor."

"Mrs. Hamilton?" Mr. Franklin smiled. "Are you from Lancaster?"

"Indeed! Lady Hamilton allowed me to borrow books from their extensive library. Don't tell Sam," William said, and grinned at his brother. "I spent many an afternoon reading in that great room instead of mending heels. That's where I read many of your works."

Sam shook his head and smiled. He always knew his brother spent more time with his head in a book than with his hands on the lady's shoes.

"My word!" Mr. Franklin said, and gulped from his ale. "A well-read soldier! Now I truly have seen it all! I've met generals who could barely read their own names!"

"I don't consider myself much of a soldier," William said softly.

"Books are for priests and scholars," Fritz belched.

Mr. Franklin ignored him. "You must come to my home before your departure, William," he said. "I shall give you some old volumes. I can't bear the thought of a young man of letters parted from something to read in the interior. I simply won't have it."

Sam watched William strain his face with an enormous smile. "Yes, Mr. Franklin," William said. "Thank you, sir. You do me a great kindness."

Mr. Franklin smiled and shrugged. "Call me Ben. Where is your company headed again?"

"Michilimackinac," Sam said slowly, as if the syllables didn't belong in his mouth. "Between the lakes Michigan and Huron."

"The French call it the *Pays d'en Haut*," Ben said with a gleam in his eye. "The Upper Country. The edge of the world."

"*Das arshloch* of the world," Fritz slurred.

Ben once more ignored the ever-drunker sergeant. "I've heard many a tale of the beauty of the lakes. Inland seas, more like as not. I should love to see them someday," he said wistfully.

A smirk came to Sam. "I'd gladly hand over my place, Mr. Franklin. You'd owe His Majesty two and a half more years, then we'd split the fifty-acre bounty," he said.

Mr. Franklin boomed with laughter. "You cheeky devil! I'm afraid I wouldn't last the first winter's eve in the interior. I'm coming up on my fifty-seventh year, I'll have you know. I could drop dead tomorrow."

Sam doubted that very much as he laughed with the virile gentleman. "Well," he sighed, "if you happen to change your mind, and want one more grand adventure before the grave takes you, we take ship for Quebec in three days' time."

"Quebec?" Ben intoned. "Seems a rather roundabout way to get to the interior. Why don't you take the road to Fort Pitt, then head north to Lake Eerie?"

"It is meant to be a show of force for the Canadians," Sam answered. "We'll be dropping off companies in Quebec and Montreal along the way."

"It's to scare *die wilden* as well," Fritz slurred.

Ben tipped his mug at something across the room. "There's one of your savages now, Sergeant," he said.

Turning, the soldiers saw a man sitting half hidden by shadow in a dark corner of the tavern. The only light that penetrated the gloom came from a dying candle sitting on the table in front of the still man. Flickering flame reflected in dark eyes that stared back at the group. Sam was unable to hold the man's gaze, and he turned back to find his fellows had similarly surrendered.

"*Monsieur* Charles Michel De Langlade," Ben said, the foreign words flowing effortlessly from his mouth.

"*Ein Franzose?*" Fritz hissed, his guard coming up.

"*Oui*," Ben answered, "but also so much more. *Monsieur* Langlade's mother is the sister of Nissowaquet."

"She's the sister of what?" Sam asked.

"Not a what, my good man." Ben smiled. "But a who. Nissowaquet is one of the prominent chiefs of the Ottawa." Franklin nodded to Langlade. "That man's uncle is one of the very Indians your company is traipsing into the hinterlands to watch over."

"Why is he in Philadelphia?" William asked. "Did he serve the King during the fighting in Canada?"

"The King?" Ben guffawed. "Yes! Just not *our* King, my good lad. That man has not been long for the service of King Louis!" Ben plunked down his ale, spilling foam over the table. "Ensign Langlade served in the French Marines." He leaned in conspiratorially, dropping his voice. "It is rumored he was present at the catastrophe that was Braddock's licking at Fort Duquesne, and that he had a heavy hand in the planning of our defeat. After that, he ranged up and down the frontier, causing trouble and stirring up the other tribes. Then they say he led an Ottawa war band outside the gates of Quebec."

Sam's eyes flashed to Fritz. The German slammed down his ale loudly and made to stand, his eyes locked on the figure in the corner.

Benjamin had to reach across the table and grab Fritz's arm to restrain him. "No, no, no, my good Sergeant," Franklin chided. "The *Monsieur* is here under a flag of truce."

Sam looked quickly to the dark corner. The black pools no longer stared back. Now they passed over the room with a too-bored look that fell everywhere except their table. Sam knew there was no way the man had failed to notice the outburst of the red-coated sergeant, and he couldn't shake the feeling that a cocked pistol was held ready underneath the Monsieur's table.

"Truce?" Fritz spat, slowly lowering himself back into his seat, his eyes never leaving Langlade.

"As we speak," Ben answered, "King Louis' representatives are discussing peace with King George's men in Paris. All this war is quite bad for commerce, you know?" Ben added airily. "It won't be long, maybe another year, before a treaty is signed. The French have already abandoned their possessions in Canada. *Monsieur* Langlade knows which way the wind blows, and he knows that it's unlikely King Louis will fight hard for the cold north at the negotiating table when he needs to bargain for his islands in the Caribbean."

"He'd give up half the continent for a few piddly islands?" Sam asked, puzzled.

"Those islands are worth their weight in gold," William said. "Sugar," he added, answering Sam's dumb look.

Ben stared at William with a mixture of surprise and regard. "Quite right, William," he said, and nodded.

William practically floated from the table at Ben's affirmation.

Leaning in towards Sam with the relish of one who liked nothing more than imparting wisdom to ignorant youths, Ben smiled and said, "My good lad, those piddly islands yield more income to King Louis' treasury than a dozen Canadas, and they cost half as much to defend. All one needs is a governor who can escape the fever for a year or two, a few companies of Regulars to keep the slaves from rebelling, and the threat of a squadron of warships over the horizon..." Ben held open his hands. "And your return on investment is hundredfold.

"Commerce, Sam!" Ben thundered. "Commerce! That's the word that has the ability to bring kings to their knees. Louis would part with a million wild, trackless acres for the few plantations that provide the sugar for his cakes."

"Could be shortsighted," William said.

Ben's smile grew. "It very well could be, my lad. Very well could be. Who knows what those vast lands could become? But if King George takes them, will he run into the same problems as Louis?

How does one who resides on a small island on the far side of the globe pay for the defense of an empire that spans a continent? All very captivating questions that I hope I'm around to see the answers to."

Bored with the weighty talk, Sam asked, "So, is this French Indian pledging loyalty to King George?"

"Why don't you ask him yourself?" Ben grinned.

Sam made to say something, but Ben cut him off and called, "Charles! Would you join us for an ale?"

The man didn't hesitate. He quickly stood and moved into the light as he crossed the tavern floor. Sam watched his every step.

Taller than Sam, Langlade was in his late thirties or early forties, with the wide shoulders of a man who was no stranger to physical toil. Ink black hair pulled back into a queue framed a thoughtful face that bore the lines of one who'd spent a great deal of his life squinting under the sun.

Just then, their eyes connected. Langlade took in Sam's uniform in an instant, and a flash of recognition seemed to cross his face. Sam could have sworn the man almost came to a dead stop before managing to put his foot down in front of the other.

Turning from Langlade's scrutiny, Sam saw William looking positively thrilled at the prospect of speaking with the man. Fritz looked as if Ben had just invited the Devil himself to share their ale. Ben made room and Langlade pulled up a chair to sit next him.

"May I introduce Sergeant Meyer and Privates Sam and William Avery," Ben greeted, pushing forward their pitcher.

"*Monsieurs, bonsoir,*" Langlade said. He nodded curtly to each of them before sitting. As he poured his drink, his dark eyes lingered uncomfortably on Sam.

"These fine fellows are with the King's Royal Americans, the Sixtieth Regiment of Foot," Ben explained. "I believe you will be sailing with them on your journey home to Michilimackinac."

Langlade raised his dark eyebrows thoughtfully and took a sip of ale, but otherwise didn't respond.

Studying the newcomer, Sam thought the only things betraying Langlade as half European were his finely tailored jacket and impeccable French. His chestnut coloring, black hair, dark eyes, and smooth jaw were undoubtedly the gifts of his mother's blood.

"Are you from Michilimackinac?" William asked, leaning forward.

Langlade nodded thoughtfully. "The most beautiful place in the world," he said, his English tinged with a Gallic flow. "I was born and raised at the fort, and made my living in the trade of furs and metals up and down the lakes before I was..." Langlade paused, searching for the right words. "Taken away, on the business of my sovereign."

Fritz stared hard at the man. "You were at Quebec?" he questioned.

Langlade gave a slight nod.

"Beauport?" Fritz asked.

Langlade took a long sip of ale, his eyes drilling into Fritz over the rim of the pewter mug. Finishing with a sigh of content, he set the mug on the table and wiped foam from his lip. "*Oui*," he answered casually.

After a long, uncomfortable pause, Fritz said, "I don't drink with frogs. Much less a half-frog, half-savage. I'd just as soon be scalped."

Ben's eyebrows shot up. He looked to Charles, aghast at what had just been said. Sam's fists clenched of their own accord in preparation for a brawl. William sat stunned at the insult.

A small smile came to Langlade's lips. "*Mon petit sergent*, even if you fought like Hector himself before I took your heart out, I would never design to take that ugly, *Allemand* scalp from your bald dome," he said.

A gasp escaped William. Ben smiled uncomfortably, in disbelief that two men could share such an exchange. Sam just readied himself for the table to flip and the blows to start landing.

After a maddening, drawn-out silence, Fritz finally nodded. "I can drink to that," he said, raising his mug.

Langlade nodded and raised his mug. William took a gulp of air, finally allowing himself to breathe. Sam unclenched his fists and Ben chuckled in relief. They all raised their glasses.

"To King George!" Ben thundered.

"To a new world," Langlade countered.

"Here, here!" Ben approved.

After long pulls, the men slammed their mugs down. Sam wiped foam from his lips and looked up to see Langlade studying him again. The man's brow was scrunched in confusion, like he couldn't believe what his eyes were seeing.

"You look at me as if I were a ghost," Sam couldn't help but say aloud.

Langlade cocked his and opened his mouth to speak, but Fritz abruptly stood and started belting an old German drinking song, cutting off his words. Half a dozen other *Deutsche* in the tavern, and even Ben and William, stood and joined in.

When Sam looked back to Langlade, the man was pointedly ignoring his existence.

***

Captain Etherington's horse whinnied loudly as the beast swung over the chasm separating the wharf from the three-masted merchantman. The soldiers watched the poor animal travel as they boarded from the gangplank. Sam ran into William's now book-laden pack as his brother stared after the horse's progress.

"Thunderbolt will be fine, William, but we'll be sleeping in the bilge if you don't get a move on," Sam admonished, pushing his brother up the gangway.

William went forward reluctantly. The brothers made the deck, only for William to stop cold once more. Sam ran into him for the second time.

"Bloody hell, William," Sam cursed. He stopped himself from rapping his brother over the back of the head when he saw the reason for the paralysis.

A beauty – a goddess – stood bathed in gold on the sun-drenched deck of the merchantman. If she hadn't moved just then, Sam would have thought her a statue of honey-colored stone. Her face looked as if it had been discovered hiding in a block of marble by one of the old masters. The rich skin of her arms and the inky blackness of her pleated hair set off the radiance of her white dress. Her brown eyes swept over the group of tongue-lolled soldiers frozen on the deck, and her ample lips turned up in a smile at the disarray she'd caused.

Sam reckoned that even the toughest sergeant would have had a hard time looking into her kind eyes without his heart fluttering a few beats.

"*Schnell!*" Fritz barked at his dumbstruck soldiers, lashing out and catching a poor private with his pike.

The soldiers unstuck themselves and pushed off under further threats from the Hanoverian, moving towards the main hatch that led to the hold that would be their barracks for the journey. Only William and Sam lingered as the men shuffled by.

Charles Langlade stood not far from the goddess, with his Ottawa wife next to the ship's master. Madame Langlade, draped in a dress that would have turned appreciative heads in any European court, was barely eclipsed in beauty by the girl who could only be her daughter. Charles saw the Avery boys admiring his progeny and gave them a long, withering look that would have buckled their knees if they'd seen it.

"Averys!" Fritz thundered, "*Schnell!*"

Sam tore his eyes from the young beauty. "Come on, William," he said, practically dragging his brother toward the hatch.

Pushing William down the stairs to the hold, Sam risked one more quick glance back.

The raven-haired beauty was smiling in his direction. Sam didn't know if it was directed at him or William, but he couldn't tear his eyes away.

Fritz's red face appeared and blocked out the beauty. The sergeant smiled devilishly before his booted foot struck out and kicked him square in the backside, sending Sam tumbling into the dark hold as peels of feminine laughter rang out across the deck.

Ch. 5

The North Atlantic. August 1762

Avery blood ran down from men who'd ranged beyond the shores of little islands and icy fjords to cross the world and bring kingdoms and continents to heel. Longships had delivered Vikings to Ireland a thousand years in the past, where they'd taken or married local Gaelic girls and sowed their seeds. Shannon Avery passed that same blood on to her two boys. Ancestors of Samuel Avery had pillaged the treasure fleets of the Spanish Main with Queen Elizabeth's sea dogs, and had explored the American coastline from the Atlantic to the Pacific. But Sam's stomach was ignorant of his illustrious heritage, and his feet had known only the steadiness of dry land since they'd first had the strength to support him.

  Heaving his guts out, Sam expelled his meager breakfast into a bucket dangerously close to overflowing, the hardtack they'd been fed for days tasting even worse on the way up. The *Brindisi* pitched in a violent summer storm, swaying the rows of hammocks that dangled like chrysalises containing pupae of soldiers. Groans of agony rang throughout the hold. Sam wasn't the only subject of the King to have lost his sea legs, or never had them, and bile and vomit erupted from several victims with every degree of pitch.

  Sam knew he had to get out of this stinking hell or his guts would never settle, and he'd be liable to cough them up. He waited for an opportune list of the ship and rolled himself from his canvas hammock. His feet plopped down on the hard deck and his stomach almost flipped. The bucket sloshed precariously in his grip, but the contents thankfully kept to their container. Sam took a moment to steady himself in the dark hold as the hammocks of his compatriots bumped and jostled him with each swell.

  "Hello, Sam," William greeted cheerfully from his swaying hammock nearby.

  Sam turned to see his reclining brother's big smile. One of Mr. Franklin's books was propped in front of his face as he read in the meager light. William's chipper attitude had much to do with how the seas that had brought low his elder brother had not affected him in the least. Rarely could William ever gloat about being stronger than Sam at anything, and he'd relished the opportunity these last few days.

"You're going to go blind reading in this light," Sam managed.

William's smile only grew. "Then I shall get a pair of Ben's bifocals!" he said.

"And I can knock them off your smug face."

William laughed, and asked, "Taking some air?"

"If they let me out of this tomb."

William returned to his book, his rock-solid constitution bringing some redemption to the Avery name. "Good luck," he sneered.

Finally feeling as if he could move, Sam started through the dark hold. Fire being the scourge of all wooden vessels, the only light came from shielded lanterns. Low beams and hanging hammocks gave the space the feel of a cave full of sleeping bats. Some men lay on the floor, covered in their own discharges as they groaned from seasickness. A few men of iron stomachs tried to carry on a spirited dice game in the low light. Sam envied them as he lurched towards the main hatch.

Corporal Kane – with his orders to keep the lads confined to the hold – sat with his face bathed in soft lantern light, his back against a spar near the stairs up the main hatch. His eyes were closed, and he appeared to be asleep. Just when Sam had steeled himself to slip by the corporal, the Irishman's eyes opened with the omniscience that all NCOs seemed to possess.

"Sam," Kane greeted, evidently unaffected by the violent seas.

"Corporal," Sam replied. "Any chance I can take some air and empty my bucket?"

Kane cocked his head. "You know the rules, lad. Exercise for two hours in the morning, two after supper. These seamen hate to have us landlubbers rolling across their deck. That's why they keep us in this boggin place. Use the heads at the bow."

The thought of being perched over a small hole at the front of the ship held no appeal to Sam.

The ship seemed to tip down the slope of a small mountain, and Sam's stomach lurched. He turned his head to spew mostly bile onto the deck, for lack of a bucket with the space for it.

Kane recoiled and looked pityingly on him. "Alri, lad. Keep your guts in. Go on," Kane said, and gestured up the stairs. "But if you're caught out and my name crosses your lips, I'll toss you to ol' Davy myself."

"Thank you, Corporal," Sam choked as he made his way past.

Gray storm clouds filled the frame of the hatch, weakening the evening light. Sam spilled onto a deck awash from spray and slick as ice. Seamen scurried about their tasks and ignored his wobbling form. He half ran, half fell into the starboard gunwale, his bucket spilling slop as he struck it. With effort, he managed to heave its contents over the side, then he purged what remained in his stomach to Neptune, much of it blowing back in his face from the strong offshore wind.

Wiping his mouth, Sam looked out on the vast Atlantic as he held on to a lifeline with the strength of a man one slip away from death. The sixth rate *Siren,* their escort, cut through the seas a quarter mile aft. Sam's belly seemed to follow along with the frigate, heaving up and down through the rolling swells. Cold sea spray struck him in the face and he shuddered, wiping the salt-water from his eyes. A bolt of lightning arced down into the sea some miles to the west, the peel of thunder following shortly after.

Sam's knees buckled at so vast a sight. It felt as if their little boat was sailing around the rim of a swirling whirlpool that wanted nothing more than to swallow them whole.

A hand hooked him under his armpit and brought him to his feet. Sam turned to see Charles Langlade's dark eyes staring into his.

"Look to the horizon," Langlade called over the wind. "It helps with the sickness."

Sam gazed toward the dark horizon, making every effort to focus on the one piece of world that offered some semblance of stability. After several minutes, all the while supported by Langlade, Sam's stomach settled. He was finally well enough to support himself against the gunwale, and Langlade withdrew his support.

"Thank you," Sam called.

Langlade nodded.

"Spent much time on the sea?" Sam asked over the wind.

Langlade shook his head. "My first voyage," he said. "I came to Philadelphia over Forbes' road."

"By God, you have the stomach for it."

Langlade shrugged. "I've spent my life on the lakes. Storms there blow up quickly, and many sailors say the inland waters are more treacherous. Not enough space for the waves to spread." He pointed to the *Siren* tumbling down a swell. "On the sea, a ship can ride the swells." He demonstrated the smooth up and down with his hands. "The swells on the lakes are spaced much closer. A captain gets no respite, and his ship can break its back between waves."

Sam smiled. "Well, I never thought I'd be thankful for an ocean tempest."

"Here," Langlade said, thrusting a small paper envelope into Sam's hand.

Sam looked up questioningly.

"It's ginger root," Langlade said. "Put it in your tea or rum ration. It will help with your stomach."

"Thank you, sir," Sam said.

Langlade smiled. "You may call me Charles." With that, he turned on his heel and made his way to the aft cabins.

***

The sea's surface had smoothed to the stillness of a placid, inland pond. Brilliant sunshine soaked the *Brindisi* as she plodded north on barely a whisper of wind. The men of Captain Etherington's company sweated under its rays as they did their slow orbits along the deck, stretching their weary legs and sucking in as much fresh air as their greedy lungs could hold. Sam walked with Fritz and talked of nothing in particular. William was in his usual spot, sitting against the main mast with a book in front of his face. All the while, Charles Langlade's daughter looked down on them from the quarterdeck.

Her presence during the company's exercises had become as reliable as the watch bells. She talked with her father or strolled the quarterdeck with her mother. She watched the sailors at work in the rigging, looked out to sea, or cast her gaze over the bedraggled soldiers, straightening backs and putting springs in steps. The men would steal a hundred glances up at her before being forced back into the dark hold, where they awaited the blessing of her presence with more longing than they held for that next touch of sun upon their skin.

Late at night, in the suffocating darkness, discourses on the presence of the mademoiselle during the company's exercise could be heard from one end of the hold to the other. Some thought that one amongst them must have caught her eye. Some poor fools even proclaimed that they were the chosen one, only to be shouted down by their compatriots, and their compatriots to be shouted down by the corporals and sergeants. Many could only summon the audacity to dream of her, and some poor wretches not even that.

But Sam believed he'd finally solved the mystery of the mademoiselle's interest, and it was indeed because of a young soldier that she never left their exercises unattended. Over several days of diligent observation, Sam noticed the girl never scrutinized any one thing or individual for too long, propriety permitting her only cursory glances about the deck. But there was one exception. Every so often, he caught her eyes lingering on the base of the main mast, the very spot where gangly William reposed during every exercise. The lad had made plenty of excuses about just wanting to enjoy the fine light to read by, and that he could pace the hold while the other men lay in their hammocks, though he never did. But Sam's suspicion of his brother's supposed laziness was finally proven correct on this day.

From the corner of his eye, Sam watched William while Fritz droned on about the queerness of navy life. He saw his brother's eyes dart up from the page of his book and focus upon the quarterdeck, right where the mademoiselle happened to be standing. A smile flashed across William's face. Glancing quickly to the quarterdeck, Sam caught the end of a smile and an almost imperceptible nod of the girl's raven-haired head.

Looking back to the mast, Sam saw a practiced, casual movement from William. The lad reached into a deep crack in the deck and removed a small sheet of parchment. The sheet disappeared between the pages of his book before another was slid from the volume and stowed where the first had been withdrawn. It was over so quickly that nobody but Sam had noticed.

Smiling, Sam shook his head and listened as Fritz complained about the piles that afflicted his tender *arsch*.

There was mischief afoot on the *Brindisi*.

***

William reclined with his book in the shaft of sunlight the main hatchway provided. Engrossed in the words in front of him, he was unaware that he was being stalked from behind. In a flash of movement, a hand snatched at the letter he'd secreted between the pages and had been reading for the dozenth time. He lunged instinctively after his chortling brother. Sam held him off with a strong left arm as he held aloft the parchment with his right.

"Give it back, Sam!" William yelled.

Sam only held the letter further away and redoubled his efforts to keep back his rangy brother. "What do we have here, eh?" he asked.

William realized a physical struggle for the letter was doomed, so he tried to lie. "It's from Ben."

Dropping the parchment in front of his face, Sam cleared his throat as if to read.

Horrified, William finally relented, "It's from Domitilde!"

"Domitilde!" Sam crowed. "Is that the beauty's name?"

Every face within earshot perked up at that.

"We've been writing each other," William said quietly.

Word that a miracle had occurred passed from the bow to the stern with the speed of a shipborne fire. The sounds of booted feet landing on the deck echoed throughout the hold as men spilled from their hammocks. It wasn't long before the entire company seemed to be pressing in on the brothers. Oaths of disbelief and jealousy were sworn back and forth as the news of William's triumph was passed to the latecomers.

Sam was beginning to regret the scene he'd created, when a strong hand snatched the parchment. Fritz took the paper and playfully slapped it across Sam's surprised face. "What's this nonsense?" he growled.

William clammed up under the gaze of his fellows, helpless as to what to say.

Sam, realizing the men wanted a show, bowed theatrically to his brother and said, "It seems we have a budding romance on this fine ship."

Fritz looked down at the parchment and squinted, unable to decipher the neat words. "*Mademoiselle* Langlade?" he asked.

Sam beamed. "*Oui!*" he said for all the hold to hear.

A ripple of energy passed among the men.

Fritz turned to William with a look of confusion. "How?" he half demanded, half begged.

Bringing his chin up, William mustered his courage and said, "I've been running the company's sick call to Captain Etherington on the quarterdeck every morning. I bade Domitilde a good morning on our second day at sea. She smiled back."

The men gathered round let out exhalations at their own stupidity. William had volunteered for a rather bothersome duty that none of the senior men had wanted. None of the veterans – a crafty and cunning bunch if there ever was one – had had the wherewithal to realize running sick call might put them in proximity to the lovely maiden. How could they have let such an opportunity escape them, they wondered?

"I wrote her a poem not long after," William said, smiling despite himself.

Desperate to hear how this beanpole had done it, the necks of the men extended as if they were turtles.

"She returned her own and we've been corresponding since," William finished, pride dripping from his voice.

Shaking his head, Fritz said, "That man, Langlade, will skin you alive if he finds that you've cavorted with his daughter."

William shrank a bit and shrugged hopelessly. "They're just letters."

Fritz crumpled the parchment and dropped it, stepping forward to look up into the boy's eyes. "For the next two and a half years, *Wilhelm*, the only woman you'll be holding is Bess," he said, referring to the British Musket.

All the lads guffawed at that.

"If!" Fritz silenced the men. "If after two and a half years you wish to present your head for scalping by that red savage, that is your own choice. Until then, it is *verboten* to see her, to write her, or ride her, or I'll scalp you myself."

Fritz pushed past William and stalked off as the hold erupted in laughter. Several of the men came forward and patted William on the back, saying he was a braver man than they. Some encouraged him that the prize was worth the danger. Others could only shake their heads in jealousy.

Standing quietly, William took their friendly jabs in the hope that they would soon grow bored, which they did. The men slowly dispersed to the tedium of their shipboard lives, leaving Sam standing with his glum brother.

Sensing William's sadness, Sam leaned down and picked up the crumpled parchment. He unfolded it gently, taking his time to smooth the sheet with great care. When he'd finished, he presented it to his brother with a smile. "Be careful, William," he said.

The lanky boy nodded gravely.

***

The *Brindisi* docked at Quebec in the last weeks of summer. The men of the 60th Regiment – those who survived the voyage – took up residence outside the battered stone walls of the fortress city, the chasms gouged by British cannonballs still not repaired from the battle some three years earlier.

The company spent its first few days in the newly conquered land drilling from dawn to dusk. Sergeant Meyer, having stated the men needed whipping back into shape after the long voyage, marched them up and down the Plains of Abraham until they finally started to resemble soldiers of the King. Once they were back in form, the men were awarded a rare morning off. Many planned to catch up on sleep, mend kit, and do laundry. Some planned to walk the lanes of the city. Sam would use the morning to complete an undertaking that had weighed on him since the company had been informed that their journey would take them to Quebec.

Begging William's pardon, Sam slipped out of the small tent they shared with five other privates. His breath steamed in the dawn light as he breathed in the day's first taste of fresh air. Turning and stretching, he saw a shimmering of frost covering the canvas of their tent. It seemed that winter was not as far off in the northern climes as the calendar declared it to be. Sam felt thankful for his heavy regimental coat for the first time in months.

He made his way through the stirring camp to the great stone walls of the city. He nodded to the sentries manning the pickets at the fortress's gate and entered a town wholly Gallic in character. The appearance of the buildings, the words of the inhabitants, the feel of the narrow streets and the smells of baking pastries transported Sam to a country he'd never seen. Most of the Canadians he passed did not deign to look him in the eye or acknowledge his greetings, their eyes passing over his red coat and quickly moving on. They were a proud people that had yet to swallow the bitter morsel of defeat their ancient enemies had served them.

Sam marveled as he came to the hollowed ruins of the great cathedral. The massive stone building had presented too ripe a target for the British gunners of the fleet, and it had been destroyed during the siege. The Catholics of New France would not soon forget this act of blasphemy their new Protestant overlords had committed. Sam continued on, passing wharves that bustled with the loading and unloading of cargo. Furs from the interior were loaded onto ships bound for the old world, while fineries forged in Europe were unloaded to be dispersed into the new one. Ben Franklin's words on commerce failed to cross Sam's mind as he passed on and the morning warmed.

Sam exited the city's eastern gate and payed a boatmen to row him across the Charles River. Consulting the hand-drawn map that Fritz had provided him the day before, he followed its directions and headed east on a dirt lane toward the village of Beauport.

The sun rose higher in a near cloudless sky, and the day's heat increased with each stride. The broad St. Lawrence flowed by on his right, and a cooling breeze blew off it every now and then. A group of farmers leading an ox-drawn cart laden with produce for the city trudged towards him. Sam had left his musket back at camp, but his hatchet hung visibly at his side, giving him comfort as the rather rough-looking fellows approached. Some of these men could have fought on these very bluffs years before, and Sam knew they might look upon a wandering British soldier as an excellent target for revenge.

He needn't have worried. The farmers were intrigued to see a redcoat out and about and exchanged pleasantries in their halting English. They were much friendlier than their metropolitan brethren. The fellows let Sam pass on his way, unmolested.

A mile outside of the city, it got hot enough that Sam stripped his regimental coat and carried it over his shoulder. The few wisps of clouds darting overhead provided only fleeting shade from the sun. Sam squinted up at the ball of fire and wiped the sweat from his brow, hoping that his destination was not far off.

As his feet rose and fell, he studied the earthen fortifications the French had thrown up along the north bank of the river during the siege. They'd been his constant companions since he'd left the city. With a soldier's eye, he admired the positions, each bastion seeming more formidable than the last. The road and fortifications ran along high bluffs that dropped down to the river, and Sam knew it wouldn't take many men to defend the heights from a river landing below.

The country village of Beauport rose in his vision as he plodded along. The village folk were inquisitive of the passing soldier, but didn't stop his determined strides with questions or greetings. It wasn't long before he passed the last outbuildings and was back in open country. Half a mile further on, Sam believed he'd finally reached the X marked on Fritz's map.

Leaving the road, he worked his way through the French trenches protecting the bluff's crest. The trenches were already filling in and the embankments had started crumbling from the march of time. Wooden spikes used to slow infantry sat at canted angles as they'd worked their way loose from the soil. Weeds and other manner of flora had invaded the ditches, slowly reclaiming the land for the wild.

Reaching the lip of a trench, Sam looked down the bluff. Fritz's memory hadn't eroded along with the fortifications. His map had led Sam right to the spot.

River flooding had scoured the redoubts below to shapeless mounds of mud. They looked no more formidable than a child's play fort, but Sam imagined they would have been difficult nuts to crack years ago, especially from a river assault. Knowing he had to climb down to see them closer, he dropped his regimental coat and even stripped off his waistcoat, piling them on the rim of the trench.

Carefully, Sam worked his way along a worn trail that wound down the bluff. The occasional dull glint of rusted metal drew his eye. Bent bayonets, musket balls, buckles, and even an officer's sword were scattered about as he made his way through the beach grass. The plate of a mitre cap confirmed what he'd suspected. He was traversing the spot where Fritz had told him the grenadiers had died in great numbers while assaulting the bluff. These scraps of metal were the only testaments left of their forlorn charge.

Scrabbling down the last few feet of slope, Sam came to a rest against the embankment of the first redoubt. He rounded the earthen walls and came to a stop on the river side of the fortification. He pushed back his tricorn and let his eyes scale the bluff. The soldiers would have been under a murderous fire from above. Shivering involuntarily, Sam shook his head as he thought of his father standing near this spot, weathering the storm of lead.

Fritz had told him that the second redoubt would be further along the beach. Sam unknowingly followed the path his father had trodden those years before. He approached, just as Samuel had, using the folds of ground to shield himself from the second redoubt. Bits of metal and scattered cloth told him that fighting had occurred here as well. Fritz had shared that it was somewhere between these redoubts that it had happened, but Sam felt nothing as he passed the spot where his father had met his end.

Coming over a fold of ground, the second redoubt appeared. No militia waited to greet Sam with a volley, but he could almost feel the musket balls brushing past his ears. No Indian war cry rang from the grass, but he turned as if to meet an ambush just the same. He gave ground in the face of phantom warriors while grasping an imaginary musket. After smiting a brute only his mind could conjure, Sam turned on his heal and retreated, running as if a demon pursued. It wasn't difficult to let his footing fail, and he sprawled onto the sand in a heap. Slowly, he rolled onto his back and looked skyward.

Is this where it happened, he asked himself?

The hairs on his neck stood up. Someone was watching. Was it a spirit from beyond spying on him? In a quick movement, Sam rolled to his knee and withdrew his hatchet from its loop. Charles Langlade stood ten paces away.

No turn of chance had brought them together on that obscure shoreline. Sam had felt the tug of fate the first night he saw the man in the Tun Tavern, when Langlade's eyes flashed recognition upon seeing him. Since learning that Langlade had fought at Beauport, Sam had swallowed a dozen questions for lack of opportunity to ask them. But he chose to remain silent now and let the newcomer speak first.

"Sam," the half Ottawa, half Frenchman greeted.

"*Monsieur* Langlade," Sam greeted, without dropping his hatchet back through its loop. He stood and brushed the sand from himself methodically, then looked at the newcomer. "I would say I'm surprised to see you out here, but that would be a lie."

"Charles, please."

Sam gave a mocking smile and twirled his hatchet with a flourish. "Very well, Charles. To what do I owe the pleasure of your company? This isn't exactly the *Place-Royale,*" he said, referencing the city's square. "But I believe it's a spot you know quite well."

"I saw you walking," Langlade offered. "I've been looking for a moment to speak with you, and I thought I'd found it. But when I saw you leave the city, I suspected that you might be coming here, so I decided to follow."

"Back to your old hunting grounds?"

Langlade looked over the ground as if he was stepping into a memory. "I've been here before, yes."

Sam nodded and looked down at his hatchet, running his thumb absentmindedly across the blade to test its sharpness. The steel was honed to a lethally fine edge. "I've also been wishing to speak with you for quite some time, Charles."

Langlade said nothing. It was his turn to wait patiently for the other man to speak.

"You led an Ottawa war band on this ground during the siege," Sam said flatly, needing to fill the void.

"*Oui,*" Langlade confirmed after only a moment's silence.

"An Ottawa war band that killed many British soldiers."

"*Oui.*"

"One of whom..." Sam sighed. "Was my father."

Langlade's chin rose, and he gave a firm nod, making it clear this was no revelation to him.

"It does not surprise you to find that my father fought here?" Sam asked, keeping his emotions at bay.

Langlade didn't answer. He turned his back and walked towards the river a ways, where he knelt and scooped a handful of coarse sand, letting it drain through his fingers to be carried away on the breeze. Finally, he said, "I've seen his face many nights, when I lie awake looking for sleep. It was a face I never imagined I'd see again in this world, especially not in a tavern in Philadelphia."

A tremor went through Sam. "You sound like a haunted man, Charles. I pray you tell me why that is."

"Haunted?" Langlade ruminated. "*Non,* I would choose a different word."

"And what would that be?"

"*Je suis mystifie*," Langlade said, his eyes taking in the ground.

"I'm sorry, Charles," Sam huffed, "but if you wish to speak French, I'm not the man to converse with. Perhaps my brother can decipher your words. He's much more worldly than I."

"Would you like to know how he died?" Langlade asked, his tone light as a feather.

Though he could see the storm coming, the question still hit Sam like a thunderclap. His knuckles turned white around the hatchet's haft, and he took a step toward Langlade before checking himself. "I would tread lightly, Charles. No good may come of this."

"From the truth? I disagree."

It was a question Sam dreaded hearing the answer to, but the desire to know moved his tongue. "How?"

"He died a brave man," Langlade answered.

Thoughts from black recesses pushed Sam to take another step toward the vulnerable Langlade. Staring at the man's back, images of the hatchet buried in the muscle and sinew between the shoulder blades played in Sam's head. He could see the blood spilling in the sand as the life escaped those dark eyes.

"Did you kill him?" Sam asked, his hatchet rising as he stepped forward.

Langlade brushed the sand from his hands and slowly stood, keeping his eyes on the river. He chose to ignore Sam's slow approach, and the weapon he held ready.

Nobody would ever find him, a voice whispered to Sam from nowhere, as if it had carried on the wind. He tried to ignore it, but the voice grew steadier and clearer as he neared Langlade. *He killed your father. You can't be blamed for revenge.* Until it finally screamed, *Kill him!*

"I did not kill your father, Sam," Langlade said softly.

The voice returned to its dark hole. Sam was left standing in confusion behind Langlade. He held the hatchet poised as if to strike, frozen in the air. Tears he didn't know he was shedding ran down his cheeks. "What?"

"Your father." Langlade turned, not at all alarmed by the position he found the young man in. "He took his own life before capture."

The hatchet fell to Sam's side. With a pleading look, he asked, "Before capture?"

Langlade nodded. "I saw your father lay low a great warrior of my tribe, a man who had taken the scalps of many English and Iroquois. I wanted nothing more than to avenge this man and come to grips with your father, but I was first engaged in the dispatch of some poor souls. *Les Anglais* started their retreat before I could cross the killing ground. I cursed, for the warrior he'd killed was a close friend. But a shot brought your father down as he retreated. I saw my chance to take his scalp."

Sam felt a flash of fear. The thought of this man stalking down the beach would freeze the blood of the Devil. "Then he killed himself?"

Langlade didn't answer. Instead he turned and moved to another spot, crouching down again. "When I came through the grass, he was here," Langlade said definitively, running his hand over the ground. "His companion had fled, and he was waiting with a small pistol at the ready. The barrels were pointed here." Langlade prodded his heart. "I knew he would not miss from such a short distance. Our eyes met, and we looked at each other for what felt like minutes. While I waited for the trigger's pull, his face took root in my soul. But he never fired."

"He spared you," Sam whispered.

Langlade nodded, slowly standing and turning to Sam. "I was covered in war paint, my hair greased, my knife poised. He could not have mistaken my intent. He could not have thought me anything else than what I was that day: a warrior of the Anishinaabek, the people. Yet he did not fire."

Langlade gestured to a spot. "Another warrior came through the grass there, his war club in hand. Your father didn't hesitate for one beat of his heart. He turned his pistol and shot the man down in an instant."

"Then?" Sam asked, his voice catching.

"Then..." Langlade sighed. "He had one more barrel. He could kill me or use it on himself. I gave him the time he needed to choose. He chose to escape the fate that awaited those we captured. It was the right choice. I do not say that because it spared my life. Prisoners do not fare well under our custody, nor do they in yours."

Sam had long dreaded that his father's death had been a slow and cruel one. That was to be expected for anyone caught alive. The rules of the great game played by the white man and the Indian along the frontier were written in the blood of the tortured. Now that he knew it was a sharp, merciful death, a great weight lifted from Sam's soul.

"Did you desecrate his body?" Sam asked, knowing the horrors committed on the dead by both sides in the heart of this vast continent.

Langlade didn't hesitate. "*Non*," he said. "A warrior takes only scalps he has earned."

"But you would have?"

"*Absolument.*" Langlade bore his eyes into Sam. "If I had killed your father in battle, it would have been an honor to take his scalp for my belt. He denied me that honor."

The longing in Langlade's voice for a lost trophy touched a nerve of fear in Sam. He looked around the empty beach, then up to the vacant bluffs. There wasn't another soul in sight, and certainly not one within the distance of a scream. He felt the weight of the hatchet in his hand. It gave him some confidence. He would at least have a chance if the man had a mind to strike.

Tears still running, Sam asked, "So are you going to take my scalp, Charles, because he deprived you of his? The son's will be adequate compensation for the father's?"

Langlade's face softened, and a look of sorrow filled his eyes. It was the first emotion the man had shown. "Your father held my life in his hands. For reasons known only to him and the Great Spirit, he did not take it," Langlade said, and put his hand to his heart. "I bear no ill will to his surviving blood."

The tension in Sam's arm slackened. With a sense of shame at thinking the man capable of so petty a revenge, he dropped the hatchet back through its loop and looked out on the river. "How long have you known he was my father?"

Langlade turned with him to look at the water. "I told you," he said. "I saw his face on you in Philadelphia. I knew that instant. You are your father's son, Sam."

"In image only," Sam said, mortified at the thoughts that had risen within him. "My father was the kindest, most virtuous man I have ever known. He would be destroyed by what went through my head only minutes ago." Sam turned to Langlade. "I think I may have been of a mind to kill you, Charles."

Langlade could only shrug. "I can't blame you. Revenge is every man's privilege. But I'm afraid I'm not so noble that I would have gone quietly."

Sam nodded, and said, "I would never have thought you would."

After long moments of watching the river, Sam said, "Thank you for telling me how he met his end, and for not mutilating his corpse. But that is all I can muster. I doubt you seek forgiveness for being his foe, and I cannot give it."

Langlade said, "I owed it to the man to tell his son that he died bravely. I have done that. I seek no pardon for acts commited in war, and only the divine can truly forgive us of our sins."

"Are you a Christian, Charles?" Sam asked, facing him.

Langlade looked Sam in the eye and smiled. "*Oui*. And a pagan, and a heathen, and many other things. My mother told me of the old stories, of Gitchi Manitou, the Great Spirit, and the forming of the world. My father taught me of Christ on his cross. The woods taught me of the divinity of nature. I choose to be many things."

"You make it sound as if a man can be anything here."

"*Oui.*" Langlade nodded. "A man can be anything he likes in this place, away from the old world."

The pair turned back to the river and watched it flow for several more minutes, each thinking his own thoughts. Langlade finally cleared his throat and said, "There is something else I must speak with you about."

Sam wiped his eyes on his sleeve. "I feel I've had enough conversation for one day, Charles. Forgive me if I wish to be alone now," he said.

"It's about your brother."

Sam chuckled. "Are you worried that he will seek revenge if I tell him of your proximity to our father's death? You've seen the boy. You'd be in more danger from a strong gust of wind."

"Never underestimate a man's fortitude when it's fed by dealings of the heart," Langlade answered. "But that is not my concern."

"Then what?"

"It has to do with my daughter."

Sam laughed loudly at that. Langlade did not.

"You've noticed, then?" Sam asked.

For the first time, anger filled Langlade's voice. "Do you think me blind?" he asked. "Do you think a man with such a daughter cannot see the wolves circling? And what's worse, one of the wolves seems to have drawn her fancy."

"William! A wolf!" Sam guffawed. "More like a puppy dog."

Langlade nodded. "Perhaps. Perhaps that's why she's so stricken by him."

Sam shook his head. "I think you are a father who sees more than what's there. It's just a harmless dalliance between two young people stuck aboard ship together."

"I pray that may yet be," Langlade allowed, "but I have seen countless letters written in your brother's hand."

Sam smiled. "William has always been dangerous with a quill."

"What I've read casts a shadow over plans that have been in place since Domitilde was a babe, plans of greater consequence than the happiness of two young fools, especially with all that's befallen my home these past few years."

"Plans?" Sam asked, his intrigue rising.

"Domitilde has an important role to fill. She is to marry."

Sam shrugged. "Most young women do."

"She is to marry the son of Minavavana on the coming summer's solstice."

Sam scrunched his brow. "Am I supposed to know that name? It means nothing to me."

Langlade smiled at Sam's ignorance of the man who commanded the respect, or fear, of all throughout the Upper Country. "*Le Grand Saulteur*, Minavavana is a great chief of the Chippewa. His son, Kinonchamek, is a proud warrior. Many scalps have adorned his belt. Kinonchamek's union with Domitilde will ensure the continued peace between our two peoples, tightening the bond between the Chippewa and Ottawa for another generation. That bond needs to remain intact. The coming years will not be easy for our people, even less so if we're squabbling amongst ourselves." Langlade stared directly into Sam's eyes. "For the sake of your brother's life and my peoples' future, Domitilde must marry Kinonchamek."

Sam shook his head, annoyed. "As I said, it's a dalliance. Nothing will come of it. Your daughter will tire of the beanpole soon enough."

It was Langlade's turn to chuckle. "I wish I were as foolish as you," he said, causing Sam to redden. "I was once young, and remember the fire that burns inside when we see the one we covet." He looked back out onto the river. "The one I coveted was forbidden to me through arrangements much like the one Domitilde is in. That only seemed to increase the desires on both sides."

Sam sighed, frustrated with the conversation. "And did you come to your senses?" he asked.

"*Non*." Langlade turned back to face him. "I made her my wife and the mother of my daughter."

Sam winced. "And *Madam* Langlade's betrothed?"

A hard look filled Langlade's dark eyes. "He did as any man with honor stained would. He challenged me to fight."

Sam swallowed and turned away. The man who would openly challenge Langlade was more foolish or more courageous than he. "And?" Sam asked, knowing the answer.

"And his scalp was the first to grace my belt," Langlade informed him, not a touch of boastfulness in his cold voice. But the implication was clear. William would pursue Domitilde at the risk of his life, be it from Langlade or Kinonchamek, or both.

Knowing he needed to try a different tact, Sam turned back and said, "My brother is drunk on the looks of a pretty girl. Such is nature. It's a story so old it's written in stone. But nothing more will come of it. You have my word."

After several breaths, Langlade nodded, aware that was the most assurance he'd likely receive. "I hope so. I have already spoken with my daughter and forbidden contact between the two of them."

Sam shook his head and smiled. "Now you're playing the fool, Charles."

Langlade frowned in anger.

"You yourself said that the forbidden fruit is often the most pleasing to the eye," Sam explained.

Recognizing his error, Langlade gave a begrudging nod. "That may be," he said, "but if you warn your brother of the consequences, maybe William will see some reason. He seems to have a sharp mind. Inform him that Minavavana and Kinonchamek are not ones to be crossed." Langlade paused. "Nor am I."

And there was the threat, finally spoken. It had to be answered.

Summoning all his courage, Sam took a deliberate step and closed the distance between them, coming within arm's reach. "There's only one thing I have left in this life, Charles, and that's my brother," Sam said. "I will do everything in my power to assure his continued health. Any man who wishes him ill will have to step over my corpse to do so."

Sam waited for an outburst, perhaps even a physical strike. None came. Langlade's expression remained frozen.

Exhaling in relief, Sam added, "Now, I *will* quash this inconvenience for you and your people. I do it because I see no benefit in the remnants of my family forming any attachment to the godforsaken country we travel to. Do not presume my efforts are made out of fear of this Indian prince, his illustrious father, or you."

That last part was a lie.

Langlade actually smiled. "I would never presume to think such a thing," he said.

"Good," Sam said, and nodded, backing away to once more look out on the river.

After a drawn-out silence filled with contemplation, Sam asked, "What was done with the corpses?"

"They were given over to the river," Langlade answered flatly.

Sam nodded, then dug into a pocket he'd sewn on the inside breast of his shirt. He withdrew the small silver medal that Fritz had given him in the graveyard, and held it aloft. The worn image of the man bearing the child shown in the sunlight.

"St. Christopher," Langlade said.

Sam turned to Langlade. "You know this image?"

"The Christ bearer," Langlade answered. "He was said to have carried the baby Jesus across a river on his shoulders. He is the patron saint of soldiers and travelers."

Sam scrunched his brow.

"Are you Catholic, Sam?" Langlade asked.

Shaking his head, Sam examined the medal. "There have been no Avery papists for generations. But my family has passed this down since before anyone could tell," he said.

"And your father left it for you?" Langlade asked.

"Yes."

"And you do not wear it," Langlade said.

"I haven't been able to bring myself to don it," Sam said. "I'm not my father. In truth, I was of a mind to return it to him." Sam gestured to the river.

Langlade made a clicking sound. "*Non.* You mustn't. Your father passed it on to you. You must keep it."

Sam thought in silence for a long moment.

"You must watch over your brother," Langlade said, "and St. Christopher will watch over you."

Sam nodded once, then left Langlade's side and walked to the shallow riverbank. Looking out over the sun-flecked water, he gave a silent prayer of hope that his parents were at peace with each other, and that they would watch over him and William.

Then he dropped the medal over his neck.

***

The bateau struggled against the current as it pushed upriver towards Montreal. Sam and William sat together on the same bench, heaving against the same oar, in rhythm with their compatriots. A squadron of small boats surrounded them, spreading for almost a mile as the two companies pushed further into the interior. Sam sweated from the strain even though the early fall weather was quite pleasant.

Sensing an opportunity for a semblance of privacy while the other men were lost to their daydreams as they pulled at the oars, Sam said, "I need you to do something for me, William."

"I'm already doing most of the pulling," William said merrily, feeling the elation that came with hard work on a fine day.

Sam scoffed at that as he heaved. "I wish your back was as strong as your wit."

"What may I do for you, brother?"

Not relishing the task at hand, Sam spoke the words quickly. "You need to stop your correspondence with Domitilde."

Only the sound of the oars and the heavy breathing of the men greeted that for several moments.

"Do you hear me?" Sam huffed.

"Why?" William asked, with an edge to his voice.

Tempted to say something sharp, Sam took a breath before saying, "She is betrothed to another."

"She's told me."

Sam looked at him. "And you persist?"

"Of course I do." William smiled. "You've seen her."

Sam couldn't argue with that. He nodded. "I have. But it's useless to pine after something you can't have. *Monsieur* Langlade has come to me personally to request that you leave his daughter alone."

"He knows?" William asked in surprise.

"Of course he knows," Sam said, raising his voice. "The entire company knows. I believe the entire garrison of Quebec knew. I wouldn't be surprised if Lieutenant Colonel Bouquet is aware of your efforts to win the pretty Domitilde from all the way back in Lancaster."

William sat quietly for several minutes, until he finally whispered, "She doesn't love him."

"Hah!" Sam exclaimed. "Since when has that ever mattered?"

"She's told me she might love me."

"Through her letters? Did she admire the way that apple in your throat bobbed up and down while you read, as she looked down on you from the quarterdeck? Moving awfully fast, this little lass."

"We have had liaisons," William said. He smiled, more to himself than anything.

The oar almost dropped from Sam's hands. He looked at his brother with wide eyes. "Have you lay with her, William?"

William returned Sam's hard stare. "If I have, I would never tell you."

Sam shook his head in disbelief. "By Jove, William, has it occurred to you that this trollop might only be entertaining you because she does not want to marry this Kinon…whatever his name is?"

"Do not call her a trollop!" William leaned his boney shoulder into Sam.

Restraining himself from physical violence, Sam looked around the boat. It was clear their conversation was drawing the attention of others. Several of the men feigned indifference as they pulled at their oars, their eyes wandering along the wooded shoreline. But their ears were cocked to take in every word.

Sam lowered his voice and said, "She is promised to an important man, a man who from everything I've heard of him would be more than capable of shortening your lanky frame by the length of a head. It is my duty to protect you and I will do so by keeping you out of danger of your own making. You will stop your correspondence, and by God you will not meet her again."

Only the sound of splashing oars met that declaration. Sam thought about telling the boy of Langlade's involvement in their father's death. Maybe that would turn the lad off of Domitilde. But no, he decided William didn't need to be reminded of that pain while feeling this new one.

"Do you understand?" Sam asked.

Dropping his voice, William said, "You're not father just because you now wear his medal."

Sam stared into his brother's face. "I am not. But I am all you have left."

William looked to the shoreline, clearly finished with the conversation. Sam looked to the lead boats. He thought he could just make out the dress of the beauty Domitilde. A feeling of sorrow gripped him. He took no joy in depriving his brother of such a girl, but if it would keep William's head on his shoulders, that was what he had to do.

***

As the air chilled with the onset of autumn, so too did Sam and William's encounters. They said no more than two words to each other as the party reached the great lake Ontario. William made sure to take the oar of a boat without his brother each morning. Each night, William slept at the far end of the tent that he was compelled to share with his brother. The sleeping forms of their tentmates served as a barrier to any effort of reconciliation Sam might make.

All the while, Sam kept watch over his brother's movements as best he could. He stayed awake deep into the chilly northern nights to assure himself that William made no nocturnal wanderings. He volunteered to be on the woodcutting parties that William had been picked for on the chance he'd use them for a tryst in the deep woods that edged up against the lake. He followed his brother from a distance as William took walks along the shore after their evening meals. He watched as William read his volumes, always vigilant for a slipped letter or the drop of a note. William, meanwhile, was always aware of his brother's surveillance, and angered by it all the more.

As the party arrived at Fort Niagara, the chill between the brothers warmed with the arrival of an Indian Summer in the Upper Country. The pleasantness of the weather encouraged a few pleasantries to pass between them. The first real words exchanged, beyond the minimum necessary for their daily interactions, occurred as the party left behind their boats and portaged around the massive falls. The raw power of the Great Lakes draining before them left Sam and William reverent in front of the altar of nature, and they couldn't help but share in the moment of awe together, as brothers should. By the time they reached Lake Eerie, Sam and William were joking and laughing as if their unpleasant conversation on the St. Lawrence had never occurred. It seemed that William – as Sam was sure would happen – had lost his youthful passion for the Indian maiden, or at least had seen some reason. Sam had even convinced himself that all was right as the company boarded the sloop *Huron* for the journey to Detroit.

***

Late one night, as the sloop pushed along under a covering of stars so brilliant they'd be thought unfathomable if not witnessed, Sam awoke from his slumber on deck. The blanket that his brother slept on lay next to him, but William was not there. Using the light of the numberless stars, Sam made out the form of his brother leaning against the gunwale.

Sam tried to tell himself that his brother was only taking in the bounty of beauty glistening over the sloop. He tried to tell himself that William was only admiring the work of the Creator as the boat seemed to sail through the heavens, the stars shining above the vessel while their reflections danced below.

But that wasn't where William's gaze fell. William was looking across the calm water, his eyes never leaving the sloop that held Domitilde.

Sam lay his head back down on the hard deck. He closed his eyes and tried not to think of the dangers that awaited the Averys on the other side of the star-filled horizon.

Ch. 6

Detroit. October 1762

Major Henry Gladwin looked out over the parade ground in front of the commandant's quarters. A pine pole with a Union Jack hanging limply from its top rose from the mud between him and the few hundred residents and Indians who had decided to come and witness the theatrics. To his right, the skeletal remains of two companies that had garrisoned Detroit since its fall stood at attention with smiles on their hallow faces. These men would soon be bound for England. Those who survived the journey – and Gladwin would have wagered then and there that not more than half would make it – would go from the fringes of civilization to its very bosom. No wonder the wretches looked so happy.

To his left, the slovenly but good-natured Captain Campbell squinted in the dull light of the gray fall day. Campbell would be staying on as Gladwin's second-in-command. If the man held any rancor that his exile in the wilderness would continue, he did not show it.

"These Frenchies look as if they've gone native," Gladwin remarked to Campbell in a half-whisper, making the polite conversation required of a gentleman.

The observation rang true. Many of the French citizens dressed in a way that made them hardly distinguishable from the Ottawa, Chippewa, and Huron mingling among them. Several brats that had to be of half Indian blood darted about, and Gladwin spotted more than one Frenchman leading a native wife with a baby on her hip. Only a few of the wealthier citizens could be described as wearing anything close to European dress, and even they would have been deemed positively savage if they'd dared to stroll down the Champs-Elysees in their outdated garments.

"A hearty, honorable people, Major," Campbell said, and beamed. "The French have given us almost no trouble since the *Fleurs-de-lis* came down. I would never have thought it in a thousand years. They've taken to King George's rule better than we could have possibly hoped for."

"Surprising, for such a rough-looking lot," Gladwin remarked.

"They know who controls the trade now," Campbell explained. "Their furs will have to sail on our ships to our markets. Control a man by his purse strings, eh, Major?"

"And the Indians?" Gladwin asked.

Campbell cleared his throat to give himself a moment. "We've had no major issues, sir."

"No *Major* issues? That would imply that there have been minor issues."

"Indeed, sir. To be expected with this sort of thing. These Indians have known the benevolence of only King Louis or his father the Sun King for the past hundred years. They are nervous about how His Majesty King George plans to rule over his new empire. They want to know that the old traditions will be kept. They want to know that the gifts their European fathers bestowed for generations will still be given."

"They'll have to take that up with General Amherst," Gladwin said dismissively.

"Sir?"

A flash of annoyance crossed Gladwin's face. "General Amherst has seen fit to end the practice of gift giving to the natives. A terrible waste of money, don't you see?"

"I don't see, sir," Campbell said, and shook his large head.

"These savages," Gladwin said, and nodded in the direction of some Indians, "have been playing us off against one another for far too long. King Louis was scared of old Georgie and young Georgie, and they of him. All the while, the Indian sat in the middle and traded his tomahawk to the king who gave the most. I don't blame the fellows. It was a very profitable enterprise, especially when the French had us over the coals early on."

Gladwin looked at Campbell. "But that's over now," the major said firmly. "The French are beaten. The colonists are overflowing with gratitude that we have vanquished their old enemy beyond the mountains and kept the savages from their doors. There's no one left on this bloody continent to fight. We don't need the Indians' tomahawks anymore."

Campbell thought for several seconds, forming his response. "The Indian way is for the heads of the clans and tribes to bestow gifts and favors upon the men who fight for them. The French wisely chose to replicate that system," he said. Then he gestured to several Chippewa warriors leaning against their muskets. "These men do not farm for their livelihood. They hunt and trap pelts to trade for powder and muskets so as to be ready to make war. They are only kept in passivity by the practice of tribute."

"I agree with you wholeheartedly, Captain," Gladwin said dully, "but General Amherst, from the comfort and bliss of fine houses and late-night soirees in New York, does not."

"I fear that is a grave error, sir. There have already been rumblings among the natives. There's been tell of a Delaware prophet stoking the people–"

"Yes, yes, Captain, I've heard all about him. There's always some prophet in some backwoods inciting the savages to throw us into the sea." Gladwin smiled at Campbell. "Yet here we are, a thousand miles from the nearest civilized hearth."

Campbell ignored that. "A Chippewa chief has come down the lake from the north. He has made it clear that he intends to speak with you. I fear much of it will have to do with the grievance I've already put forward."

"I shall see him in my own time," Gladwin answered. "In the meantime…" The major gestured to several warriors staring back at him with looks of boredom. "I think it's high time these natives learned to submit their backs to the plow and make something of this land they were given, instead of letting it rot in neglect. Enough squabbling and carousing and drinking. These lads need to become diligent, God-fearing subjects of His Majesty."

Captain Campbell made to say something, but the sound of fifes and drums stopped him.

"Ah!" Gladwin smiled. "My companies have disembarked."

***

The Averys marched into Detroit through the west gate of the palisade. Sam and William stepped in time with their mates down the Rue Ste. Anne, marching ramrod straight for the sake of the citizenry. Through their peripheral vision, they took in what had been the western bulwark of the French Empire in North America.

The fortified village had been hewn out of a cedar forest that spread to the east bank of the river that joined the lakes Huron and Eerie. The felled trees became the gray spines, bones, and skins of the buildings that made up the settlement. The place looked as if it could hold several hundred souls comfortably within its walls, and in times of trouble it might be able to accommodate a couple thousand from the surrounding countryside. The soldiers passed guardhouses and magazines, a large Catholic church, and storehouses that butted up to gardens surrounding small cabins. Chickens scattered from the company's path as they tramped down the packed earth street. Dairy cows mooed in their pens next to rough hovels, begging the newcomers to relieve their swollen udders.

The residents watching the troops' entrance looked as rough-hewn as their dwellings. These were not the more refined folk of Quebec, nor even Montreal. These people lived on the edge of the world, and they looked as if they could not only survive the wilderness but also prosper there. Sam couldn't help but notice the large amount of Indians within the walls. They mingled easily with their French counterparts.

It didn't take long for the companies to reach the parade ground that was surrounded by onlookers. Major Gladwin's company smartly wheeled left until their ranks were at the far side of the flagstaff. Etherington's company marched on until it took up the south side of the parade ground, to the left of Major Gladwin and Captain Campbell.

"*Kompanieee*, halt!" Fritz barked.

The men's left feet fell softly one more time, then their right feet slammed to the dirt, the sound rippling through the courtyard.

"To the left face!" Fritz ordered.

As one, the company pivoted to face left.

Sam couldn't help but feel a sense of pride at the show they'd given the locals and the rabble of King's soldiers across the way. Those men, in their tattered and faded uniforms, looked as if they'd been lost in the wilderness for much too long. *That should help keep the frogs in line,* he thought.

If he'd really bothered looking, all he would have seen on the locals' faces would have been looks of mild amusement, with boredom bordering on contempt from the Indians.

Campbell turned deferentially to Major Gladwin as their men looked on at attention. The bovine captain bowed gracefully and saluted with his hat. "Major Gladwin, I transfer the command of His Majesty's garrison of Detroit to you, sir," he said.

Gladwin looked as if he'd been presented with a gift he had no interest in receiving, one that would soon be exiled to the deepest recesses of his largest closet back in London, but he managed to smile with forced grace. "Thank you, Captain Campbell," he said, and offered a slight bow.

The companies snapped their muskets in front of their faces in salute. Major Gladwin gave a weak wave of his hand, which could have been taken as an acknowledgment by some. The major was just about to dismiss the men when a scene he never would have imagined conceivable unfolded in front of his eyes.

An Indian, a noble looking Indian but an Indian, regally strolled onto the parade ground, followed by a handful of lackeys. The vein in Gladwin's temple seemed about to burst as he hissed, "What is this, Campbell?"

Campbell's jowls quivered as he searched for words. Sam heard the Captain say, "It's Chief Minavavana, sir, of the Chippewa. It appears he's leading several notables from the local tribes. That tall fellow there is the Ottawa War Chief Pontiac, and there's also–"

"I didn't ask who!" Gladwin spat. "I asked *what*! What is this nonsense?"

"It looks as if he means to speak with you, sir."

Looking as if he were close to ordering a bayonet charge, Gladwin struggled to straighten himself and regain his composure. He stepped forward and puffed out his chest, meaning to make a good first impression with these important men. He chose to remain where he stood, forcing the Indians to cross the vast ground between his men's muskets. The weathered Indian Minavavana came to a halt five paces from the major.

So this is Domitilde's soon-to-be father-in-law, Sam thought, *or whatever it is the Indians call it*. Not so much imposing as he was stately, the man looked placid as he stood before the King's representative.

Much more imposing were the two warriors behind him. Both were over six foot, and well-muscled to boot. Their firm chests were bare but for the ceremonial blankets they wore almost as togas. Their pates were shaved in the manner of their tribes, and what hair remained was done up with feathers and grease. Their features, in line with the inherited traits of their people, were clean and sharp. Sam correctly guessed that the younger warrior had to be the great chief's son – Domitilde's betrothed – Kinonchamek.

Seeing the man in the flesh, Sam could only pray that his brother's pursuit of Domitilde had truly ended. No good could come to the Averys if that giant was even aware of William's existence, much less the boy's overtures to his woman.

Sam's eyes fell on the Langlade family, who stood with the other prominent French citizens of the settlement. Unsurprisingly for a woman who had engaged in a summer tryst or two with a lowly private, Domitilde showed no signs of joy at seeing her future husband. She pointedly avoided Kinonchamek's many attempts to catch her eye, much to Sam's dread.

The name Pontiac meant nothing to Sam, and he hardly wasted another glance on the man as he continued to size up Kinonchamek.

Gladwin and Minavavana looked each other over in frosty silence. It seemed as if they might be trying to outlast each other as to who would speak first, or perhaps the Indian waited for an exchange of gifts, which by order of General Amherst would never come. The hundreds of people – white, red, and in between – could only wait as the two men faced off. A gulf of mere paces separated the major and the chief in the physical world, but leagues and leagues divided them in everything else.

"Englishman!" Minavavana bellowed, his voice confident and loud.

Gladwin flinched a hair, but recovered quickly.

"Englishman!" Minavavana continued. "You know the French King is our father. He promised to be such, and we, in return, promised to be his children. This promise we have kept."

If Major Gladwin was shocked by the chief's words, or the eloquence and fluency of their delivery, he showed no sign of it. Sam figured the gentleman was just struck dumb by the whole occurrence.

"Englishman," Minavavana said, and pointed to the major's chest, "it is you that has made war with our father. You are his enemy; and how then could you have the boldness to venture among us, his children? You know that his enemies are ours."

Sam's eyes, along with the rest of his company's, nervously wandered to the assembled French and Indians. Though they were a rabble-looking lot, they outnumbered the Regulars by a margin of perhaps three to one. It would be an easy thing for them to mob the soldiers. Many of the rabble's muskets were probably loaded, and steal glinted at their belts in the weak sunlight. Thinking they were marching into a pacified village, the soldiers' muskets were unloaded, and they didn't even have their bayonets fixed. Every Royal American on the parade ground could be slaughtered within half an hour if the Frogs and Indians put their backs into it.

"Although you have conquered the French," Minavavana continued, "you have not yet conquered us! We are not your slaves. These lakes, woods, and mountains were left to us by our ancestors. They are our inheritance, and we will part with them to none."

It might have been his imagination, but Sam thought that several of the native warriors in the crowd had coiled into more aggressive stances. Major Gladwin's hand, through its own accord or that of its master, grasped the hilt of his sword.

"Our father, the King of France, employed our young men to make war upon your nation," Minavavana continued. "In this warfare, many of them have been killed, and it is our custom to retaliate until such time as the spirits slain are satisfied. Now the spirits of the slain are to be satisfied in either of two ways. The first is by spilling of the blood of the nation by which they fell. The other is by covering the bodies of the dead, and thus allaying the resentment of their relations. This is done by presents."

"Sam," William whispered, his voice full of fear.

"Easy, William," Sam soothed, while his own knees shook. "Hold steady."

"Your king," Minavavana scoffed, "has never sent us any presents, nor entered into any treaty with us. Until he does these things, must we consider that we have no other father, nor friend, among the white men? Must we consider that we are still at war?"

The question settled heavily over the ground. Not a soul seemed to move, nor even breathe, as all waited for the answer. Fritz's knuckles were white around the shaft of his sergeant's pike. In the deep silence, Sam thought he could hear the hearts of his comrades as they rattled in their rib-cages.

"If you do not come with the intention to make war," Minavavana sang in a softened tone, "if you truly come in peace, you will trade with us, and supply us with the necessities of which we are in want. If you lay presents over our slain warriors, we shall regard you as a brother. You may sleep tranquilly, without fear of the Chippewa, if you pledge to do these things. Until then, as a token of our friendship, we present you with this pipe."

Pontiac appeared at Minavavana's side with a packed tomahawk pipe. A collective sigh escaped from the soldiers as Minavavana lit the pipe with a match cord. Many of the French citizens looked just as relieved as the soldiers. A way out had been provided. All Gladwin had to do was keep his bloody mouth shut and smoke from the pipe. The man was at least smart enough to do that, Sam hoped.

Hesitantly, Gladwin accepted the pipe that had just graced Minavavana's lips. It seemed only a great effort kept him from wiping the tip with his sleeve, and he cautiously pulled from the long stem. The major spasmodically coughed the smoke from his lungs while the Indians tried not to notice his shame.

There would be no slaughter on the Detroit parade ground that day.

***

With one last swing of his ax, Sam felled the old cedar. His fellows immediately swarmed it and began chopping at its various branches. Sam joined William in attacking a rather thick limb while Fritz watched over the woodcutting party, the sergeant's epaulet on his coat saving him from manual labor.

William, his queued blond hair matted from sweat, leaned in close to his brother. "I'm leaving, Sam," he whispered.

Sam didn't flinch. "Fritz will have your hide if you feign sickness. These trees need to be cleared back from the fort. Might as well break our backs now and get it over with. We don't want to linger here till winter. That Indian chief's words set my hairs on end," he said.

"That's not what I meant."

"What did you mean?" Sam grunted, swinging his ax into the cedar.

"I'm leaving the Army."

"To go where?" Sam laughed, still concentrating on the wood.

"Anywhere," William huffed.

Sam tried to choose his next words carefully. "I know you don't like the Army, William, but it's only two more years. We'll get through it together. I won't let them skin you like they did me. I promise."

"It's not only that. Domitilde wants to leave."

Sam shook his head in frustration. "I knew you'd still been seeing her. You've been too happy of late. Damn me for letting it continue."

William ignored him. "She wants to marry. She says she loves me."

Sam sneered. "Christ."

"It's true!" William croaked, causing several lads to look in their direction. William dropped his voice down to a whisper. "She'll not marry Kinonchamek. She does not love him. She says she'd rather take her own life."

"This girl sounds as if she's made for the theater," Sam grunted, swinging a heavy blow. "Or perhaps you've just filled her head with too many of those silly stories from your books."

William tried to ignore him.

Sam continued, "Even now, after seeing that brute in the flesh, you'd dare try to take his woman from him? I think he'd hardly break a sweat snuffing out both our lives."

"I will not leave her to that man," William vowed.

Sam nudged his brother down the trunk of the tree, where the pair began hacking at another limb. "So," he said, and sighed, "you'll drag that poor girl off into the wilderness? Will you find some cave to make a home? Will you survive on nuts and berries?" Sam laughed at the thought. "You'll be dead with the first freeze."

William straightened. "We will go to the Iroquois lands in New York. Otayonih said that he would take me in if I ever chose to leave the Army."

"Said that during one of your long talks, did he?"

"*Wilhelm!*" Fritz barked.

William flinched and returned to chopping at the cedar. After a few moments, he said, "He did. The Iroquois have taken in many deserters."

"Nice of them," Sam scoffed. "They'll just turn you into a bloody savage for the trouble."

"You know they're not savages."

Several minutes passed where the only sounds were the grunts of the men and the strikes of ax heads. Sam finally asked, "You would leave the Army, leave me, for a girl you barely know?"

"Come with us," William begged.

The words rattled in Sam's head longer than they should have, but the stupidity of deserting and the tightness of the scars on his back soon flushed them out. They would be caught. They would be striped. They would likely die from their wounds. Sam certainly would, it being his second date with the Cat.

"They'll run you down in half a day," Sam said.

"I can run better than any man in the company," William said proudly.

"Aye, but can your woman?"

William had no answer for that.

"And it won't be men of the Sixtieth chasing you," Sam added. "Kinonchamek will be after his woman, and Langlade after his daughter. You'll not outrun them."

"We shall try!" William said.

"And if by some miracle you do make it to New York, you'll live the rest of your lives as rogues. No, I will not be part of such folly."

"Sam," William said, and turned to his brother.

"Private Avery!" Fritz screamed.

William started and went back to swinging his ax.

Sam didn't look at him, but he said, "If you leave the Army, you leave me. You're going to abandon your only family for some cunny?"

Only silence greeted that.

The pair redoubled their efforts against the wood, both of them using their axes to release their anger. Sam tried to forget his brother's words, attributing them to a young man struck dumb by the first pair of tits he'd seen. He hoped the threat of their separation would be enough to forestall William's desertion. He convinced himself it must. William could never survive without him.

***

William made to desert only three nights later. Sam awoke to the sound of the tent's canvas flap being furtively drawn back. In the thin light of a half moon, William slipped from the tent and was gone. Sam knew this was no nocturnal stumble to the latrines. William was leaving the Army, leaving him.

Sam rolled from his blanket and dropped his regimental coat over his shoulders. Without thinking, he pulled his hatchet from beneath the straw he'd been sleeping on and slipped it through the loop he'd sown specially on the coat's inside breast. Quietly, so as not to spook his brother, he pulled back the tent flap and entered the night.

The cold of the air sent a shiver through him as he watched William's faint form duck from view down an alley abutting the parade ground that had been the company's temporary bivouac. Exhaling, Sam stepped through the vapor of his own breath and stalked after him, passing the permanent soldiers' barracks that housed the yet-to-depart former garrison. Keeping William in view but staying at a distance, Sam followed through the dirt alleys between the meager buildings of the sleeping settlement. William never suspected he was being followed as he approached the palisade.

The light of a torch ahead caused Sam to slow. He ducked behind a rain barrel just as William shot a glance over his shoulder. Counting ten breaths, Sam finally risked a peek around the barrel. A torchlit sally port in the south wall of the palisade framed William's retreating lank. A rough looking corporal and a dirty private from the old garrison waited in the glow of the flame, and they greeted William as if they were expecting him.

"Hullo, gov," the corporal called merrily. "Build up your courage then?"

"She shouldn't be long," William responded, ignoring the taunt while looking about like a spooked hare.

Sam ducked back and sighed. He could hear the fear in his brother's voice, as he should. The two ruffians – like most men in the Army who hailed from the home islands – looked as if a city jail would be a known and comforting accommodation for them. *What have you gotten yourself into, William,* Sam thought? He peeked around the barrel again to get a good look, trying to decide if he should step out and end this madness before it had a chance to go further.

The arrival of a figure in a black hooded cloak stopped Sam from revealing himself. "Domitilde," he whispered to himself.

"Well, well," the corporal chortled, "this ain't the flea infested camp-follower I'd thought she'd be. Come, luv." The corporal stepped forward and reached for her hood. "Give us a proper look-see."

William swatted the man's hand away and pulled Domitilde behind him. "We had a deal," he growled, removing a coin purse from his pocket. "Are you to honor it?"

There was nothing of honor in the corporal's eyes. Sam doubted there ever had been in all the man's life. But the fury on the corporal's face at the impertinence of this pipsqueak was slowly masked over by a leering smile. The corporal finally held out his hand for the purse and said, "Alright, sonny. The coin, then we open the door."

Sam ducked back when the bedraggled private cast a skulking eye about the surroundings, but he heard the clink of metal when the coins fell.

"Right," the corporal said. "Off you two love-birds go."

The sound of the heavy door's bolt being withdrawn drew Sam to peek again. William pushed Domitilde through the small door and was gone as soon as that. But the sentries did not shut the door and bolt it after their departure.

"I can't believe you let that stripling lay hands on you, Bill," the private teased.

The corporal lashed out with speed born from a boyhood spent in the shadows of London's allies, striking the man's ear hard.

"Blimey, Bill!" the private screeched in pain. "I just can't believe you let the little twat out, is all, especially with a filly like that."

"Shut your bleedin' hole!" the corporal spat.

The private hushed and rubbed his pained ear.

"Now," the corporal said, his voice softened, "we ain't letting those two go nowhere. The forest is a dangerous place at night. And I think it's our duty to see them off."

Sam shivered.

The private squealed, "Are we gonna have some fun, Bill?" in revolting delight.

"I'm gonna have some fun," the corporal said, looking out the sally port. "If there's anything left of her when I'm through, you're welcome to it."

"What about the sergeant of the guard?"

"The sergeant's in his cups, it being our last night of watch. He won't be round to find us gone. Besides, this won't take long." The corporal eased a buck knife from his belt. "Follow me."

Sam watched the pair leave their muskets behind and slither out the sally port. He had only seconds to decide his course of action. If he alerted the sergeant of the guard, William would face the Cat for desertion and, if he survived, would hate him for the rest of his days. Sam couldn't bear that. He rounded the barrel and left the fort with all the noise of a whisper.

The red coats of the hunters bobbed through the darkness and over the open ground outside the palisade. Sam stayed close to their heels and plunged into the wood line not far behind them. The hunters, with the hubris of predators, kept their focus on the prey in front of them, allowing Sam to keep pace with little threat of discovery. The hatchet came from its loop and into his hand without thought, and he dropped his red coat in a bush as he stalked.

The pair were following a well-used trail now, and Sam was sure they were right behind William and Domitilde. They moved with increased stealth and care. Using the tricks that Otayonih had taught him, Sam slid to within yards of the pursuers. They were now well into the woods, and any screams would be muffled by the rustling of the dry, dead leaves on the surrounding trees.

The pair suddenly stopped, and Sam crouched behind a thick tree trunk.

"Who goes there?" William's fearful voice pierced the night. "I'm armed."

Sam heard one of the men step from behind cover.

"You ain't armed, sprat," the corporal said. "I got a good look at ya."

William, you damned fool, Sam thought, shaking his head that his brother hadn't even remembered to bring his hatchet, much less his musket.

"You followed us?" William choked.

The private joined his master. "We just wanted to make sure you got along safe, is all," he giggled.

"Stay back!" William barked.

"Come now, sprat," the corporal drawled, sounding as if he'd moved to the left. "If ya give us the girl, we might just let you walk out of this wood. Hell, Ol' Bill might even give ya a turn if you help hold her down."

William gasped. "You're animals."

"Aye, that we are," the corporal agreed, in a voice that would have held sorrow if there had been a soul behind it. "These woods is full of animals, boy. You just haven't lived in 'em long enough to learn which ones are dangerous."

"And never will," the private giggled louder.

Sam's hatchet sliced through the tendons and gouged into the bone of the private's left knee, cutting his tittering short. A gasp of pain escaped the man as he dropped onto the dead leaves. Sam desperately yanked at his weapon to free it from the now writhing private, but it was lost in the tangle of the man's flailing limbs. Domitilde let out a scream of terror that seemed to fill the black woods.

The corporal, a man well acquainted with violence, recovered quickly from the interruption. Sam had to give ground as the man advanced towards him.

"Come close to me, lad," the corporal soothed. "I've got something for you."

Moonlight glinted off the buck knife's huge blade. Sam had nothing to defend against it, not even his heavy coat. With the confidence of a true killer, the corporal closed the gap between them.

Too quickly, the corporal lunged and sliced a furrow in Sam's thigh. Sam gasped in pain as he struggled back.

The corporal knew to give a wounded enemy no respite. He made to close again, when something he'd not expected happened. The lanky sprat who had shown little spine all night lunged from the darkness and took out his legs. The knife flew from the corporal's hand as he fell.

Sprawling in the leaves, William used his long limbs to entangle the beast of a man. But the corporal had wrestled for his life before, and he quickly gained the upper hand with a few moves and a bit of leverage. The corporal found the spindle's windpipe in his hands and started to squeeze.

"It's alright, boy" the corporal wheezed. "Go to your maker. There's a good lad."

Like a feral cat, Domitilde flew at the man killing her love. She latched onto his back and closed her teeth around the stump of cauliflower that was the man's ear. A quick yank saw the flesh ripped from his skull.

"You fucking bitch!" the corporal screamed in pain as he released William. He threw the she-devil off before she could claw out his eyes.

Domitilde shrieked as she tumbled into the darkness.

Sam, fighting through the agony in his thigh, used the opening to send a mighty kick into the corporal's face. The corporal sprawled off of William, and the lad skittered over and grabbed onto the man, wrapping his legs around the corporal's waist. William then rolled them both onto their backs, making them appear like a giant overturned turtle squirming on its shell.

"Hold him, William!" Sam gasped, moving to straddle the man.

Sam landed a hard right against the corporal's jaw, taking much of the fight out of him. Then he sent another blow into the grimacing face, then another. The fight ebbed further from the man with each landed strike. Warm blood streaked against Sam's face with each thump. He went about it as if he was chopping wood – steady, rhythmic blows.

Knuckles aching, lungs begging for breath, Sam finally stayed his hand. He stood and stepped back, looking at the charnel he'd inflicted. William sucked in air while the limp corporal pressed down on him. Sam could see his brother's face covered in blood, his eyes full of fright and his features a mask of horror.

"What are we going to do, Sam?" William choked.

The man on him still breathed quite steadily.

The answer was given to them. Domitilde had found the knife lying in the dried leaves where she'd landed. She picked it up and pushed past the huffing Sam. Before he could stop her, she plunged it into the corporal's chest. The pain brought the man to, and he let out a guttural groan. William had to redouble his efforts to hold him as he gave his last mighty struggle.

Needing to end it, Sam pushed Domitilde aside and grasped the knife. It came free with a hideous sucking noise. Sam leaned into the terrified, bludgeoned face in front of him. "It's alright, boy," he taunted, drawing a shudder from the corporal, or perhaps from William. "Go to your maker like a good lad."

The corporal's dim eyes brightened one final time as Sam raised the knife and plunged it through his heart.

Sam held the knife for a long while, looking into the dead man's face. He could hear Domitilde weeping softly over the rustle of dry leaves. He could hear his brother's sobbing. He could hear the agonizing groans of the wounded private. He could hear his own labored breathing finally slowing.

Knowing he had to look away, Sam tore his eyes from the corpse and released the knife. He feared what he'd see, but he looked to his brother. His fears were realized when he saw William looking at him with a mix of fear and sorrow, as if he was some monster from one of the sad tales the boy read.

"This is all your fault, William," Sam sighed, dropping to his knees in exhaustion. "You've made me a murderer."

Domitilde stopped her weeping. She sat in the leaves in silence, staring at the knife's hilt buried in the chest of her attacker. William struggled to get out from under the body. Sam chose to let him struggle by himself. He hoped the boy could at least manage to get out of that on his own.

"What are we to do now?" Sam asked himself.

"By God, help me," the wounded private gasped.

Sam let his eyes fall on the struggling man. "What are we to do with him?"

"Kill him," said Domitilde.

Sam looked at Domitilde in horror, shocked at how easy the words had come. "We can't," he managed.

"We must," she answered.

William finally freed himself from the body and stood, panting from the effort. "Maybe he'll die of his wound," he said hopefully.

The private let out a whimper and begged for their forgiveness. "It was all Bill, it was!" he shrieked. "I'd have left you alone if it weren't for him!"

Domitilde stood and moved to the body, planting a moccasined foot on the wide chest and clasping her hands around the knife's hilt. With a mighty heave and a grunt of exertion, she pulled the blade free. William began to shake as she approached him with the bloody knife outstretched. "*Tu dois, mon amour*," she comforted.

William hesitantly closed his long fingers around the hilt. He looked into her eyes as if hoping this was all a dream he'd soon awake from, but she nodded down to the private and said, "*Finis-le*."

With a gulp, William took a few tentative steps toward the wounded man, who screeched in terror and tried to pull himself away through the dried leaves. He didn't make it far. Standing over the writhing figure, William grasped the knife in both hands and raised it. Tears streamed from his eyes as he searched for some area to plunge the blade and end the man's squirming so the nightmare would stop.

Sam snatched the knife and in one quick movement sank it into the throat of the wriggling private. One sharp gasp, a few convulsions, and a torrent of blood brought an end to it.

Sam looked into his brother's watery eyes and said, "This is all your fault, William."

***

The young Chippewa watched the trio move off into the night after their whispered conversation. They'd made no attempt to hide the bodies of the dead redcoats before departing in a hurry. *Strange indeed,* the warrior thought to himself for the dozenth time.

The Chippewa – a scout tasked by Pontiac and Minavavana to keep watch on the comings and goings of the fort – had seen the young couple dash from the palisade under the half moon. He'd thought they were no more than doe-eyed lovers seeking the privacy of the forest, and he'd been of a mind to let them enjoy themselves in solitude. He could certainly relate to their quest to find a place to enjoy each other away from prying eyes. But the two figures that skulked after them had turned his stomach. The appearance of the third figure trailing the preceding two eliminated any chance that he could let the odd party go unobserved.

It was simple enough following the crashing herd. White men moving through the woods could be heard over thunderstorms. But he did see that the last fellow moved through the forest with a care close to that of an Indian, but not quite. The group had finally stopped in a small clearing, with the stealthy figure remaining hidden, and the warrior hidden from them.

English words were exchanged, but they meant nothing to the Chippewa. He knew a bit of French, but only enough to make himself understood during a trade. But the exchange made it clear that this was not a gathering of friends. He didn't need to understand the words to pick up the fear and anger on the voices.

The stealthy man had decided to act first, and had crept from the darkness and buried a hatchet into one of the redcoats' legs. The Chippewa warrior could now admit to himself that he'd leaned forward in fascination, eager to watch a fight he had no stake in. But that was when everything changed.

The girl's shriek of horror had drawn his eye. Her hood had fallen back, and the moonlight revealed a face that every young warrior in the Upper Country could describe from memory. Domitilde. The Chippewa had cursed his rotten luck at being in the wrong place at the wrong time. He'd half thought of slipping into the woods, leaving the scene behind and feigning that his watch had been filled with nothing but a sleeping fort and falling leaves. *Kinonchamek will peel your skin off if he finds that harm came to Domitilde and you did nothing,* he'd reminded himself. He'd sighed in irritation, hefted his war club, and prepared to intervene if it looked as if injury would come to the girl.

It was a damn near thing. The gangly redcoat and the sneaky one had barely been able to overcome the real killer in the group, and only then with a timely intervention by Domitilde.

And now it was only the warrior and the dead that remained. *I must tell Minavavana and Pontiac,* the scout told himself. He looked towards the fort, unable to see it through the trees. *And I must tell Kinonchamek that his woman might have her eyes on another man, and a stick of a man no less. The poor fool of a redcoat.*

The warrior shook his head at the queerness of the night, then pushed off into the darkness.

***

Charles Langlade heard the creak of the cabin's door in his dreams. He awoke with the ease of a man who'd spent a lifetime being wary of the dark and the enemies it concealed. Silently, he crawled from the bed he shared with his wife and took the candle burning low at his bedside. His other hand closed around the knife kept under his pillow. He opened his door softly and closed it gently behind him, then turned to find Domitilde standing in the cabin's main room.

Immediately sensing something was wrong, Langlade stepped forward to comfort his daughter. But he recoiled in revulsion at what the candle's flame revealed. Domitilde's dark eyes were wide over a mouth covered in dried blood, and the dress under her cloak looked like the apron of a butcher. Memories of the stories his grandmother had told him on fall nights like this, the ones about beings from the forest who would suck the blood from the young in the depths of night, flooded back to Langlade. But a whimper escaping his daughter's lips told him it was truly Domitilde who stood before him.

Regaining his senses, he dropped the knife and stepped forward to wrap his daughter in a hug. "*Mon enfant?*" he asked.

She buried her head in his chest and wept, "*Papa, aidez-nous.*"

***

Sam and William waited in the darkness outside the sally port. Looking east, Sam thought he could just discern the first sliver of gray on the horizon. Morning was not far off. "Where is he?" he said impatiently.

"The man will kill me, Sam," William whispered.

"Aye."

"Why do we need his help?"

"Because I can think of no other soul who *would* help us, William. Not after the mess you've led us into."

"Fritz–"

"Fritz will have your back for desertion, murderers and rapists be damned. The only way we get out of this is with Langlade's help. We don't know the country well enough, nor do we have the time to make the bodies disappear proper. Reveille is not far off, and we will certainly be missed."

"Langlade will take my scalp."

"I can't say I'd do any different if you'd put my daughter in that spot."

"I would never have let those monsters hurt her," William said, his breath catching.

Sam looked at him. "I don't think you had much say in the matter, brother."

William choked back a few tears.

"What was the plan, anyway, William?" Sam asked. "Make it to New York on foot? You didn't even bring a damned knife."

"Domitilde placed a cache in the woods with two of her father's pistols and a few knives. That's where we we're headed before…" He couldn't finish the sentence. "I didn't want to take any of the King's weapons lest we were caught."

"Two pistols and some knives," Sam repeated, shaking his head.

"We would be together," William said, and sniffed. "That's all that mattered."

Sam was about to call him a damned fool when the gate opened and Charles Langlade stepped out. The man made right for William, and the boy yelped as a quick hand slashed him across the face. William covered his head for protection as more blows fell.

Sam let the father land a few more swats before he pulled him off. "Charles!" he whispered, restraining him. "It's not the time, Charles! We have business that needs doing, then I'll give you my leave to kill the fool."

Langlade restrained himself with effort, until William peeked up and asked, "Where's Domitilde?"

Sam had to redouble his efforts as the father went back for seconds. "Charles!" he whispered. "Enough!"

Langlade pushed Sam off of him and pointed a finger at William. "Domitilde is with her mother, where she should have been this past night," he said.

"We must tend to the bodies," Sam whispered, looking at them both. His eyes settled on Langlade. "We don't know where to bury them, and doubt if we have the time before the first drum-roll."

Langlade peeled his stare from William and looked to Sam. "Show me where they are. Then you will go back to your tent. I will make sure they are never found. And we will never speak of this again. And you." He again pointed at William. "You will never lay your eyes on my daughter again, or I will pull them from your head and pop them within my fist."

Sam shuddered at the image, but said, "I think that's a damn fair trade, eh, William?"

William said nothing.

"Alright," Sam said, and nodded, "this way."

He led them across the open ground and into the woods. He soon found the path, and his red coat, which he plopped on his shoulders, and led them toward the clearing. Sam's feet almost carried him past the spot, but he stopped and looked about them. He scanned the bare ground, turning in circles several times and scrunching his brow.

"This is it," he said, but not with confidence.

Langlade held his hands open and spoke the obvious, "It can't be. There are no bodies."

Sam did another turn. "I'm certain of it. I hid behind that tree." He pointed. "And this is where I felled the private."

Dropping to a knee, Langlade overturned some dried leaves. He dug through several layers, then brought up his finger and held it under the weak moonlight. Sam saw what could have been fear cross the man's face.

"We must go back immediately," Langlade ordered.

"Where are the bodies?" William asked.

"Someone has already done our work for us," Langlade answered. He stood and started back for the fort at a trot. "Come!"

Sam and William followed, confused.

Sam called out, "This is no bit of luck for us?"

Langlade's silence was all the answer needed.

***

Kinonchamek could not just let these men pass by him unmolested. Not after the shame one of these Englishmen had covered him in. Raising his tomahawk and pulling his knife from the sheaf at his chest, he made to step from the woods and confront the men as they returned to the fort.

A firm grip on his forearm stayed him. "No, brother," Pontiac assuaged.

The tomahawk quivered in Kinonchamek's hand, and Pontiac could see the fury behind the man's eyes just looking for a release. But he knew that Kinonchamek could not turn his ire on him. Pontiac was too powerful among the tribes, too respected by all the warriors to go against. Kinonchamek, seeing no alternative, dropped his tomahawk and his stare, sheathed his knife, and pushed down his anger so it could erupt at some future date.

"Two English are already dead," Pontiac explained. "We cannot have another two vanish from the garrison. That will put them on edge."

"You said the bodies would not be found," Kinonchamek said softly.

"They won't be," Pontiac affirmed as he watched the trio of men slip back into the fort. He looked up at the lightening sky. "And you will have your revenge for the shame brought to your name."

Kinonchamek did not respond.

"But not today, my friend," Pontiac continued. "Your father and I's plans are much too important to be squandered because of a woman."

"She is promised to me," Kinonchamek said.

"And so she still is. Langlade will never allow his daughter to take an Englishman. And when our plans come to pass…" Pontiac looked at the young warrior. "You can roast those English on a spit and eat their hearts in front of the lovely Domitilde, if that's what would please you."

"What would please me," Kinonchamek said evenly, "is seeing every Englishman gone from the Upper Country." Kinonchamek looked to the fort. "But until then?"

Pontiac took a breath. "Until then, we will act as the supplicant children our English *fathers* take us to be."

***

The lieutenant ticked off the names of the men as they shuffled by him and up the gangplank. The last of the scarecrows touched his cap in salute, and the lieutenant consulted his list. Two men still unaccounted for since yesterday. *Not like the rogues to make a dash so close to a journey back to England,* the lieutenant thought, annotating his list with a quill. *Maybe the daft fools fell in love with this godless wilderness.* It would be a problem for the new garrison, not for him.

The sloop's sailors were eager push off and head downriver to Lake Eerie. The lieutenant boarded, allowing them to take in the gangplank, and he turned to take in Detroit one last time. *I won't miss the place*, he thought. *But I hope those two poor devils find what they were looking for.* The sloop slid away from the wharf and the current took her downriver as her sails began to unfurl.

Three miles south, Ol' Bill and the private, their bodies wrapped in old blankets and weighted with heavy stones, stared up sightlessly from the river bottom as the keel of the sloop bearing their comrades homeward slid overhead. The fish pecking at their vacant eyes and delicious lips paid no mind as the hull slipped by. Soon only a wake remained on the tomb of water pressing down on them. Then all was still, except for the incessant nibbling of the fish.

Ch. 7

Michilimackinac. November 1762

The November storms that lashed the lakes had yet to fall from the frozen north. The sloop bearing Etherington's command approached Michilimackinac on calm water under a blanket of cloud. The little *Huron* tacked against the cold west wind, passing Bois Blanc Island and entering the four mile straits where the mighty lakes Huron and Michigan met. Dead and dying leaves set the shorelines of the strait ablaze in the reds and oranges of fall, giving color to an otherwise gray world.

The boom of a cannon carried across the water. Those aboard the sloop strained their eyes and saw a timber fort clinging to the south shore, smoke curling up from a corner bastion. This was Michilimackinac, the guardian of the straits. The *Huron's* crew answered the greeting with a pop from their tiny deck gun as they beat by the graying fort and turned. The boat's master used the wind to push her towards the landing beneath the fort's palisade. Sails were brought in as they glided toward the shore and finally thumped gently against the landing. Lines were thrown and the *Huron* was secured.

A sentry called down a friendly greeting from atop the Water Gate as the wooden doors beneath it were thrown open. The men of the garrison flooded from the small fort, eager to see the men who would replace them and the conveyance that would bear them back to civilization before another long winter fell over the straits. The men's faces showed the cheer and relief of those who could see an end to some great length of hardship.

The new arrivals – thirty privates, two corporals, one sergeant, one lieutenant, and one captain – walked down the gangplank with the blank faces of men about to endure some lengthy sentence.

"It doesn't look so bad," William offered.

Sam leaned against his brother for support and grunted in pain as they navigated the gangplank. His feet finally hit the ground and he looked up at the gray palisade. A violent shudder passed through him, but it wasn't from premonition or a feeling of despair.

"I need to get warm, William," Sam sputtered, clutching at the thin blanket that covered him.

William looked on his brother with worry. Sam's face was pale, and a sheen of sweat glistened on his features, despite the cold. He'd been getting sicker and sicker with every league sailed up the lake. Now he stood shivering in the chill, barely able to keep his feet under him.

"I must take you to the surgeon," William whispered.

"No!" Sam said, and grasped at his brother's collar. "They'll find my wound. They'll know something happened."

"Then what am I to do?"

Sam's eyes fell on Charles Langlade, who was disembarking with his family. Seeing no other option, he said, "You must ask him to quarter us. We've been told we can find our own lodgings if able. Tell him we will pay him all we have. And remind him that he has as much to lose as us if any knowledge of Domitilde's flight with you spreads."

"Threaten him?" William choked.

Sam grasped the back of his brother's neck. "Persuade him. Use some of that knowledge you fill your head with, for once."

The prospect of speaking to Langlade stole the color from William's face.

"Swift and bold, William," Sam said.

After a moment's thought, William raised his chin and repeated, "Swift and bold," then strode across the crowded landing.

"*Mein junge,*" Fritz said as he came up from behind Sam.

Sam tried to straighten his back and smile. "Fritz," he said. "What do you think of our new home?"

Fritz took in the fort with one sweep of his head. "*Winzig,* tiny. But the walls look high and the garrison seems to have maintained her well. She'll keep out the wolves."

A cough rose in Sam's chest. He couldn't suppress it, and he hacked violently into his elbow.

Fritz patted him on the back, looking concerned as he waited for the fit to pass. "You need to go to the surgeon," Fritz scolded.

Sam gained his breath and tried to smile. "Why on earth would I do anything so dangerous as that?" he asked.

Fritz laughed. "*Ja,* but it might do you some good to get the bad blood out. Just a pint or two will see you revived."

"I think not, Fritz. I'd like to keep my blood in my body. I just need some rest and a warm lodging, which I think my brother is securing as we speak." Sam nodded to William, who was in whispered conversation with a very angry looking Langlade.

"Smart," Fritz said. "It will get very crowded in the barracks over the long winter. There will be much sickness."

"Will you be finding outside lodgings?" Sam asked.

"*Gott ja.*" Fritz nodded. "But be careful with that *Franzose.* You might wake with a blade across your throat."

Sam shook his head and laughed. Fritz would forever be a good French-hating German.

A barrel of powder being rolled down the gangway fell and spilled its black contents over the landing.

"*Scheisse,*" Fritz hissed. "I must see to these *idioten.*"

Fritz stomped off, yelling threats in German and English. Sam turned his eyes back to the conversation across the landing. William pointed in Sam's direction and made a pleading gesture.

Just then, a cold gust blew off the straits. Sam shivered and pulled the blanket tighter around him, hunching his head to keep warm. The wound on his thigh throbbed with each beat of his heart, and he knew he wouldn't be long for the grave if he didn't see to the cut properly. When he looked up, Langlade was standing before him. "Charles," he greeted.

"I believe your *chiot* of a brother just tried to threaten me," Langlade said.

Sam smiled. "Did he succeed?"

Langlade paused long enough to make it clear he had not, but then said, "As much trouble as you two have caused me, I still remember that I am only here because of your father's actions, or lack thereof." Langlade looked Sam up and down, taking in his sorry state. "I don't want your father's ghost to haunt me because I let you die in some dirty barracks. You will lodge in one of the cabins I use for visiting traders. You will stay until you get better, then you will leave. Understood?"

"*Absolument,*" Sam said, and smiled wider.

"Follow me," Charles ordered.

William appeared and hefted Sam's pack and musket for him. The trio walked through the crowd and into the fort. They entered a well-ordered space of timber buildings and gardens, but Sam didn't look around much as he fought to stay warm under his blanket.

In no time, Langlade stopped in front of a rough door. Sam looked up to see a tiny cabin with a small stone fireplace poking up. Langlade pushed open the door to reveal a dark room. Sam followed, eager to get out of the cold. Langlade opened the shudders of the only window in the place, a small, glassless opening. The faint light revealed a room barely big enough for the two sleeping pallets and small table with wash basin that took up the space.

"A fire, William," Sam said, nodding to the stack of wood and tinder near the hearth.

William dropped their meager belongings and went about getting a fire going. Sam eased himself down on one of the pallets, hissing in pain.

Unable to hide the concern on his face, Langlade asked, "Your wound?"

"A gift from Ol' Bill that just won't go away," Sam said, wrapping more blankets around his shivering body.

A strike of flint and sparks on tinder brought the fire forth, and Langlade closed the window to the cold. In the firelight, he took down a hanging lantern, checked its oil, and lit it with a smoldering stick. Langlade hung it back up, then turned to William in the warmly lit space. "William, some water," he said.

Without protest, William grabbed the bucket resting near the hearth and opened the cabin door. Sam shivered as a gust of wind invaded the warming space. His brother disappeared into the late afternoon.

The door closed, leaving only Sam and Langlade, who knelt down next to the pallet. "I must see it," he said.

Sam nodded, and lifted the blankets from his leg, then he pulled aside the skirt of his regimental coat. A red blossom of blood was plain against the blue of his breeches. "Bled through again," he said with a sigh.

"How often have you changed the bandages?" Langlade asked.

"As often as I could without drawing suspicion." Sam looked into his eyes. "Not often."

Langlade nodded, and brandished a knife from his belt. Sam didn't even flinch, aware that the man meant him no harm. Carefully, Langlade cut away the fabric over the wound. A foul smell emanated from the blood-soaked dressing, and Sam could see Langlade's face pinch. With even greater care, Langlade slipped the knife between the skin and the dressing. Delicately, he cut the dressing and pulled it from the wound.

Ol' Bill's knife had cut a deep furrow along six inches of Sam's thigh. Grisly though the wound was, its damage was nothing compared to the trauma infection now wrought. The skin around the wound was an aggravated red, and Langlade imagined that he could feel the heat pouring from the skin. The hasty stitching that William had sewn oozed a yellow pus, and the skin surrounding the thread was inflamed and straining against the sutures.

"You are burning with fever," Langlade told him.

Sam smiled weakly and said, "And I thought I was fit as a fiddle."

"I must open the wound," Langlade said flatly.

"Must you?"

"Well…" Langlade sighed. "I could leave it, but then you'd be a corpse within days."

"Then I suppose you must open it."

The door banged open, and William entered with a sloshing bucket. Langlade stood and ordered, "Heat the water, William. I will be back shortly." Then he was gone.

William looked after him for a spell, then turned to Sam. "What's happening?" he asked.

"I believe you are about to be promoted to assistant surgeon, William," Sam said faintly, before falling back onto his pallet.

Time stretched and squeezed as he lay shivering. William went about the cabin with purpose, stowing their belongings and tidying up. Every now and then, he cast a worrying glance at his brother, but Sam barely noticed. He was just about to slip off into a fever dream when the door opened again.

Langlade entered with Domitilde in his wake. Sam used what strength he had remaining to rise on his elbows. He saw that the beauty carried a pile of fresh linens in her cradling arms. William shot up from the fire, looking from father to daughter in shock that the man had allowed her to come.

"Where are your manners, William?" Sam asked with a rattling chuckle.

William looked to Sam, then to the linens. With the care of a mouse sneaking by a sleeping cat, he slipped past the stern Langlade and relieved Domitilde of the linens. The pair exchanged a long look before the piercing eyes of Langlade finally forced them to tear their gaze from one another.

"The door," Langlade ordered.

Nodding dumbly, William set the linens down and shut the door. Langlade and Domitilde quickly knelt beside Sam and started prepping the area around them. Their efficient movements made it obvious that they'd done something like this many times before.

Langlade, the space in front of him clean and covered with fresh linen, took a thinly-bladed knife from his pocket, then a flask from his other. "Drink some," he offered to Sam.

Sam tried to disentangle his arms from the blankets he was wrapped in. Domitilde stopped his struggles with a hand to his chest and took the flask from her father. She brought her free hand behind Sam's head and propped it up, then carefully tipped the flask so he could drink. The harsh whiskey stung his throat, but he choked down as much as he could knowing the pain that awaited.

When he was done, Domitilde handed the flask back to her father. Langlade poured the rest of its contents into a bowl, then dropped the knife into it. Looking to William, he said, "You will need to hold down his legs."

William's green eyes widened, but he stooped down and put his hands on the ankle of Sam's wounded leg and used his shin to cover the unwounded appendage. Sam winced, but a calming hand from Domitilde wiped the hair from his face and eased the pain.

Langlade spoke commands rapidly in French to his daughter, who took it all in. "*Oui*," she said when he was done. She stood and moved the fire poker into the hottest, reddest bed of coals, then returned and took up her spot next to her father.

Looking to his helpers, Langlade made sure they were ready, then his eyes fell on Sam's. "This is going to hurt," he said.

Sam nodded and said, "It is."

"If you feel as if you're about to slip off, my advice would be don't fight it. Better to not be awake for what's coming."

Sam shivered. "I'm ready."

Domitilde brought forth a wood dowel and gently placed it between his teeth. The knife appeared in Langlade's hand and the man hunched over. Before Sam could draw in a breath or offer any hesitation, the sharp blade passed over the first stitch.

A gasp of pain escaped around the dowel as pus burst from the wound with a pressure that was hard to believe. William redoubled his efforts as Sam's leg jerked violently. The rancid cheese smell of infection filled the room as the knife traveled up the wound and cut more stitches, releasing more of the vile pus.

"*C'est bon, c'est bon,*" Domitilde soothed, her hand running over Sam's quivering cheek. The girl's serene face, showing no revulsion to the sickening sights and smells, was almost enough to distract him from the pain coursing from his leg.

Langlade cut the last stitch, then squeezed the wound between his hands, releasing more of the stinking pus. Sam convulsed in pain, but Domitilde's eyes quieted him.

"*Nettoie,*" Langlade ordered.

Domitilde wiped the pus from the leg as Sam shuddered.

Langlade looked to William. "Keep a tight grip," he said. Then he poured clean water over the wound, washing out the last of the pus.

Sam's leg jerked again, but William held firm.

"Whiskey," Langlade said.

Domitilde took the whiskey bowl and tipped it over the wound. A scream so bestial that it brought tears to William's eyes erupted from Sam, and William was almost thrown by the mighty jerk his brother gave.

Domitilde sprawled over Sam's chest, trying to comfort him. "*C'est bientot fini!*" she whispered. "*C'est bientot fini.*"

In a delirium of pain, Sam spat out the dowel and gasped, "Finish it!"

Domitilde stood quickly and went to the fire, withdrawing the white-hot poker from the coals.

Langlade added his weight to Sam's chest and grasped his hands, then turned to his daughter and said, "*Fais le!*"

Without pause, Domitilde knelt and touched the poker to the wound. The sizzle and smell of cauterizing flesh filled the space, bringing a gag to William's throat as he struggled against his brother's efforts. Sam's screams buffeted Domitilde as she slowly ran the poker up the cut, making sure to burn out all the infection and close the wound. Sam issued one final groan of agony, then heeded Langlade's advice and let himself slip away.

***

He awoke from dark dreams to a face filled with light and life. Domitilde sat over him, her eyes filled with concern. Sam blinked several times to make sure he was lucid. The girl was still there when his head cleared.

The sudden urge for water burned in his throat, and he gasped for it. Domitilde quickly brought a ladle filled with clean, cool water to his lips. He drank its contents in one gulp, than begged another. When he finally gasped for breath, he looked around the small cabin that he remembered being brought to after their arrival.

"Where's William?" he asked.

Domitilde set the ladle down and said, "*En garde.* It is his watch."

Nodding, Sam tried to move his injured leg. A heavy ache of pain greeted the movement. A very much different feeling than the suppurating agony he'd walked in on. He removed the thick blanket covering what he now realized was his naked form. Domitilde looked away to give him privacy while he removed the thin bandage over his thigh.

A pink, puckered knot of flesh and scab occupied the space where Ol' Bill's knife had done its damage. The wound was still healing, and the poker's burn still secreted some fluid, but the angry red streaks of infection had disappeared.

"It looks as if you and your father have worked a miracle," Sam said.

Domitilde brought her eyes to the wound, taking in his nakedness with the indifference of someone who'd seen it all too many times to count, which Sam reckoned she probably had over the past however many days. Her hand found his thigh, but she touched him with the tenderness an artisan would use when handling one of their wares.

She inspected her handiwork and said, "You need to keep it clean. *Deux fois par jour*, twice a day. I'll show you how."

Sam nodded and covered himself with the blanket, easing himself back down on the pallet. "How long have I been out?" he asked.

"*Une semaine,* uh…" Domitilde searched for the English words. "A week." Her hand found his forehead, and she nodded to herself in satisfaction. "William said your fever broke two nights ago."

"And your father has let you tend to me all this time, in the lion's den?" Sam smiled.

Domitilde shrugged, annoyed. "I come when William is on watch. My father comes when he is not."

"Does Fritz know?" Sam asked, suddenly fearful. Questions that could not be answered would be raised about the wound, and it wouldn't take one of William's men of science to draw a line from the missing soldiers to a knife wound hidden by another.

"He knows you are sick. But half of the garrison came down with the fever after our arrival. Two of your redcoats have already died. Fritz has been in to check on you, but he is much busy. He doesn't know of your wound," Domitilde explained.

"Well," Sam breathed, "I must thank you for what you and your father have done." His eyes fell on a stinking bucket overfilled with soiled rags and blankets in the corner. "And especially what you have done. It can't have been easy. In fact, it must have been horrid."

A smile crossed Domitilde's lips. "I have been around death and wounds and *merde* and *pisse* all my life. Such is life in the *Pays d'en Haut*."

"I thank you all the same," Sam said.

Domitilde only shrugged in reply, but the smile remained.

"And what of you and William?" Sam asked.

A defiant look fell over the girl's face, telling him all he needed to know.

"You're still corresponding," he said, and sighed.

Domitilde stared down at him and said, "*Oui.*"

The laugh that escaped Sam surprised her, for she probably expected a haranguing. Sam shook his head with a smile. "You two will be the death of me. If not Ol' Bill's knife, it will be your father's bare hands around my throat. If not that, I'm sure this Kinonchamek's tomahawk will seek out my skull for a good paring."

Domitilde looked at him with a mixture of sadness and gratitude. "I know you will always protect your brother," she said, "and I thank you for that. Know that I will do everything I can to protect him."

Sam's face grew serious. "Then leave him be. If you care for him so, don't put him on the wrong side of so many dangerous people."

Domitilde offered a sorrowful shrug. "That is the one thing I cannot do."

Seeing there was nothing to gain by pressing her, Sam turned his head. "I think I shall sleep a little more."

"*Ridicule!*" Domitilde huffed, throwing the covers off of him and standing. "You have been on that pallet and in this cabin for too long. You need to get moving, get your blood pumping." She threw a new set of breeches and his shirt at him. "*S'habiller rapidement!*" She smiled. "I will show you your new home."

***

Stepping from the cabin, Sam entered a world that had been transformed since he'd last seen it. Several inches of fluffy white snow blanketed everything in sight, covering the drab gray wood of the buildings in the garnish of winter. The sun shone low in the sky, betraying that the longest night of the year was not far away. The air was cold but pleasant, and Sam filled his lungs with the stuff, relishing being out of the small, stuffy cabin.

"*Allez,*" Domitilde ordered, trudging forward through the snow.

Sam hugged the blue greatcoat she'd given him tighter around himself, then set off after her, his leg aching with each stride.

They were in the southeast corner of the fort, an area occupied by a dozen small cabins just like the one he and William had sheltered in. Domitilde informed him that the traders used them as lodgings for important guests and business partners, but now most were occupied by the NCOs and soldiers who had spare coin to rent them.

In only a few dozen steps they came to the Rue Dauphine, the main thoroughfare that ran the length of the fort. The snow there had been packed down by traffic, and mud showed through the white in spots.

"*La Porte Terrestre*, the Land Gate," Domitilde said, and gestured to the gateway at their left.

Sam looked at the gate, a strong set of timber doors mounted by a covered platform that had firing slits looking outward. A sentry stood on the platform above the open gate, and he called down a few jibes to Sam about shirking duty of late, which Sam took with grace. He assured the private that he was back on his feet, and that he would soon be freezing his ass off on guard duty just the same.

Domitilde faced him north and pointed the length of the thoroughfare. A few soldiers meandered along the street, and a few residents cleared snow from in front of their cottages, but the place had an empty feel for such a large space. Over a hundred and fifty yards away, a similar gate opened onto the beach that led to the cold waters of the straits.

"*La Porte D'eau*, the Water Gate," Domitilde shared. She turned and gestured left, to a long rowhouse. "Several families live here, and there is space for trade goods as well."

Before Sam could ask any questions, she started north down the street. They passed a few small cottages and gardens before coming upon another long rowhouse, which housed more families. Past that, there were dormant gardens lined with neat little fences made of sticks, and then a small building emanating the welcome smells of bread.

"*La boulangerie,*" Domitilde said, confirming it was the baker's. Pointing right, Domitilde gestured beyond several more rowhouses and cabins to a large, low mound of snow-covered turf. "*Le magazine.*"

Sam could see the heavy iron door at the bottom of the stairs that led into the half buried building. He could just make out the large padlock that protected the King's powder.

Further on they came to what had to be the soldiers' barracks, a long, low building with several smoking chimneys and a few windows. A private hoisting his musket and donning his tricorn spilled from one of the doors. The private eyed Domitilde appreciatively, then greeted Sam with a smirk. Sam gave a cool greeting in return and looked back to the barracks. The squat building, with the warm light of lanterns and interior fires filling the windows, looked almost cozy under its dusting of snow. But Sam knew the place was packed to the roof beams with privates, and he had the urge to thank Domitilde again for her and her father's kindness in quartering him and William.

Domitilde gestured across the small thoroughfare in front of the barracks. "The parade ground," she said.

Sam looked up to see the Union Jack fluttering from a tall pine poll in front of the snow-covered space. The fairest residence within the walls took up the north end of the ground. That was where Captain Etherington would reside during his command of the fort.

Domitilde led him behind the barracks. The tallest building within the walls – within hundreds of miles – lay in front of them. "*L'eglise de St. Anne,*" Domitilde said, and gestured up to the wooden spire of the Catholic Church of St. Anne. The wooden cross was comforting to see, even though Sam had not spoken to God since he'd been on the bank of the St, Lawrence.

"You're alive then, lad," a voice hailed.

Sam turned to see Corporal Kane on the porch of a small building. The heavy door and small windows told Sam this must be the guardhouse.

"Just barely," Sam called back, straightening so as not to be seen favoring his leg. "I've heard many are sick."

"Aye," Kane said, and nodded, "this infernal place is already cutting us down."

"Hopefully more will recover."

Kane looked over Domitilde, then smiled at Sam. "Many would, if they had a nurse such as that."

Sam chuckled and nodded. "I believe many a man would spring from their graves at the prospect of Domitilde seeing to them."

Kane bellowed a laugh. "Aye! I believe they'd even have the blood to do a little jig."

The girl shook her head in feigned annoyance, but smiled and blushed none the less.

"I'll be able to muster tomorrow, I should think," Sam affirmed.

"You'd better, lad, or I'll stripe that backside of yours!" Kane roared.

Leading Sam away from the rowdy corporal, Domitilde brought him to a row of comely little houses built in the French manner. "*Le maison de mon pere*," she said, and swept her hand over the nicest looking home in the row.

"Your father's house," Sam said, and smiled, pleased that he'd gained a little French along the journey through Canada.

"*Oui*," Domitilde smiled, looking over the garden, it's beauty still discernible under the blanket of snow.

"Let's move away before your father takes a shot at me from one of the windows," Sam only half joked.

The pair moved on, taking in another rowhouse, several cabins, and the smelly latrines in the northwest corner of the fort, where Sam excused himself and made a rather large deposit while Domitilde waited. Business done, they moved on and came to the King's storehouse, where the garrison's supplies were kept. Beyond that was the Water Gate. Sam looked through the open portal to gaze upon the straits. The vast expanse of water undulated with low whitecaps in the timid, cold breeze.

Domitilde led him out the gate and onto the beach that was the landing. There were only a few snow-covered canoes and a couple bateaux pulled up below the walls. They walked east, past a small platform that could hold artillery if the straits needed defending. The gray timber of the cedar palisade rose over their heads, fifteen feet above the snowy ground. Rounding the fort's northeast corner, they passed under a small blockhouse that formed a bastion. The fortification held a 6-pounder that bristled from its firing slit.

The east wall was devoid of a gate and featureless except for the tricorn and musket of a soldier pacing along the sentry's walk inside the palisade. When they were halfway along the palisade, Domitilde gestured to the open clearing on their left. "In summer, this whole space is filled with traders from every corner of the lakes. Indians, French, English, even Spaniards have been known to venture here from their lands far to the south," she said. The remnants of wigwams, lean-tos, old tents, and the husks of bare, simple cabins dotted the field. "This field becomes a village that can rival Detroit, if only for a few months."

Sam had to laugh at the way she said that, as if Detroit were some metropolis. "So, hundreds of folk?" he asked.

"*Oui*," she said seriously. "Many hundreds. All of them here to trade."

"Furs come in. Powder, steal, rum, and the fineries of Europe go out to the wilderness."

"*Absolument*. So it has been ever since *le Francais* arrived and you people began wrapping yourselves with the skins of our animals in an effort to outdo one another on the streets of London and Paris."

"Never been to London," Sam said. "Certainly not Paris. The only skins I've ever known are buckskins." He looked at her as they walked. "You speak of the French as if you aren't one of them."

Domitilde stopped and smiled at him. "Look at my skin. If I wasn't wearing this dress and speaking your horrid tongue, you'd think I was nothing but an Indian."

"What's wrong with being an Indian?"

"Nothing at all," she retorted, continuing to walk. "It's you heathens from Europe that seem to think there's something wrong with being anything but white as a lily."

Sam chuckled and nodded. "I'm not one them. This is the farthest I've ever been from old Penn's woods."

"So what do you consider yourself?"

"A Pennsylvanian." Sam held his hands open to the country around them. "An American, I suppose."

They rounded the southeast bastion and saw several outbuildings south of the fort. "Stables," Domitilde indicated, "storehouses, and a few workshops. That is all of Michilimackinac. It might not seem much, but it's the surrounding country and waters that truly make this place home."

Sam saw an opportunity. "This place is no home for my brother and I," he said.

Domitilde blanched, but said nothing.

"When our time in the Army's done," Sam continued, "we'll be on our way east. Out of this wilderness. The both of us."

A mirthless smile crossed Domitilde's lips. "*Qui vivra verra*," she said.

"Meaning?" Sam asked curtly.

"Time will tell."

Annoyed, Sam asked, "Is Kinonchamek such a monster?"

"*Non*," Domitilde said quickly. "Just a man."

"A man of some stature. A man any maiden would do well to marry."

"But a man who never listens," Domitilde retorted. "I've told him since we were children that I do not love him."

Sam sneered. "What does that matter?"

Domitilde looked at him with pity. "It matters more than anything, Sam. I hope one day you find that out."

"Why William?" Sam asked. "Why not some Ottawa prince? Why not anyone else but my daft brother? None of the girls around Lancaster ever deigned to look in his direction. What do you see that they didn't?"

"*C'est simple.*"

"Simple?" Sam huffed.

Domitilde's face softened. "I see a man who listens. Ever since his first letters, all he has wanted is to know me. I have never had that. Not even my own father…" A tear welled in her eye, but she quickly brushed it away. "Not even my own father," she continued, "has ever listened to me. I am only told what to do, where to go, and whom to marry."

A defiant look fell over her face, and she stood taller. "Now *I* will be listened to," she said.

Sam opened his mouth to say something harsh, but he was cutoff by a voice hailing, "Who goes there?" He looked up to see William's smiling face staring over the parapet. His brother's expression cooled his anger.

"Don't shoot," Sam said, holding up his hands. "She was only showing me around the fort."

"Is that the truth, *mademoiselle*?"

Domitilde's face flushed and her eyes seemed to sparkle. "*Oui, mon amour*," she said.

Looking upon the faces of the two young fools as they gazed at each other, Sam realized that any efforts to douse their feelings for each other would be hopeless. It would be as futile as trying to keep the moon and stars out of the same night sky.

They were truly in love.

"How's the leg?" William asked him.

Sam gathered his thoughts and said, "I'll have a bit of a limp for a few days, but nothing I can't hide."

William nodded and asked, "What do you think of the fort?"

"Small," Sam said with a shrug. "But welcoming."

William looked off into the forest, a smile crossing his face. "It truly is beautiful country, Sam. Fritz has taken me on a few ranging parties away from the fort. The woods are filled with more deer than could feed an army. And there's plenty of pleasant streams and lakes filled with fat fish. A man could be happy here."

"If he still had skin on his back and a scalp on his head."

William looked down at him with hard eyes. Slowly, his smile returned. "Aye. That would certainly help."

Ch. 8

Michilimackinac. December 1762

"I need to speak with you, Sam," said William.

"We've been speaking all night," Sam said. He smiled, his features bathed in the light of the brazier keeping the worst of the cold from the two. They'd drawn sentry duty on the night watch, their posting the southwest bastion of the fort. They stood on the sentry walk outside the bastion as Michilimackinac slept behind them under an ever-deepening blanket of white. The dark forest beyond the palisade stirred with the nocturnal wanderings of a few critters trudging through the snow, but no danger.

William looked over the parapet towards the boundless forest and tried to order his thoughts. Sam warmed his hands over the charcoal of the brazier and stomped his feet to keep the blood flowing, bracing himself for whatever was coming. William let out a long sigh and finally looked him in the eye.

"Domitilde thinks she's with child," he said.

Sam could only blink a few times as he rocked on his heels, the pain in his thigh a reminder of William's last blunder. The revelation was not entirely unexpected. After all, a new life was usually the outcome of two young peoples' affections. But the news still struck him like an icy blast blown off the cold straits.

"How?" Sam asked.

William smiled sheepishly. "Don't tell me you need your little brother to explain the ways of nature," he said.

"You know what I mean!"

William sobered. "It happened in Detroit, we think."

"She told you all this by note? Her father practically watches her every move, and Fritz and I yours."

With a conspiratorial glance around their surroundings, William said, "Her father has a smuggler's tunnel that runs from his root cellar out beyond the palisade. He believes nobody knows of it, not even his own daughter."

"And she meets you when you draw sentry duty for the stables," Sam continued for him.

William's downward gaze confirmed that.

"I was wondering why you were so eager for such a bland posting," Sam added. "Always one step ahead of the rest of us, aren't you?"

The two fell quiet. Seconds or minutes passed as this calamitous news tumbled through Sam's mind. Countless scenarios started shooting off to imagined ends, running through his head one after another. Each conjured path seemed to end in a destination worse than the previous. This could be nothing but dangerous for them both.

"What are your thoughts?" William asked, unable to bear the silence.

"My first thought," Sam said, "is to throw you off this palisade."

William didn't react to that, expecting as much from his brother.

"My second thought," Sam said evenly, "is that that probably won't kill you, at least not with my fortune. It would only maim you, and it being an attempt at mercy, I'd have to find some other way to do the work that other men in this country would carry out in a much grislier fashion." Sam shook his head. "When word spreads of this, your head will be a sought-after ornament."

William could only stare, overwhelmed with the weight of everything that would soon be crashing down upon him.

"I must assume," Sam continued, "that because you are still drawing breath in front of me, that Charles Langlade does not yet know that you have defiled his only daughter and planted a bastard in her belly."

"He does not know," William confirmed. "Domitilde is to tell him tomorrow."

"In that case, may I have your possessions after you are killed? I do hope the Army will reward me with your fifty acres, but I won't hold my breath."

"If he means to kill me…" William nervously fingered his musket. "He can try."

"He will succeed," Sam said. He tore his eyes from William and looked on the forest, weighing the options left to them. "Can she end it? I know some Indian women are knowledgeable of certain plants—"

"She cannot, and will not, and I agree," William said, cutting him off.

"Why not run now?"

"And go where?"

"To your dear friend Otayonih."

"We can't, not with a baby coming. We might have had a chance just the two of us, but we'll not make it with her pregnant."

Sam couldn't argue with that. He shook his head and said, "You just couldn't leave well enough alone."

William puffed out his chest. "We're in love, Sam. I know you don't agree or understand, but that's the plain truth of it."

"You're in love and I'm left to clean up the mess, as I am with every other mess you've created! What shall I do?" Sam asked himself.

"I'm not asking you to do anything," William said softly.

"But here I am, making every effort to do something."

"It's because you love me as your brother." William smiled, trying to break the mood.

Sam couldn't suppress his own smile at his brother's cheek. The simple truth was this lanky young man standing before him was all he had left. All that was left of his father, besides what parts resided in him. All that was left of his mother, who loved them all so deeply that she couldn't bear the pain when one of her boys was taken from her. The lad could have walked into hell and spit in the Devil's face, and Sam would have been right behind him.

"God help me, I do love you," Sam said, and sighed.

"And I love her," William said, serious once more.

"So." Sam wiped his nose. "I suppose I'll have to look after the both of you now."

William put a hand on his shoulder. "You'll help us then, with her father?"

Sam looked up at the low clouds scuttling by in the moonlight. "Will I keep Langlade from killing you? I'll try my best, but I don't believe Hercules himself could keep that man from squeezing your skinny neck if he had a mind to. But what's worse, he is the least of our worries now."

"How do you mean?"

"Kinonchamek," Sam breathed the name.

William's eyes widened. The lad had spent his waking hours and dreams fearing what Domitilde's father would do to him when he found out. He had completely forgotten about what horrors her betrothed might try to visit upon him. "Oh yes," he croaked, "I'd quite forgotten all about him."

"Well," Sam said, "don't let him slip from your mind again. He certainly won't forget about you after he learns your name and what you've done."

"The Army will protect us from him," William said hopefully, "if they don't have me whipped first."

Sam thought for a second. "Fritz may have you skinned, but I doubt that. Half the privates in the regiment have fathered pups with camp followers at some point or another, even though it's against regulations. You'll probably get nothing more than a tongue lashing."

"I can handle that."

"And the Army will keep this Chippewa from walking into the fort and cutting the scalp from your daft head in the light of day. But look around us, William." Sam gestured over the walls. "We are but a few soldiers in a wilderness filled with Indians. If he wants you bad enough, which he will, he'll find a way." Sam lay his hand on one of the sharp points of the palisade. "These thin walls won't hold him back for long. You'll be hunted from now until the end."

"The end?"

"Until we leave this wilderness," Sam answered, "or somehow this Kinonchamek meets his own end." A grimace crossed his face. "Or your scalp is fixed to his belt."

A long exhalation escaped William. "I don't think that will matter much. I'm sure that Charles will do the deed for him on the morrow."

Sam put his arm around his brother. "We'll see, William. And we will meet what comes, together."

***

The crash of the cabin door pulled Sam from a dream about a warm summer day. He shot up to find Charles Langlade framed in the doorway. He'd come for William already. Sam reached for the hatchet he kept at the side of his pallet. Langlade lunged across the small space and stomped his foot onto the hatchet's head. Several other bodies spilled into the cabin.

"William!" Sam yelled to his waking brother, but the others went for William, pinning him to his pallet before he could rise.

Sam tried to move but Langlade forced him down. Several Indians carried the struggling William from the cabin.

"Sam," William shrieked in terror.

Sam redoubled his efforts, but Langlade was stronger and had the upper hand. The man pinned his arms and dropped his knee onto his chest, leaving Sam only the ability to kick his legs. "You mean to murder us in the fort, Charles!" Sam yelled, struggling against the man's strength. "The Army will hang you for this!"

Langlade didn't answer.

Three more men entered, and Sam noticed that two wore the red coats of soldiers. What was more perplexing, they had wide grins on their faces.

"Bind him," Langlade ordered the new arrivals, who pounced on Sam as he struggled.

"What are you doing?" Sam spat, mystified as the men flipped him and bound his hands behind him.

"Easy, Sam," one private said.

"He means to murder my brother!" Sam screamed.

"Oh, his life be ending today," the other soldier crowed.

The soldiers laughed and picked Sam up from his pallet. Sam wore only his breeches, but they put his moccasins on his feet and dropped his regimental coat over his naked shoulders, then they led him from the cabin. They emerged into daylight surrounded by the smiling faces of most of the garrison. Fritz's red German face beamed at Sam as he was pushed towards the Water Gate.

"Fritz?" Sam called.

Fritz held up a hand in a calming gesture. "Don't struggle," he said.

Sam could only stare at the man with wide eyes. *What in God's name is happening,* he thought?

A couple of Indians and a Frenchman carried the still-struggling William, who called for Sam's help. Domitilde emerged from the crowd and unleashed a French tirade at her father, who walked behind the queer parade. Langlade ignored his daughter's pleas as the troupe tromped on and exited the fort.

Outside the Water Gate, the mass spread out on the half-frozen beach sand. William was dropped and forced to his knees at the water's edge. Sam made to break the hold upon him to reach his brother, but the men regained their grips and held him tight.

Captain Etherington and Lieutenant Leslie stood with amused grins as they watched William, naked but for his breeches, whip his head this way and that. "Sam?" he cried out.

"What madness is this!" Sam yelled at the officers, who only chuckled in response.

One of his captors gave him a playful slap to the back of the head and said, "Enjoy the show, Sam."

Langlade slowly made his way forward and stepped in front of the shivering young man. "William Avery," he said in a hollow tone.

William looked up at Langlade. After a long swallow, the lad stiffened his back and pushed most of the fear from his eyes, replacing it with something approaching defiance. He puffed out his rangy chest in challenge. "What is this, Charles! I demand you release me," he said.

Sam couldn't help but feel a bit of pride at his brother's courage. It was a side of William he was getting more used to seeing.

"Have you been baptized, William?" Charles asked.

Sam's mouth opened in puzzlement.

William's shoulders sagged in confusion. "What?" he asked.

"I asked if you have been baptized," Langlade repeated.

William looked back to Sam, who could only offer him a perplexed grimace. Turning back to Langlade, William lifted his head and said, "I have not."

"This must be done, though you are no Catholic, and never will be," Langlade said, and turned to the crowd. "Father."

The Jesuit priest of the Church of St. Anne came forward to stand in front of the confused William. The bearded Frenchman shared the rough-looking characteristics of most French settlers. His dress made it clear that his flock called home a rough wooden church on the edge of a forest, not a grand stone cathedral along the banks of the Seine. His black cassock had faded to a dismal gray after countless days under the sun, and the fabric he'd used to patch its tears and holes had been chosen without care to uniformity of color. But the man's white collar was clean and stiff from devoted attention.

"*Se lever*," the priest said, and gestured for William to stand.

After a moment's contemplation, William slowly rose. The priest turned and walked toward the straits, entering the freezing waters as if they were a summer-warmed pond. Langlade motioned for William to follow, which he did when he realized he had no choice in the matter.

William put one bare foot in, then the other. His skinny frame began to shake again, the remaining color in his skin leeching into the straits. Bone-white, he slogged through what had to be piercing agony to join the priest in waist deep water. William took up station next to the priest and looked back to the shore, his eyes falling on Domitilde as his teeth chattered.

The priest began to drone in that thick tongue that could only be Latin. The French looking on grew solemn. The soldiers, nary a papist among them, looked on with the scrutiny of those watching some mysterious, mystical rite only known to them through rumor and hearsay.

After many minutes – and many worries on Sam's part that his brother would freeze to death before the priest could complete his incantations – the priest turned to William and spoke to him in Latin. William could only reply with a blank stare. Unperturbed, the priest put his hand on William's forehead and in one swift, strong movement pushed the youth back while simultaneously tripping him. The stunned William plunged backward and was immersed in the freezing water. The priest struggled against the flailing William, waiting a bit longer than necessary before raising the gasping lad for a breath.

William, ignorant of his purification, stumbled forward cursing, desperate to leave the cold water and escape the clutches of the crazed holy man trying to drown him. Sam broke free from his laughing captors and intercepted his freezing brother, wrapping his regimental coat around William's shaking frame.

"What was that?" William sputtered, blowing water from his nose.

Langlade's tall form appeared beside them. William recoiled only slightly. With an unreadable gaze, Langlade said, "In four days' time, you will accompany me to L'Arbre Croche. There you will be joined with my daughter in accordance with the old ways and the new." With that, he strode away, past his now smiling daughter.

Domitilde waited respectfully for her father's exit, then burst forward with an exuberance and relief that could hardly be believed. She wrapped her arms around both Averys, spouting French so quickly it was indiscernible to even the fluent, but the feeling was unmistakable. Caught up in the happiness radiating from her, Sam wrapped his other arm around her. He looked up to see William's head above the tangle, his features frozen in stupefied amazement as Domitilde clung to them both.

"You are one daft, ungrateful, treacherous lank of an idiot," Sam laughed. "But you've survived this day. Why not a few more, eh?"

Looking down to Sam, William finally seemed to register what had just befallen him. Slowly, a smile spread across his pale, handsome face.

***

To the bald eagle flying towards the morning sun at a height of 5,000 feet, the canoes and bateaux cutting west out of the straits below caused no great arousal of interest. His keen eyes were much more intent on spotting the telltale signs of carrion along the shore, or the glint of a fat fish in the still ice-free waters of Lake Michigan. His gaze lingered on the party of red-coated soldiers, bundled Indians, and traders for no more than a moment before passing on in his unceasing search.

5,000 feet below, Sam paddled next to another private in one of the bateaux. Fritz looked on from the bench in front of them, his status as a sergeant precluding him from doing anything as degrading as pulling an oar. "I still cannot believe Captain Etherington has agreed to this. Privates are restricted from marrying," Sam said.

Fritz gave a loud *harrumph* as Sam pulled. "*Die armee* also has regulations against gambling, whoring, fighting, and desertion, yet you louts do plenty of that," he said.

The private next to Sam chuckled and said, "That we do, Sarge."

"But marrying?" Sam said, and gaped. "Especially an Indian." Sam dropped his voice. "And a Catholic no less."

Fritz shook his head at the lad's simpleness. "*Herr* Langlade is going to be an important part of the King's plans for this region," he said. "Through his *vater*, he's a prominent member of the *Franzosen* community, and one of the leading traders on the lakes, a position that holds much weight in these parts. Add to that his success against us in the war. He is a man the frogs will follow. With his mother's blood, he's related to the local chief of the Ottawa, a man I'm told is held in high regards by the tribes throughout the lakes."

Fritz opened his hands. "You see, Sam, we cannot rule these *Franzosen und Indianer* without help from their chosen men. Langlade happens to be chosen by both at once. He's as much a savage as he is a frog. Two birds with the same stone, as you English say. Why else do you think he was in Philadelphia meeting with *Jeneral* Amherst?"

"If he's so important to the King, why not just let Langlade strangle the beanpole, as he surely wished to do?" Sam asked.

"Remember your own words." Fritz held up a pointed finger. "Langlade is *Katholisch,* or as close as one can get in these wild lands. His daughter having a pup out of wedlock is *verboten*. The locals can forgive a bastard so long as the child is made right before God with a marriage. And it probably would be no great honor in the heathen religion of his *Indianer* blood to have a grandson with no father.

"No, no, Sam. Langlade wanted this marriage as much as our poor *dummkopf, Wilhelm*. He practically demanded it when he spoke to Captain Etherington. The good captain didn't want to upset such an important figure by denying it. We couldn't have the local Ottawa and the filthy frogs ready to string us up because *Wilhelm* could not keep his *schwanz* in his breeches."

Sam could only row on as Fritz's words ran through his head. The wind was thankfully low and the temperature not too much below freezing as the boats threaded southwest. The vastness of Lake Michigan spread from the gunwale of the bateau to the western horizon, broken only by the humps of a few wooded islands poking through the frigid water. The coastline to their left marched south, its sandy beaches rising to towering dunes topped with the ever-present trees that clung to every bit of untended ground in this country of forest.

The sun had begun to dip towards the lake when Fritz craned his neck to look over Sam's shoulder. "We are close," he said.

Turning, Sam could see pillars of smoke rising into the graying sky, the fires feeding them hidden behind trees. The flotilla rounded a bend and entered a great bay. Sam strained his neck, spotting a huge, bent tree on the north shore. This was L'Arbre Croche – The Crooked Tree.

Many years before, the local Ottawa settlement had been right up against the walls of the French fort at Michilimackinac. The fields where traders now camped in the summer used to be full of corn stalks, but the soil soon became exhausted and, in the Indian way, the settlement was easily abandoned and moved south to The Crooked Tree.

Resting on a high dune, the massive bent oak tree that gave the area its name towered over the flotilla as they passed beneath it. Its long arms were bare of leaves in winter's coldest depths, but its mass still loomed over them like a giant making ready to reach out and pluck the soldiers from their oars. Langlade had earlier told Sam that this tree was of great importance to the Ottawa. Even before they'd moved their settlement there, councils of war were held beneath the tentacled branches of the gnarled tree.

Rounding the high dune the tree sat on, the boats entered a smaller, sheltered harbor. Now they could see the fires and wigwams of the Ottawa. The village spread from the canoe-lined shore towards dormant fields in the distance. There were enough bark-covered wigwams and longhouses to house several hundred souls. A French mission church was ubiquitous, rising among the low bark dwellings of the natives. Lanes were filled with running children and yapping dogs. Deer carcasses hung from buck poles, and hides and furs of every manner were stretched and drying outside every wigwam. There was no palisade, the village's only protection the tomahawks of its young warriors.

A teeming crowd of Ottawa gathered along the shore as the boats touched down. The soldiers disembarked and shouldered their muskets cautiously, nervous not to make any move that could be perceived as threatening. William found Sam and saddled up to him.

Sam smiled and gestured to the crowd. "Aren't you going to introduce me to your new family, William?" he asked.

A nervous croak was all that escaped William's throat.

Cheerful Ottawa calling his name mobbed Langlade and pulled derisively on his European coat. Langlade joked and jested back, arousing much laughter in the gathering. Madame Langlade, a full-blooded, beautiful Ottawa herself, was greeted cheerfully by friends and family. Domitilde, who had been kept away from William since the baptism, was swarmed by young Indian maidens. Fritz had to swat at a few of the escorting privates whose eyes were a little too greedy in their examination of the beauties.

A sudden hush fell over the crowd, and an Indian in fine skins stepped toward Langlade.

"This must be your new granduncle, William," Sam whispered.

Nissowaquet shared the same fine features of Langlade, with a strong nose and a cut jaw. He was of average height and looked to be only in his fortieth year, though Sam knew the man to be much older.

Langlade and Nissowaquet wrapped each other in an embrace, then Langlade introduced Captain Etherington, who made a show of bowing slightly to the Indian chief. When the introductions were done, Langlade gestured towards William and began speaking to Nissowaquet.

William tried to shirk back, but Sam would have none of that. With a firm hand to his back, he pushed William towards the inquisitive Indian. Nissowaquet looked on William while Langlade spoke, his eyes traveling up and down the lad as he seemed to take in the worth of this Englishman marrying his beloved Domitilde. William stared back with feigned confidence.

A painful silence fell over the crowd with the closing of Langlade's entreaties. Sam began to wonder if William had been found wanting by the great chief. Finally, Nissowaquet cocked his head slightly and spoke a few words.

A great eruption of joy burst from the crowd. Langlade smiled with relief. Tears came to Domitilde as her maidens chirped in excitement. A band of young Ottawa warriors rushed William and began slapping his back in congratulations at the conquest of such a renowned beauty. The color flushed back to William's face, and he smiled dumbly and nodded his head at the unknown words the warriors spoke.

Sam could only stand back and shake his head, a smile on his face.

***

A great fire burned in a stone ring under a hole in the center of the bark roof of Nissowaquet's longhouse. Sam, William, and Fritz – who William had insisted was family – sat in their uniforms on one side of the fire. Captain Etherington and Lieutenant Leslie sat to their right as sweat poured from under the gentlemen's powdered wigs, the longhouse being quite stuffy. Langlade sat with Nissowaquet, opposite Sam and William. Several of the village heads lounged to the left of the brothers. A pipe was being passed around, and its smoke added to the already thick atmosphere around the fire.

"His Majesty King George," Etherington spoke to Nissowaquet, "is much pleased that you have decided to lay down your tomahawks and join him on a new path to peace and prosperity for the lakes. He wants all his new subjects, French and Indian alike, to know that he will hear their pleas and attend to their wants as any father would for his children."

Langlade translated the English into the Ottawa dialect of the Ojibwe language the chief and his people spoke. Nissowaquet listened intently, then turned to Langlade and rattled off a long, steady stream of words. Several times, the chief pointed at Etherington accusingly, and the tone of his voice allowed for no mistaking the substance of his words.

When Nissowaquet finished, Langlade took several long beats to order his words, and said, "Chief Nissowaquet says that he appreciates the promise of a benevolent father in King George, but he is having difficulty seeing those words as anything but hollow. He asks where the gifts for his people are. Where is the powder he must use to hunt the furs he needs in order to trade? Where are the wampum belts that are given so we can tell our stories and make our treaties with the other tribes? Where is the steel for knives, tomahawks, and cooking pots? Where is the rum for our warriors?"

Etherington seemed to flinch with each question, but he raised his chin and answered, "King George thinks his subjects need to learn to make the earth fruitful from their own labors. He does not want his subjects to become dependent on his gifts alone. You must hunt for more furs in order to trade for the goods that you need."

The words were translated, and Langlade offered the Chief's response. "We would have to hunt the land until it was empty of every creature to trade for all that we received as gifts from our French fathers. Nissowaquet asks if his new English father is not as rich as his old French one. How could the English have possibly won the war if they cannot afford to give their Indian subjects goods that are only trifles to them?"

"You have to remember," Etherington responded, "that this is just but one lonely outpost in the vastness of His Majesty's new empire. It would bankrupt him if he made gifts of what you ask to all his new subjects."

Nissowaquet waved his hand dismissively, and Langlade translated his response. "If King George cannot afford the price of his new empire, King George should have been content with his little island."

Etherington choked back a hasty response to the insult. He finally managed, "*Monsieur* Langlade, please tell the chief that we are aware he is in great need of powder. In the spirit of building a lasting friendship between the Ottawa and my garrison, I have brought with me four barrels of fine English powder, as well as two hundred flints from the garrison's own stock. This is my gift to him, and I give it on behalf of King George."

Nissowaquet looked little pleased at that, but Langlade translated, "Chief Nissowaquet gives his thanks, but he knows that this gift is not given by the King, and he knows that little more of the King's graciousness will be forthcoming, and that you cannot afford to give all your powder away indefinitely."

Etherington nodded. "I cannot, and this will be the last. But you have my word that I will send your concerns along to my superior in Detroit, and I am sure he will forward them all the way to General Amherst."

The chief's features made it clear that he believed none of what Langlade translated. But he listened in silence, then began speaking slowly while Langlade translated along.

"My nephew," Langlade spoke, "whom we have followed into battle dozens of times, and traded with and prospered from for many years, has told me that we must accept that the English are here to stay, and that our French fathers will not be coming back. Because we know his counsel to always be wise, we heed his advice and accept that King George now calls us his children. We shall remain his faithful children while we wait for him to see the folly of his ways and return to giving us the gifts we need to live happily and to fill his ships with furs."

Nissowaquet's gaze bore into Etherington for the first time as Langlade translated, "But I pray we do not have long to wait for King George to see his error. I pray that his Indian subjects are not forgotten. There are already whispers being passed along the hunting trails, up through the lakes and down the mighty river to the south. The whispers speak of treachery, of spilling English blood in the hope our old French father will return to us. The whispers speak of war to defend the Indian way of life. Those whispers have even been spoken here, in this longhouse, but I will not listen to those who bear them. I tell you this, so you tell your betters in Detroit, and they tell their General Amherst, and he tells our father, King George: do not forget us."

Etherington bowed his head, then looked to William, who had been raptly absorbing the weighty conversation. "I would once again like to apologize for the circumstances of this union," Etherington began, eager to change the subject, "but I am certain that its unfortunate beginnings will prove to have brought about a fortuitous and happy partnership, between both the bride and groom and the garrison and your people."

For the first time, a smile crossed Nissowaquet's face. Langlade translated his words, "Domitilde has always been dear to my heart, just as her father is. I will welcome William into our family."

"What of the feelings of the Chippewa?" Sam asked, unable to stop himself. "Charles, you yourself told me that the union of Domitilde and Kinonchamek carried great weight for the future of your peoples."

The old Indians around the fire didn't know the English words, but they did not fail to recognize the name Kinonchamek. Dour looks crossed wrinkled faces, and several whispers were passed back and forth. Nissowaquet needed no translation.

Langlade turned to Sam and said, "My daughter's belly carries the future of my people. What is done cannot be undone."

Nissowaquet spoke and Langlade translated, "Matters of the heart sometimes outweigh matters of the council fire. Domitilde's marriage was always supposed to bring two peoples closer to one another. That is still so, just not with the Ottawa and the Chippewa. Her union will now bring the Ottawa and the English closer. That is a trade that we can accept."

"But can Kinonchamek?" Sam asked. "Will his father, Minavavana, accept this insult?"

Langlade translated, then spoke Nissowaquet's response. "Emissaries will be sent to the Chippewa. Other offers will be made. Nissowaquet has many granddaughters, some of whom he says can even rival the beauty of Domitilde." Langlade smiled proudly. "Kinonchamek may come and try to win over any he sees fit."

"I do apologize for any inconvenience this has caused in the relationship with the Chippewa," Etherington added.

"The Ottawa and the Chippewa," Langlade translated, "are as brothers of the same mother. This will not break bonds that have been in place since the creation, though they may be strained for a short while."

"Forgive me for speaking," Sam said, drawing looks from Etherington and Leslie that showed no forgiveness. "I am glad that my brother's follies will result in no great harm between the Indians, but how can we be sure that Kinonchamek will accept the offer of another bride? Everything I've been told of the man makes it seem as if William should expect retaliation."

Langlade translated, "Nissowaquet will make a personal plea for the safety of young William to the war chief Pontiac, whom Minavavana spends much time in council with. Minavavana will not risk any offense to him and Nissowaquet both. It is not in the interest of the Chippewa to make enemies of the Ottawa and the English, which would surely be the outcome if William met an untimely end."

Sam thought that was wishful thinking. Remembering Minavavana's words in Detroit, he thought the man would have no fear of making an enemy of the British. He might balk at upsetting his Ottawa allies, but he might not.

***

The morning dawned bright but cold. The wedding ceremony began under the great crooked oak. The local French mission priest and an elderly Ottawa, whom Sam took to be some sort of holy man, presided. It seemed that most of the village lined the dune under the tree, turned out in their best dress, the men with feathers in their hair and the women adorned with all manner of beads and trinkets.

The escorting soldiers stood at rigid attention, with their muskets held in front of them. Etherington and Leslie looked on respectfully as Fritz and Sam stood behind William as his representatives. William's uniform had been patched with great care and scrubbed and brushed to a state of cleanliness it had never seen before and never would again. His white dress gaiters shone in the sun. His fair hair was clean and freshly pleated, giving the tall young man a handsome appearance that drew approval from Domitilde's maidens.

In fine doeskins studded with indigo and the peculiar Petoskey stones native to the area, with her dark hair pulled back and braided, Domitilde's beauty was only rivaled by that of her mother, who stood beside her and could be mistaken for an elder sister if one looked quickly enough. The bride's maidens spread out behind them, each looking more beautiful than the last.

The fetching young pair and their companions stood before the priest and the elder in front of the massive tree trunk, the even more massive lake behind them. It was a setting of such beauty as to hardly be thought terrestrial.

The clipped hybrid of a Catholic and Ottawa ceremony was mercifully short, for Sam could decipher none of the French and Ojibwe spoken. William understood none of it either, so it was fortunate that all he had to do was stand there and nod at a signal from the priest. With a last bit of ceremony, the elder Ottawa lit a fine, long pipe and passed it to William. William took a short draw and managed not to cough before passing the pipe to Domitilde. The girl took the pipe and deeply inhaled the tobacco smoke, giving a great exhalation that caused much delight and admiration from the soldiers looking on. With that done, Langlade made a pronouncement in Ojibwe that drew great cheers from those assembled.

Sam looked on at the two young people so in love with each other. He tried to smile as he imagined their future together. No matter how hard he tried, his mind couldn't conjure anything but darkness.

Ch. 9

Michilimackinac. March 1763

The sunsets crept up cold Lake Michigan with the passing of every evening, giving those enduring winter's frigid grip the promise that spring was indeed approaching, that it hadn't forgotten about this far-off corner of the world. But the fort was still encased in snow and ice, its occupants still existing in a state of semi-hibernation. The soldiers bundled themselves against the cold as best they could as they went about their duties. The French inhabitants engaged in minor trade and late nights of wine and song by their hearths. The Ottawa men hunted and trapped, then went home to their warm fires and warmer women.

    Sam was now alone in the little hut. He paid the savvy Langlade a hefty percentage of his meager wage for the privilege of his own meager space. The roof leaked the few times the temperature had spiked above freezing, and the wind and cold penetrated the window's thin shutters and the gaping cracks in the mud insulation. But the pallet was comfortable and the space was his own, so he felt it was a price well worth paying.

    William had spent the winter in much better conditions, in marital bliss with his new bride in a lovely little cottage near Langlade's. His new father-in-law provided the accommodation, and the Frenchman charged his new son-in-law a "very fair price." The happy couple had Sam over for supper many a night, and the trio spent much of the long, dark winter in each other's company while they waited for the sun to return. Domitilde's belly grew along with the length of the days, and it was expected the baby would arrive with summer.

    Never one to commune much with the divine, Sam had taken to praying nightly that they would all still be together and in good health when the baby came. The nightly howls of the wolf pack that ranged outside the palisade reminded him of the danger that awaited beyond the gates. The wolves' howls seemed to grow more persistent and nearer as the nights shortened and the season marched on to its close.

***

A shiver shot through Sam as he splashed cold water from the basin over his freshly shaven face. For lack of a mirror, he inspected his work by running his hands over his cheeks to search out any missed stubble. *Standards must be maintained,* Sam heard Fritz's voice in his mind, even though the soldiers rarely went about with their faces uncovered by thick scarves. Only a few more passes with the razor were needed to complete the job.

A sharp knock sounded on the door. Sam wiped his face with a somewhat clean rag, not bothering to dawn his shirt before cracking the door to a gray morning. Fritz's red face greeted him.

"*Mein junge,*" Fritz said, beaming.

"Sergeant Meyer," Sam replied. He swung the door open and stood at mock attention. "To what do I owe the privilege? I have sentry duty this evening. I wasn't aware I'd be needed before then."

Fritz pushed by him and moved his stout little frame in front of the fire as Sam closed the door to keep out the cold. "The King's stores are running low, *mein junge.* Captain Etherington wishes to supplement our diet with some good venison."

"And you've volunteered me," Sam sighed.

Fritz only smiled in response as he warmed his rump.

"Why not use the Ottawa to hunt?" Sam asked. "They're much more capable than we." He moved around the thick sergeant to get to his shirt. "Just trade some rum or shot for a fresh kill."

"Where's the fun in that?" Fritz boomed. "I told the captain that you, *Wilhelm,* and I are the men for the job."

"Hah!" Sam laughed. "You think you can peel that beanpole off his new bride to go sit in the cold woods and see nothing but squirrels? I know what my answer would be."

"Well it's a good thing it's an order and not a request."

Knowing further protest to be futile, Sam slowly donned his shirt and regimental coat, then the buckskin overcoat he'd traded for some time ago. "Fine, fine, Fritz. Let's go freeze our backsides off," he relented, wrapping his face in a scarf and donning the Indian mittens Domitilde had sewn him. He hefted his musket and cartridge belt and pushed the little sergeant out the door as he adjusted his tricorn.

The two men traded what scant gossip and news they had as they slogged to William's cabin. They had run out of both by the time they reached William's door. Fritz used the butt of his musket to wrap loudly on the sturdy portal.

Much feminine protest and cursing rose from within. After a long wait, the door finally opened. William's disheveled head popped from the warm space, wearing a look of annoyance. Sam chuckled at the sight of his brother. The lad's state made it evident that Domitilde's delicate condition had not kept him from fulfilling his husbandly duties.

"What?" William asked, not hiding his irritation.

"Is that how you talk to your sergeant?" Fritz chided.

William inhaled sharply. "What may I do for you, Sergeant Meyer?"

Fritz let his chin rise in mock triumph as he looked down his nose at the boy. "Get your things and get your *arsch* out here on the quick. We have some hunting to do, *mein junge*."

"William?" Domitilde called from somewhere within the warm confines of the cabin.

William looked back inside, then back to the men standing in front of him. It almost seemed, for perhaps just a moment, that he might refuse to go.

Fritz ended any resistance when he began counting, "*Eins, zwei, drei.*"

William disappeared inside, shutting the door with a curse.

"You can't blame him," Sam chuckled, hearing Domitilde erupt in protest deep inside the cabin.

"*Nein,*" Fritz agreed, "you can't. Not with her in his bed."

William finally appeared with his necessary kit and a rotten look on his face. Fritz ignored it and happily steered them to the Land Gate. As they strode along the snow-packed lane, a particularly rough-looking Frenchman in a red knit cap stepped from his tiny, dirty cabin and hacked a particularly vile, viscous looking glob of phlegm into the snow. The bare-chested bear of a man spotted the approaching soldiers and eyed them with malice. Fritz locked eyes with him in return and never looked away until they'd finally passed.

"What's his issue?" William asked.

Fritz looked at the lad, then pulled open William's overcoat to reveal the red beneath. "This," he said, thumbing the red regimental jacket.

Needing no further explanation, the group trudged on in silence.

The Frenchman, who'd made a habit of watching the comings and goings of the tall, skinny redcoat and his little half-breed bitch throughout the long winter, watched the soldiers' every step until they disappeared out the Land Gate. Then he turned on his heel and entered the dirty hovel. He emerged moments later fully dressed against the cold, with musket, powder, and cartridge belt in hand. He hefted his snowshoes across his back and hurried for the Water Gate.

***

With their native-made snowshoes strapped to their boots, the three plodded over the long-abandoned fields surrounding the fort, only a dull ache reminding Sam of Ol' Bill's handiwork. They had many miles of hard travel ahead of them to reach rich hunting grounds, the area around Michilimackinac having been hunted to exhaustion. They chose to head southeast. Fritz had bagged a nice buck in that country at the beginning of winter and hoped to replicate his success. Soon, they entered the forest and were surrounded by ice-encased hardwoods and hearty evergreens.

"Every step we march," William huffed, his long legs struggling over the snow, "is a step we have to march back with a bleeding deer carcass on our backs."

"If we even see one," Sam added.

"Ah!" Fritz said, and swiped his hand. "Where's the fire in you, lads?"

"William's is back in his bed." Sam smiled, summoning a similar response from his brother.

Fritz tried a different tack. "I rarely see you boys anymore outside of duty. Don't you miss your old Uncle Fritz?"

"I miss Uncle Fritz," William said. "I can't say I miss that mean bastard Sergeant Meyer, though."

Sam let out a mighty laugh, scattering a few squirrels. For a split second Fritz's face reddened with anger, but he soon broke into laughter at the jest.

"*Mein junge!* Maybe that girl *is* putting some fire in your belly!" Fritz said.

"That she is," Sam agreed.

William could only smile sheepishly.

They came to a ribbon of ice that marked a wide stream. "Is it safe to cross?" William asked, using the butt of his musket to test the thickness of the ice along the bank.

"Probably," Fritz answered, "but I know a spot a little further along that is much safer."

They trudged a few hundred yards upstream, sticking to the woods to avoid the rocks and fallen branches along the bank. Fritz poked his musket at an evergreen weighed down with snow, causing a little avalanche in front of them. When the snow ceased falling, he pushed his hardy frame through the boughs. The brothers followed, popping out once more alongside the stream.

"Aha!" Fritz said, and gestured proudly at a huge fallen elm tree that spanned the stream. "Safe!"

The men removed their awkward snowshoes and took turns tying them to one another's backs. Sam went first, easily crossing the span with his musket held parallel for balance. William came second. At the midpoint, a slight teetering tied Sam's stomach in knots, but William recovered and scampered across. Fritz came last, and what a sight he made. The little sergeant shuffled his feet in such small movements that he more inched than stepped along the trunk of the great tree.

"By God," Sam burst out laughing, with William joining. "You look like a giant red snail advancing along!"

Fritz's face grew redder than its normal shade, but he wasted no concentration in responding to the insult. In his own slow time, he finally reached the opposite bank. He gave each laughing brother a playful slap and then pushed them in the right direction.

The sun reached its zenith, popping from clouds and bringing light to a forest floor that had seen precious little of it throughout the winter. The temperature rose above freezing for the first time in weeks, and Sam began to sweat from exertion. He almost regretted bringing his buckskin overcoat. But then he remembered the trek back to the fort, and how the temperature dropped like a stone when night fell in the Upper Country.

They came to a high ridge covered in bare hardwoods. Fritz dropped his voice to a whisper and pointed down to a shallow valley below them as he said, "The deer bed in the aspen and pine down there. We will take up position along the ridge. You here, Sammie. *Wilhelm,* follow me. I'll place you a hundred yards further along, then I'll take the southernmost position."

"How long are we planning on sitting out here?" William whispered. "It will be dark in a few hours."

Fritz gave him a playful punch on the shoulder. "That's when the deer come out, *mein junge.*"

"Domitilde will be worried."

"Let her worry," Fritz growled, but his face softened after a moment. "She'll greet you all the more passionately if you let her fret a bit."

"I have sentry duty tonight, Fritz," Sam reminded him.

"Fine, Fine!" Fritz huffed in defeat. "Just an hour or two, then we go back. Come, *Wilhelm.*"

Dejected, William let Fritz pull him along. They soon disappeared from Sam's view in the thick underbrush.

Finding a fat oak, Sam took off his snowshoes and diligently swept away the snow to make a more comfortable area to sit. When satisfied, he propped his musket against the tree and lowered himself down so his back was against the trunk. Then he plopped the musket across his lap. He pulled off his tricorn and let the warm sun hit his face as he gave an exaggerated sigh of comfort.

Paying no great mind to his hunting ground – he had little intention of shooting a deer and having to drag the carcass back, suspecting Fritz's motivations were more towards spending time with the brothers than bagging meat – he listened to the sounds of the forest as the afternoon passed on. Gusts of wind blew through bare branches. Squirrels chittered and skittered across the ground and through the trees. Moments of deep silence endured until they seemed unending, only to be finally broken by falling snow or the call of a bird.

Sam allowed his eyes to close, and he slipped into a pleasant doze. His mind drifted until some small sound brought him back. He would open his eyes, scan the ground to see mostly the same things, then close his eyes again, repeating the process a dozen times as the sun marched overhead.

A cold blow announced the wind was making one of its sudden shifts, reorienting from the southwest to almost right out of the north. Sam raised his collar and stamped his feet as the temperature dropped by the minute.

It wasn't long after when he heard a racket approaching from his left. He raised his musket slightly, but let it fall when he saw William and Fritz tromping toward him along the ridge. "I didn't hear any shots," Sam said, and smiled.

William gestured over his shoulder and said, "The great hunter's bum got cold!"

Sam let out a hoot of laughter. "That was barely more than an hour, *Sergeant* Meyer!"

Fritz cast his eyes upon Sam. "*Mein arsch is kalt!*" he said, and shivered. "Let us go. We'll have a spot of rum by the fire back home."

"I won't argue with that," Sam answered, gathering his things and standing.

The group made a leisurely pace as they retraced their steps, the going easier from the packed snow along their path. The boys informed Fritz of the scuttlebutt that was passing among the privates, leaving out anything that could get one of their compatriots in real trouble. Fritz told them all he knew about the goings on outside the fort and back in Detroit, which wasn't much. They soon began talking of the old days. The brothers shared stories with Fritz of their parents during their childhood, bringing a smile and a few tears to the sergeant's face. Fritz contributed stories of his escapades with their father during their time in the Army. Many laughs were had, and a couple pairs of wet eyes sprang from the brothers. It wasn't long before they reached the stream crossing.

Sam made to mount the elm when Fritz put a firm hand on his chest. "*Nein*," he hissed. "I'll not have you jackals howling at me from the far bank. I go first."

Doffing his tricorn, Sam drawled, "Very well, Sergeant Meyer. After you."

Fritz ignored him. He took off his snowshoes, had William tie them to his back, then hefted his musket and inelegantly mounted the elm. The brothers took off their snowshoes as Fritz began his slow shuffle across the frozen stream. Sam and William were ready and waiting their turn by the time Fritz reached halfway.

"It will be dark soon," Sam jested.

Fritz never had a chance to respond. A musket cracked from somewhere behind them. Sam watched the ball drive between Fritz's shoulder blades and exit through his chest in an eruption of cloth and blood and gore. The brothers looked on, frozen, as Fritz seemed to maintain his balance for a split second, then he slowly toppled and dropped to the ice with a dull thud.

The whine of a ball passing close to Sam's ear snapped him from the grisly scene. He pulled his brother down and they ducked behind the only cover at hand, a fallen limb of the elm. Looking back to Fritz, Sam could already see a bright red pool blossoming on the ice under the sergeant. Blood blew from Fritz's lips in ragged gasps, and his wide eyes looked around in bewilderment.

Without thinking, Sam rose and made to go for him. A musket's crack forced him to duck back under cover.

"Don't!" William yelled, a steadiness in his voice at odds with their predicament.

Sam locked eyes with his brother.

"There's at least three," William answered his stare, "and the other two have reloaded by now. They'll cut you down if you go out there."

The sound of movement through trees came to them over the protection of the log. Men called to one another in French. "They're bloody frogs," Sam spat, incensed that a beaten foe would dare be so brazen. More movement and snapping branches told him they were being surrounded.

Peeking his head over the log, Sam saw a figure in Indian dress dash behind a tree not more than two dozen yards away. He ducked back and gasped, "They'll soon be on us. We should stand and fight!"

"We'll die," William answered.

"We're going to die sitting here," Sam retorted. "Better to die fighting."

"There might be another way," William said, looking around. "Remember Otayonih's words on ambush: you must leave the ground the attacker chose and keep moving to have any chance of survival."

A ball thwacked into the wood above their heads, sending splinters flying in all directions. Sam instinctively flinched. "Then let's have your plan."

With a calculating eye, William swept the ground around them, finally settling on the stream. He nodded calmly towards the ice. "We'll have to make our way downstream over the ice. It's our only chance without snowshoes. They chose the spot well."

"We'll break through!"

William shrugged. "Possibly."

Sam looked out over the ice. Fritz was still alive, gasping for air as blood bubbled from his lips. "What about Fritz!"

Emotion showed for the first time on William's face. He looked out to the sergeant and tears began running down his cheeks. "Fritz's lung's been shot away. He doesn't have long no matter what aid we render. He'd want us to at least try to get away."

As if in concordance with William's plan, Fritz called out weakly, "Run!"

Sam locked eyes with his dying friend. Fritz gave him the smallest of nods as a smile came to his bloodstained lips.

Tearing his eyes away, Sam looked to William and asked, "How?"

"Wait until one fires, then you stand and fire, then run. I will follow along and keep my shot in case we need it. We run north along the stream as long as we can. It will eventually reach the lake," William explained.

"We'll never outrun them." Sam shook his head in defeat. "There's at least one Indian among them."

William put a hand on Sam's shoulder. "We don't need to outrun them, brother. We only need to get them into a different position. One of our choosing."

Sam marveled at his brother's calm. Where was the boy who yelped in fear at the sight of Ol' Bill not long before?

"Fine," Sam finally relented, "but you fire and go. I'll follow along."

"Very well," William said with a sigh, knowing his older brother would have it no other way.

Giving Fritz one last look, William called out, "I love you, you old fool."

Fritz didn't respond, or couldn't respond. He just kept struggling for breath.

"Swift and bold, William," Sam said.

"Swift and bold," William repeated. He took a few long, deep breaths, then raised himself so his back appeared over the log, then he dropped like a lead weight.

The ruse worked. One of the attackers fired off a shot, the ball whizzing through the air above the brothers.

William quickly sprang up. He leveled his musket and looked down the barrel for half a second, adjusting his aim left before pulling the trigger. The flint struck and a billow of smoke erupted from the pan, followed by an explosion from the barrel.

Before the smoke had even begun to settle, William shot off onto the ice. Sam wasn't far behind. Another musket shot belched from the tree line, but the ball passed harmlessly between them.

Sam looked down at Fritz as the brothers ran by no more than ten yards from him. Comprehension had come back to Fritz's eyes, and the little sergeant fumbled with his musket, bringing it up and aiming in the direction of their attackers. With no time to spare, Sam ran on, trying desperately to maintain his footing on the slick surface as it creaked and groaned beneath him.

A wild yell of frustration echoed from the tree line behind them. No doubt their attackers saw their victims escaping down the ice, and their own snowshoes were hindering their pursuit. Sam knew it wouldn't take long for the men to lose their snowshoes and take up the chase across the ice.

That was when another musket cracked. William flinched, but no ball whizzed by. A distant grunt of pain carried across the ice and into the brothers' ears. Sam didn't know if Fritz had felled one of their attackers, or if the scoundrels had finished off their dear friend. He just kept on running.

The going was slow as the two struggled to keep their feet. Then William slipped completely, his butt thudding against the smooth ice and sending veins of cracks in all directions. Sam's heart dropped until the lad regained his feet like a big cat during a chase. William hardly lost any of his forward momentum and scrambled on, soon finding his stride a few paces in front of Sam.

Sam came to a snow-covered, reliable patch of ice and risked a look over his shoulder. Two men were scrambling along the ice a hundred yards back. They moved with a confidence that spoke of hunters gaining ground. Fear gave way to anger as Sam recognized the lead pursuer. A red knit cap bobbed along after them. It was the brutish Frenchman who had given them such a look of hatred in the fort. An Indian followed not far behind. No other attackers had followed onto the ice.

He must have followed us, Sam thought as he turned his eyes forward.

"Two follow, William!" he gasped. "They're gaining."

"Keep pushing!" William called out. "Make the bend!"

A hundred yards ahead, the stream bent sharply to the left. "Then?" Sam choked, his breath failing him.

"As we round it," William panted, "you break off into the trees on the left."

Sam needn't waste anymore breath asking for explanation. He knew exactly what his brother had in mind. Instead, he kept all his energy on keeping his feet under him as he moved over the treacherous ice.

After a couple more heart-stopping stumbles, the brothers finally reached the bend. They turned with the stream and briefly escaped their pursuers' view. William pointed to the left bank, where a thick evergreen leaned out over the ice. Sam wasted no time, changing direction and scrambling towards it. He tumbled into the snow beneath the pine, making sure to keep his pan dry. William just scurried on down the ice, his frantic movements comical if it had been another time.

Sam came to a knee and sucked in air to regain his breath. He didn't have much time to compose himself for what was to come. He slowed his breathing and took deep inhalations, then blew the air from his lungs in long, steady exhalations. Raising his musket, he cocked it and looked down the barrel. The cold metal rose and fell with his lungs. The thundering in his chest hadn't eased, and he knew it would impact his shot, but there was nothing to be done.

William was almost fifty yards on when Sam finally heard them coming around the bend. The red knit cap of the Frenchman came around the tree, then the greased hair of the Indian. Sam could see the Frenchman's head cock slightly at the sight of only one soldier on the ice in front of him, but he didn't check his stride and kept pushing forward.

Sam tracked his barrel onto the back of the Indian no more than a dozen yards away. His labored breathing kept the barrel dancing in his eye, but every second he let pass, his target got further away.

A fine marksman could miss a standing fat man at fifty paces with the Brown Bess. That was just the nature of the fickle, smooth-bored bitch. Hitting a running man at twenty-five paces, with your heart hammering in your chest and the breath out of you, was no simple shot, especially when a miss meant the death of your brother.

With a gentle squeeze of the trigger, Sam fired, then he shot up and dashed through his smoke. The Indian ran on, seeming no worse for the wear. Sam cursed himself, thinking he'd missed. But the Indian's steps began to falter, until finally he stopped running and dropped to a knee, clutching at his stomach.

Sam was on him in seconds. The warrior looked up at his rapid approach without emotion. Sam swung his musket like a club. Knowing he was already a dead man from the gut shot, the Indian made no attempt to shield himself as the butt staved in his skull and splattered bits of his brain and bone over the white ice.

Sam never broke stride as he passed the crumpling body.

The Frenchman was only a dozen yards ahead of him now, still chasing his prey, oblivious or uncaring that his compatriot had been felled. William ran on a few dozen yards beyond the Frenchman.

Sam could see the Frenchman still wielding his musket, but his failure to take a shot at William meant the shot must have been spent earlier.

"William!" Sam called out.

Everyone skidded to a stop and froze in their tracks. William turned to see the Frenchman separating him and Sam. The Frenchman turned in tight circles, the realization that he was now the surrounded dawning on him. All stood their ground, each sucking in breaths after the long run.

The Frenchman's shock at the turn of the tables subsided quickly, and he gave each Avery a calculating eye. Then he looked to the woods. Sam shivered as he realized the man was weighing his options. If he ran, he might catch a ball in the back. If he ran and lived, half the Upper Country would be looking to cash in on the bounty his scalp would surely fetch after the two sprats made it back to Michilimackinac with their story. If he fought, he'd probably die, but maybe not. Maybe he could kill them both. That was his only chance to escape the consequences of this day.

Knowing what conclusion the Frenchman would reach, Sam dug into his coat. He cursed himself when he found the loop that normally held his hatchet empty. It was one of the rare times he'd forgotten it. The musket would be his only weapon. He hefted it confidently and started forward.

"Load, William!" Sam commanded.

Unwilling to wait and be shot down like a tethered cow, the Frenchman dropped his empty musket and drew an old but lethal spadroon – a short sword popular among the frogs – and made for what he thought the easier target.

William faltered and dropped his cartridge as the Frenchman charged at him. Turning and running was out of the question now, so he braced his musket in front of him and readied himself.

The Frenchman's blade slashed forward, only to be caught by William's musket. But the frog used his momentum to crash into the lanky soldier with all his weight. They landed together heavily, a bloodcurdling crack issuing from the ice. Each man froze as a spiderweb of cracks scarred surface beneath them. It held for only a moment longer, then shattered.

William gulped in a breath just before he plunged into the cold water. His body felt as if it had burst into flame as the stream pulled at his heavy clothes. He did the only thing he could, clutching at his attacker, who remained half out of the water. The need to breath drove William toward the daylight, and he squeezed and clawed his way up the clothes of the Frenchman until his head burst from the water. He gasped in a breath of air, getting much water in the process.

Fighting for his own life, the Frenchman tried to scramble from the hole in the ice, but he found little purchase on the smooth surface. In a rage, he sent several elbows flying into the face of the man dragging him back into the cold stream. One landed, and the soldier's grip slackened but did not fail altogether.

William, his nose broken and pouring blood, fought desperately to maintain his grip and keep his head above the water. It was a losing struggle. His heavy clothes and the Frenchman's efforts forced him down to the stream's bottom.

The Frenchman knew he was only one more strong effort away from ridding himself of the soldier and being able to struggle his way to safety.

The brass butt plate of Sam's musket cracked the Frenchman across the bridge of his nose. The brute froze like a stunned fish. Sam stomped down on the man's coat collar, pinning him in place so both William and he wouldn't be swallowed by the slow current.

William felt the Frenchman's body go limp against his struggles. With all his remaining strength, he climbed the man as if he were a ladder. His head broke the surface, and he filled his lungs with life-giving air. Sam stood over him. A musket's butt dropped in the water next to his head and William clung to it. Sam gave a mighty heave and pulled William from the water like a landed catch.

With William safe, Sam turned back to the Frenchman. The big man was regaining his senses, clawing at the ice and struggling to pull himself from the frigid pool. But the water's cold and Sam's musket butt had taken their toll. There was barely any fight left in him.

The two locked eyes and the Frenchman ceased his struggles. They looked at each other for a long moment, the only sounds the gasping breaths William took as he lay on the ice next to them. With hardly a thought, Sam stood tall and raised the musket.

Sorrow filled the Frenchman's blue eyes. A pleading, "*Non!*" escaped his lips.

Sam swung the musket and cracked it across the frog's red cap. The Frenchman's eyes rolled back and his body went lifeless. The cold, slow current drew him down under the ice. Sam watched the man's body disappear. The red knit cap lingered on the surface for only a moment longer before it too sank and vanished.

"Sam," William gasped.

Sam dropped his musket and knelt beside his brother.

"I'm cold," William chattered, his lips a deathly shade of blue.

The cold was now as dangerous an enemy as any they'd faced that day. Sam began working at his brother's coat, his numb hands fumbling with the heavy fabric. Against William's weak protests, he stripped off the wet clothes clinging to his brother. It wasn't long before the lad was completely naked and shivering on the ice. Sam doffed his overcoat and draped it over William before he sprinted back the way they'd come. He reached the dead Indian and began pulling and tugging at the man's buckskins, liberating every dry article down to the already stiffening corpse's moccasins.

Loaded down, Sam rushed back to his brother. It was difficult getting the lad's shaking limbs into the clothing, but Sam worked with a speed that spoke of how dire the situation was. He knew William only had moments left if he was not warmed soon. And there could still be other attackers lurking in the woods. Movement and the sanctuary of the fort were their only hopes.

"Come!" Sam gasped, lifting his brothers dead weight.

William let out a groan but let himself be lifted from the ice.

"We must keep you moving!" Sam cried as he started forward, half carrying, half dragging his brother downstream.

After only a few hundred yards, William, his teeth rattling in his skull, said, "I don't think I want to go on, Sam."

"Nonsense!" Sam huffed, bearing the lad on. "Domitilde is waiting for you back at the fort. She'll have a warm fire in the hearth and a big tankard of rum ready for you."

"I don't know if I can." William fumbled, stumbling over the ice.

Sam caught him and brought him back up. To push him, he said, "You're going to be a father, William! Are you so ready to give up and never see your babe born?"

William didn't respond, just struggled on.

Sam kept talking. "A father must fight for his children from the moment they're born to the day he draws his last breath. Your day to start fighting just came a little sooner, that's all. Your fight begins today. Start fighting, William!"

William continued to drag on him, not responding. This would do for no more than a few hundred yards before Sam would collapse himself. *Could a fire be built*, Sam wondered? No. He'd have to go back for the muskets and gather tinder from the frozen forest, then only God knew if he could get it going. And a fire would be a beacon if any attackers remained. It was the fort or nothing.

"What would father think of you giving up on your child!" Sam tried again. "He never gave up on us! He'd have crawled home from Quebec if he'd had a quarter the strength left in you!"

Only labored breathing answered, but Sam noticed his brother raised his back ever so slightly. His strides seemed to strengthen, and the burden weighing on Sam lightened with each step downstream. Soon they were moving at a steady pace, and the flowing blood undoubtedly warmed William. It wasn't long before they both fell into the trance-like state that soldiers embraced on the march. With what felt like the last reserves of strength left to them, they each lifted one foot and placed it in front of the other. Then they did it again, and then again. Their minds wandered, but not far enough to let their feet stop churning forward. They slogged on.

The ice began to thin noticeably, pulling Sam from his trance. He looked up to see a break ahead in the unending trees. "The lake!" he gasped.

"Thank God!" William panted.

They left the thinning ice and turned northwest. Deep snow slowed their pace, but they pushed through until they reached the beach. The straits' relentless winds had scoured the beach of snow, and the frozen sand was as fine a roadway as any on the continent. The sun fell into the lake in front of them and brought twilight, but they kept moving forward.

Smoke rose over the horizon and the brothers smelled it well before they laid eyes on the fort, putting strength into their remaining steps. It wasn't long before the gray wood of the palisade rose from the shoreline in the failing light. Sam pointed them toward the sentry's brazier that burned like a beacon of life outside the Water Gate.

"Who goes there!" a nervous voice called at their approach.

"The Privates Avery!" Sam hailed.

A private with musket in hand stepped into the light of the brazier. "Sam?"

The brothers pushed past the confused soldier with no explanation, their stride not breaking as they made for the guardhouse just inside the gate. Sam threw the latch on the heavy door and they tumbled into the warm space. A blazing fire burned in the hearth only paces away. Sam used what strength he had left to drag William as close to the fire as he could without scorching the lad, then he dropped next to him, exhausted.

Someone stepped into the guardhouse, but the brothers took no notice as they warmed themselves before the fire like lizards on a sun-soaked rock. "Where's Sergeant Meyer?"

Sam turned to see Corporal Kane's concerned face. William began to sob gently into his sleeve. Kane looked at the state of the brothers, then let his eyes linger on the sobbing William.

He needed nothing more to know that something terrible had happened.

***

"This is the spot," Sam said.

Lieutenant Leslie and Corporal Kane drew level. Fritz's body lay in front of them, still where it had fallen the day before. The two pushed past Sam and cautiously made their way over the ice toward the body. Sam stood and stared as the other five soldiers accompanying them brushed by.

Langlade, who'd stuck to the rear of the group, stopped at Sam's side. He took a long look over the ground and nodded appreciatively. "A good spot for an ambush," he said.

"Very good," Sam agreed, unable to turn away from Fritz's corpse.

"Come, Sam," Langlade finally said.

They joined the group circled around the sergeant's body.

Kane pointed to a frozen corpse on the stream's bank. "Did you fell him?" he asked Sam.

Sam took in the fallen Indian, then looked to Fritz. His musket lay along his side, as if he'd just fired it from his back. His right hand was still frozen around the grip, his index finger still in the trigger guard. Sam bent over the body. The hammer had fallen into the pan.

"Fritz must have shot him down as they pursued us," Sam choked, trying to hold back tears.

Langlade joined him, crouching over the body. "It would have been his last act," he said.

Sam looked into Langlade's eyes.

"A good death," Langlade consoled.

"But still a death," Sam said.

"And this fellow?" Leslie asked, prodding the fallen Indian with the tip of his sword.

Langlade stood and answered, "A Chippewa," as he walked over to the corpse.

"How can you be sure?" Leslie asked, his eyes never leaving the dead Indian. "They all look the same to me."

Langlade paused and glowered at the lieutenant. "Could you tell the difference between a dead Englishman and a dead Frenchman?"

Leslie looked up at Langlade as if he were a fool. "Of course!"

After a long look of disdain, Langlade finally pointed down to the dead man's feet. "Look at his moccasins."

Leslie barely deigned to look.

Langlade explained, "The Chippewa cure their moccasins over the fire. The Ottawa do not do this. It's as plain to me as it would be to you if he were a Frenchman with a *fleur-de-lis* growing from his asshole."

Leslie reddened, but made no retort.

"I knew," Langlade continued, "that they were Chippewa last night, when I saw the moccasins Sam scavenged for William."

"We must bring Fritz home," Sam said, caring little for the conversation.

Langlade and Kane supervised the other privates' effort to build a crude travois out of two large birch logs. They lashed smaller sticks between the two and made to gather up Fritz's body. Sam had to look away when the corpse was peeled roughly from the ice and placed on the sled. Langlade thoughtfully covered Fritz with a blanket from the dead Chippewa.

"And he?" Kane asked, nodding to the Chippewa.

Leslie shrugged and said, "Leave him for the wolves."

Ignoring the officer, Langlade went forward and knelt over the body. The soldiers watched as he said a few words in his native tongue, seeming to perform a little ritual. Then he drew his knife, gripped the Chippewa's long hair, and ran his blade across the skull, yanking with all his might. The frozen scalp tore away with a hideous ripping noise as the soldiers winced in shock. One of the privates lost his breakfast over the ice.

Langlade stood and brought the gruesome trophy to the travois. He moved the blanket aside and tied the scalp by the hair to Fritz's cartridge belt. He said a few more words before pulling back the blanket. When he'd finished, he looked to Leslie and said, "Shall we continue on?"

Not waiting for a response from the horror-struck lieutenant, Langlade started off downstream. Sam didn't hesitate to follow. Two privates took up the poles of the travois and started off after them, with Kane following. Leslie and the rest needed a few more moments of recovery.

They soon reached the second dead Chippewa. Langlade looked to Sam and pulled his knife, nodding to the naked, frozen corpse. Sam took his meaning and quickly shook his head. He needed no trophy. Langlade merely shrugged and sheathed his knife as they moved on.

The hole that had taken the Frenchman already had a thin skin of new ice, and the soldiers eyed the ground warily. They moved as if trying to be light, slowly dropping each foot. The men with the travois stuck to the bank as close as they could.

Leslie finally arrived and bent over the Frenchman's discarded musket. He picked it up and made a show of studying it. "It's certainly French," he declared.

"How can you be so sure?" Langlade mocked.

Leslie gave him a hard look, but chose not to do anything.

Sam sighed. "As I've said a dozen times, he was from the fort. I don't know his name but I've seen him often, and he watched us leave yesterday morning."

"From your description," Langlade answered, "you describe Boucher. He has not been seen since yesterday. He has many dealings with the Chippewa, some of which are of the unsavory sort. He is the lowest form of trader." Langlade looked to Sam. "Or was."

"Can you track back to where he met the Indians?" Leslie asked Langlade.

"*Absolument*," Langlade answered.

"Do it," Leslie ordered. "I will escort the body back. How many men do you need?"

"Just Sam."

"Are you up for it, lad?" Kane asked.

Sam nodded and said, "I'm fine."

"Well, then, carry on," Leslie said dismissively.

***

After backtracking to the ambush site, Langlade easily found the trail the attackers had left. Boucher and his accomplices must have been quite confident that they'd eliminate their quarry, for they hadn't made any effort to hide their path. The going was relatively easy for Sam and Langlade, and they traveled quickly and wordlessly over the packed snow. The trail of the attackers gradually turned north, and the pair soon headed back toward Michilimackinac. They came to the shoreline east of the fort. In the protected saddle between two high dunes overlooking the very route Sam and William had used to return the night before, they discovered a small encampment that had seen much foot traffic.

Langlade finally broke the silence that had settled between them. "This is where Boucher came," he said, kneeling and looking into an abandoned lean-to shelter with animal hide coverings.

"Is it some sort of hunting camp?" Sam asked. "I thought most of the game around the fort had been depleted."

Langlade didn't answer. He gestured for Sam to follow as he entered the woods at the edge of the saddle. They clawed their way up the inland face of one of the dunes, using a well-worn path. Reaching the top of the great, snow-covered mound of sand and trees, Langlade pointed west. A sheer drop fell before them, devoid of trees. Through the opening, they saw the fallow fields surrounding Michilimackinac. The fort sat some miles away, but it was clearly discernible from their perch. Sam could see smoke rising from inside the gray palisade, and if he squinted he thought he could just make out the red form of a sentry moving along the wall.

"A man with a glass can see everything that happens at the fort from this spot," Langlade said.

Sam finally put the thoughts that had been going through his head since the day before into words. "This is the work of Kinonchamek," he said. "He posted men here to watch for us. He had a man in the fort to watch our dealings, to strike if the opportunity arose."

Langlade did not look convinced as he watched the distant fort. "I don't think these men were posted here just to watch for you, that this was all arranged only for revenge."

"But Boucher."

"Oh, I have no doubt that Boucher was aware of Kinonchamek's humiliation at the hands of your brother. Most in the Upper Country are, and certainly everyone in Michilimackinac. But Kinonchamek is the type to settle his accounts personally."

"The Indians who ambushed us?"

"You were in Detroit," Langlade replied. "You heard the words Minavavana spoke to that haughty major. The war may not be over for him, and it would be prudent to know the goings on of the fort if one wanted to know its weaknesses, in case fighting broke out again. I think Boucher was working with the Chippewa in this. And when he saw the three of you leave…" Langlade looked to Sam. "He saw an opportunity to ingrain himself further into the good graces of Kinonchamek and Minavavana, and he sought to use the scouts who were here to help him."

"Well," Sam said, "Fritz is dead. William was almost killed. What will happen next?"

"Indeed," Langlade said, and nodded. "What will happen next?"

***

At the very limit of the blazing fire's warming glow, Sam stood at attention in the commander's house. Langlade was just finishing presenting his findings and theories to a listening Etherington. The two men sat at a long wooden table set close to the hearth, joined by the always blasé-looking Leslie. Corporal Kane was much closer to the conversation and the heat of the fire, but hadn't been asked to sit.

"So," Etherington said. He leaned back in his chair, looking quite tired. "You seem to think that these men who attacked Sergeant Meyer's party were tasked by Minavavana with keeping watch on this fort? And that the Frenchman who aided them was in fact some sort of spy?"

Sam could see annoyance flicker across Langlade's face along with the firelight, but the man hid it quickly and said, "*Oui*. I don't need to remind you what was said by Minavavana at Detroit. Not all are happy with your presence in these woods."

"Sir," Leslie said, and looked up from his wine, "if I may?" Etherington nodded for him to continue. "I believe this simply to be a case of a few rogues seeing an opportunity to waylay some of the King's soldiers. *Monsieur* Langlade himself has already told us that this Boucher was a man of the lowest sort, with a reputation for unsavory trade practices. Maybe he fancied Sergeant Meyer's coat? Maybe he saw an opportunity to procure three fine muskets and their shot and powder? Maybe he saw a chance to avenge his humiliation as a Frenchman subjected by the British? We will never know." Leslie looked at Sam, who stood at the edge of the shadows. "Shame you didn't leave the Frenchman alive, Avery. That would have helped us get to the bottom of this."

"My apologies, sir," Sam droned with contempt.

Ignoring him, Leslie gulped more wine and turned back to the Captain. "I think a few punishments handed out to the frogs, along with a few good Indian hangings, will see this kind of nonsense stop right away."

"Hang Indians?" Langlade menaced.

The tipsy lieutenant misunderstood the meaning behind the question. "Oh, any will do, I should think. Just grab a few drunks from the closest village and string them up on the parade ground. That will cow frog and savage alike."

"Enough!" Etherington said, pounding the table.

Leslie blanched and shut his mouth. It was a good thing he did. Sam could see that Langlade would probably have killed the man if he'd uttered another word, consequences be damned.

"*Monsieur,*" Etherington said, trying to draw Langlade's dagger gaze from Leslie, who sat stupidly fiddling with his wine glass.

Only reluctantly did Langlade turn his attention to the captain.

"I can assure you," Etherington continued, "that there will be no arbitrary punishments while the Union Jack flies over this fort, to Frenchman *or* Indian."

Langlade nodded curtly, but his eyes made it clear the declaration was irrelevant. None of his people would come to harm while he had breath, British intentions be damned.

"But," Etherington added, "it cannot be ignored that a Frenchman attacked some of the King's soldiers. You have been granted several lucrative contracts and concessions by General Amherst with the belief that you would aid in seeing the transition to British rule goes smoothly, with both the French and the Indians. I need to know that you are capable of that."

Langlade's chin rose. "I have pledged my allegiance to King George, and I will do all I can to be a faithful subject to him, but I never claimed that I could sway the heart of every man in the Upper Country," he said.

"But you will do everything in your ability to keep the French under control, along with the Indians?"

Langlade nodded, too upset to repeat oaths that had already been sworn.

"Now," Etherington said, and leaned back once more, "it is my opinion, or maybe my foolish hope, that these men were indeed just rogues seeking their own personal gain after a hard winter. But I cannot overlook *Monsieur* Langlade's beliefs that this might be part of a more concerted effort by Minavavana, perhaps one that may soon spill into rebellion. I will inform Major Gladwin in Detroit of your concerns. He will do with them what he will."

Etherington looked to Leslie, who was refilling his wine glass from a decanter. Seeing the man was well on his way to inebriation, Etherington turned to Corporal Kane and said, "Corporal Kane."

"Sir!" the man said, and stiffened.

"You are hereby promoted to sergeant."

"Thank you, Sir!"

"You are to double the guard immediately and pass orders along to the sentries that no Indian be allowed into the fort unless under express permission from me. And if allowed in, they will be escorted at all times by one of His Majesty's soldiers."

"Yes, sir!"

"The gates will now remain closed after dark, and any breaking of His Majesty's laws – by Frenchman, Indian, British citizen, or the soldierly – will result in the harshest punishment."

"Yes, sir!"

"And I leave it to you to find among the men somebody suitable for promotion to corporal."

"I don't have to go far, sir," Kane said, and smiled. "I believe Avery here will do."

"Step forward, Avery!" Etherington barked.

Sam hesitated a split second while his heart dropped into his stomach, but then stepped toward the fire and stomped to attention. "Sir!" he said.

"You are hereby promoted to Corporal in His Majesty's Army."

"Sir!" he barked, hoping his dismay wasn't plain for everyone to see.

Turning to Langlade, Etherington said, "You will do your part and remind the French that they are now subjects of His Majesty King George III. Remind them of the benevolence their sovereign shows to his loyal subjects, and remind them of the malevolence he visits on those who act in rebellion."

Langlade gave no reaction. He just kept his unreadable gaze on Etherington.

Etherington's features softened and a pleading look came to the captain's face. "I need your help, Charles," he said. "I want no more blood spilled in a conflict that has already been decided, French, Indian, or British."

After a long inhalation, Langlade nodded his head and said, "*Oui*."

"Now," Etherington said, and sighed, "is there anything I can do to aid you in that endeavor?"

"Tell General Amherst to pull his head from his ass and scrap the prohibition on gifts."

The fire's crackling was the only sound as the white men stiffened at the insult. Sam looked from face to face. Etherington seemed confused. Leslie looked to be building himself into a drunken rage. Kane looked as if he was holding in a laugh.

Etherington's lips finally curled into a smile. With a burst of laughter, Kane finally exhaled, easing the tension in the room. Sam smiled and chuckled along with Langlade. The only one to not see the humor was Leslie, who could only morosely pour himself another glass of wine.

"Is there anything I can do that wouldn't result in me losing my commission and making an enemy of the most powerful man on the continent?" Etherington asked, and smiled.

Turning serious again, Langlade said, "Though you may not feel this assault's objective was the death of William, I nonetheless think it might be prudent to take measures for his safety."

Sam perked up at that.

"I am due to make my spring visit to one of my stations in the south," Langlade continued. "Having William along would serve the purposes of providing some extra protection and removing an unpleasant reminder of shame to the Chippewa. That might cool any heads that have grown too hot from the wedding."

"A wonderful idea," Etherington chimed. "We shall send a few men along with Private Avery. Corporal – excuse me – *Sergeant* Kane, who shall lead this detachment?"

Leslie seemed to shrink back in his chair and try to hide himself behind his wineglass.

Sam almost stepped forward in his eagerness, but remembered he was still but a mere corporal in the presence of such gentlemen.

With another wide smile, Kane said, "Sir, I can think of no better man to lead the detachment than our own Corporal Avery."

Etherington slapped the table in triumph. "And why not!" he said. "Sergeant Kane, pick two men to accompany them.

"Yes, sir!"

Sam beamed.

***

Fritz had never mentioned any blood family. He'd always told the boys their father was his only brother in this life. When it came time to decide where to lay his remains, Langlade mentioned to Sam and William that the great waters of the lakes inevitably made their way to the St. Lawrence, and the St. Lawrence inevitably made its way to the sea. Why not send Fritz on his way to their father? It might take ages for what was left of them to find each other, but they had until the end of time.

Langlade helped the brothers push the bateau from the frozen shore, and the two rowed her slowly toward the center of the strait. The fort's garrison stood at attention on the receding beach, their red uniforms looking much like the blood that had stained the white snow only days earlier. A few curious Frenchmen, and even some Ottawa men, stood near the rigid soldiers, watching the retreating bateau as it fought against the chop that churned the straits.

Fritz's corpse, sewn into the canvas of several old sacks, lay in silence at the feet of Sam and William, who were silent themselves except for the occasional grunt of exertion as they pulled at the oars.

"This should do," Sam finally said.

William froze for a few heartbeats, then nodded and shipped his oar. They bobbed in the chop for several more silent moments, neither wanting to do what had to be done.

With a sigh, Sam reached out and put his arm around his brother's back and said, "Say goodbye."

A groan slipped past William's lips. He leaned into Sam and began to weep softly. Sam pulled him in tighter and let him cry as they continued to drift. A few tears rolled down Sam's cheeks, stinging his face with each gust of cold wind.

After several minutes, William finally wiped his nose, looked down, and said, "Goodbye, Uncle Fritz. Say hello to father, would you? And mother."

Sam choked back more tears and gave his brother a sad smile and a nod of approval. William tried to smile and nodded in return.

Turning his attention back to the cloth-wrapped body, Sam cleared his throat and said, "Goodbye, Fritz. You were a fine sergeant and a damn fine uncle. We shall see you again, but no time soon."

Without another word, Sam stood and moved to the head of the body. William stood unsteadily in the tipsy boat, taking a moment to right himself, then bent and grabbed the feet as Sam grabbed the shoulders.

"On three," Sam said. "One, two, three."

The pair lifted Fritz and slipped him over the side. The body, weighed by a small cannonball resting in the canvas beneath the feet, slid beneath the waves with hardly a noise. The canvas disappeared in the water's gloom in only seconds, as if it had never been there at all.

A cannon shot drew their attention. The brothers looked up to see the little sloop *Huron* beating towards the fort. Several deckhands could be seen waving at the garrison lining the shore. Sam and William looked to each other, perplexed, then went for the oars.

The *Huron* beat them back easily. By the time the brothers reached the shore, sweat poured from them, and they found the mood on the beach much changed from the somber scene they'd left. Some of the men were dancing little jigs with the sailors and hugging one another. Several others held flasks of rum and offered toasts to King George. Queerest of all, the officers and NCOs did nothing to stop them. Etherington and Leslie themselves excitedly poured Sherry from a decanter. The Frenchmen had all disappeared except for Langlade, who resignedly looked on the display next to the crying Domitilde. The Ottawa men stood with bemused looks, unsure of what to make of these giddy soldiers.

Annoyed at the gaiety, Sam called to the closest private, "What news!" as he jumped from the boat.

The skeletal private grinned from ear to ear and called out, "A treaty's been signed in Paris! The war is over!"

Sam looked quickly to William. The look he wore said it all. That signed piece of parchment wouldn't bring back their father, nor their mother, nor Fritz. There would be no joy for them this day, treaty be damned. Sam reached out and wrapped the younger lad in a hug. William returned it as the garrison celebrated around them.

Ch. 10

Lake Michigan. April 1763

Two million years before the name Avery had ever been uttered, two million years before the small band piloting two bateaux and half a dozen canoes moved south along the lakeshore, ice sheets a mile thick had ground their way down from the north and carved out the landscape. The ice had retreated for the last time only fourteen millennia before the Avery brothers began making their way south, and the melting ice left behind by those frozen giants had filled in the great troughs they'd gouged in the landscape to form the very lake the young men paddled upon.

Under a sun that had burst from its winter covering of cloud and haze like a bear emerging from its den in spring, Sam stroked with his paddle from his spot at the front of the canoe. He had foregone his regimental coat and waistcoat, letting the gloriously warm spring air play across his bare forearms with each gentle puff of breeze. Charles Langlade took up the rear seat, guiding the canoe and leading the party that spread behind them over a hundred yards on the glass-flat water. The space between the two men was loaded down with as many trade goods as the little craft could manage. The other canoes and bateaux were filled much the same, loaded down with rum, powder, shot, flints, and steel.

"Is spring always so glorious here, Charles?" Sam asked, raising his face to the sun.

"*Non,*" Langlade answered. "I've seen streams locked under ice well into spring, and midsummer eves where snow still lies in the shadows of high dunes. Some springs, there's so much rain that we fear even the lake will spill over its banks." Langlade stopped paddling, and Sam imagined he was taking in the warm air. "This weather, Sam, is a gift from on high."

"From our Lord and Savior or Gitchi Manitou?" Sam teased.

"Who can say which?" Charles chuckled. "It's only for us to be thankful for the blessing."

The band paddled on under the golden sun, entering a passage between the mainland and two large islands that poked from the water like giant tree-covered turtle shells.

At the passage's south end, Sam laid eyes on a sight that froze his paddle in the air. On the mainland shore, a wall of khaki sand three miles in length rose from the turquoise water, towering hundreds of feet above the beach below. A great, tree-covered mound stood atop the wall's north end to dominate the whole area.

"My God!" Sam exclaimed.

"It's the mother bear," Langlade said.

Sam took in the great cliff of sand. It looked like some magnificent earthwork thrown up by God himself to protect the shoreline. He could barely say, "Pardon?"

"The mother bear," Langlade repeated, digging his oar in the water to make up for Sam's slack.

"I don't understand." Sam finally lowered his paddle into the water, still unable to tear his gaze from the dune as they slid beneath it.

"In the time long before," Langlade began, "a mother bear lived with her cubs across the lake, in a land that was turning barren. Many people and animals were dying, unable to find food. The mother bear, seeing her cubs starving, decided to strike out for the land of plenty that lay across the water – Michigan. The mother led her cubs into the lake, and they swam with all their strength. They came within sight of the shore, but the cubs were too tired and weak to continue, even though their mother tried to encourage them. First one sank beneath the waves, then the other. The mother could not save them. She had to continue on. She reached the shore here." Langlade indicated the great mound. "Her heart was broken, and all she could do was climb the dune and lie down, looking out over the water where her cubs had died. There she cried. The Great Spirit Gitchi Manitou saw the mother's tears, and decided to try to ease her pain. Where the cubs had drowned, he brought forth islands from the depths."

Sam turned in his seat, and Langlade pointed with his oar to the two large islands they'd passed.

"The mother bear could now look over her children," Langlade said. "She chose to lie there for the rest of time, never abandoning her cubs, watching them from her bluff."

Sam turned back and took in the mound looming over them. If he squinted, the great mass did indeed take on the form of a sleeping bear, her snout pointed north towards the islands that were her lost children. "It's glorious," Sam whispered.

"*Oui*," Langlade answered.

***

Each evening, the flotilla put into one of the countless little coves that cut into the coastline, which Sam soon learned were lakes at the terminus of inland rivers. After making camp and seeing to their duties, the brothers would explore the surrounding areas, climbing dunes, threading through thick forests teeming with deer, and staring into the depths of lakes so clear they could see fish darting along the bottoms. After a hearty meal of fish pulled from the lake and a few of Langlade's stories around the campfire, the party would retire, Sam to a shared tent with the privates, and William to the much more desirable company of Domitilde's tent. Langlade and the few Ottawa he'd brought along slept by the glowing embers of the fire, under a sky overflowing with stars.

On the fifth day, the flotilla came across a shoreline of beach grass and thick woods covering low dunes. The coastline bended in a great arc, the beach squeezing eastward before gently running back westward to form the curve of a thumbnail. At almost the midpoint of the arc, a river flowed into the lake.

The water beneath their hulls changed from blue to brown as the boats entered the river's discharge. They aimed for the river's wide mouth, which sat between two low dunes.

"*Le Grand*," Langlade called to Sam from his position at the back of the canoe.

"The Grand River," Sam said under his breath, taking in the scenery as he rowed.

The river's banks mirrored the shoreline's. Low, rolling dunes came down to the water's edge. Woods stood just over the grass-covered mounds. The river bended north, and the flotilla pushed by floating debris, some of it as large as whole trees that tumbled towards the lake. The dunes soon gave way to gentler banks lined with deep woods.

After half an hour's struggle against the current, the party came to a split in the river. The point in front of them was the tip of an island that had been cut away from the mainland some centuries before. Langlade pointed them to a sandy beach on the island's point, and Sam soon felt the scrape of sand beneath the bark of the canoe. The party hauled their boats ashore, and the newcomers took in their surroundings.

A low, moss-covered cabin took up the north end of a small clearing. The remains of several wigwams and a longhouse took up space around the rest of the beach. This was Langlade's spring trading post. Their new home.

***

All manner of Indians and backcountry Frenchmen began streaming down the Grand River in birch bark canoes. The long, skinny craft arrived barely afloat, struggling to keep their gunwales above the waterline under loads of pelts trapped during winter. Parties trekked in on foot from all over the western half of the peninsula, their backs bent from all the furs strapped to them. Sam even met a few Indians that came from the great river the tribes called the Misi-ziibi, which the French called the Mississippi.

Langlade took in fox furs, deer skins, marten hides, and the shell of every manner of creature in between. But beaver pelts were what he sought most.

Each winter, and the worse the winter the better for the quality of the fur, Indians and French trappers would set their snares at the entrances of beaver damns in ponds and streams across the Upper Country. The successful trapper would skin his prize, dry it, and stow it for transport in the spring. When the snows finally began to melt, he would load his canoe or tie his pack and set off to trade. Coming to the mouth of the Grand River, the trapper would find Charles Langlade waiting with powder, shot, steel, muskets, blankets, cooking pots, and rum to exchange for his skins. The trapper would leave loaded down with enough powder and shot to hunt for the next year and enough rum to keep him in good spirits for as long as he could ration it. The furs traveled back to Michilimackinac with Langlade, where he would store them for eventual shipment or trade them to a third party for money or goods.

The beaver furs would then travel in reverse the same path the Averys had taken the year prior, moving across the lakes, around the falls, and down the St. Lawrence. A merchant in Montreal would purchase them and send them on to Quebec, where they would be loaded on an oceangoing ship. They would then make the opposite journey that the Avery brothers' ancestors had taken across the Atlantic. Finding their way to London or some other English city, they would be purchased by a felt maker who would transform the rough pelts into something workable. Then the hatters would get hold of the fabric the felt makers had created. These men would twist the material into every manner of fashionable hat, selling the finished products to court dandies or exporting them to the continent for huge profits.

Sam tried not to think of Ben Franklin's words on commerce and kings as another Indian strode by with more pelts on his back than could be counted. He tried not to think how the little varmints' fur had played a part in bringing him and his brother to this far-off place. As another canoe landed on the island, he tried not to think how the mottled furs had played no small role in bringing about the death of his poor father outside Quebec.

At the great quantity of the stuff coming into the station, Sam had shaken his head more than once and remarked to anyone within earshot, "How can there be any beavers left?"

***

Flowers were blooming and the days were stretching longer when a spring thunderstorm rolled across the big lake one evening. Sam, in his capacity as detachment commander, sat and sipped rum with Langlade at the rough-hewn table under the low roof of the cabin. William, in his capacity as Charles' son-in-law, joined them. Domitilde, looking quite pregnant, hummed quietly by the fire and sewed a swaddling blanket of soft furs and buckskin while rain pounded against the roof and leaked into waiting buckets.

After a long, low rumble of thunder, Sam drained his mug and stood with a mighty groan. "I think I shall stretch my legs," he said.

"It's pouring!" Domitilde exclaimed from her warm spot.

"*Il doit pisser*," Langlade explained to his daughter.

"Ah." She scrunched her brow.

A gleam of drink in his eye, Sam pointed triumphantly at Langlade. "That's right! I do have to piss!" he exclaimed with pride at his understanding.

"*Tres magnifique!*" Domitilde beamed. "You are getting as good as William."

"*Oui, oui*," Sam twirled his hand in the French manner.

"The very embodiment of distinction," William jibed with a smile.

Sam could only point a wavering finger at his brother while he pushed out the door.

Rain fell in a steady pour from a sky soon to lose its last light. Thunder continued to rumble, but the worst of the storm seemed to have finally passed to the east. Sam put up his collar to the spring chill and moved off around the cabin. Smoke rose from the surrounding cooking fires in front of the wigwams and soldiers' tent, but the occupants were out of sight, seeking shelter from the cold rain. The shore of the island was littered with canoes and bateaux, so Sam worked his way upstream to a bare spot of beach.

As he fumbled with his britches to free himself, lightning flashed behind him and lit up the breadth of river. The broad water flowed lazily and empty towards the big lake. Not even the ducks wanted to be out in this deluge. The first drops of Sam's relief joined the rain falling into the river, and he shivered with content.

"Sam," a voice spoke from behind him.

Fumbling and pissing all over himself, Sam turned with fright to see an Indian in a bear-grease hood standing within striking distance. The Indian quickly pulled back his hood to show himself.

"Bloody hell!" Sam exhaled, finally getting his cock back where it belonged and realizing he was in no danger.

There were more turkey feathers sprouting from his wet hair, but the red waistcoat of a King's soldier rendered the man unmistakable. "Otayonih!" Sam gasped. "What in God's name are you doing here?"

"Hahgwehdiyu visited me in a dream," the Indian said flatly.

"What?" Sam huffed, wiping water from his eyes to see if the apparition in front of him would disappear.

"Fritz is dead," the Indian stated.

Sam froze at the name, then let out a long breath, turning his face into the rain. "How did you find out? Is that why you're here?"

"The Haudenosaunee sent me to Detroit to give warning to our English fathers. I had troubling word to give."

Sam looked over the Seneca's shoulder at the warm light streaming from the cracks in the side of the cabin. "Shall we go inside and talk? William would be glad to see you."

"No," Otayonih said firmly. "This is no place for me. I came only to deliver my warning."

"Warning?" Sam asked, still confused at the queerness of Otayonih's presence.

The Seneca blinked in annoyance. "As I said, I was sent to Detroit to give warning. And now I come to give warning to you."

"Is the warning for me or the Army?"

"Both!" Otayonih stepped forward, rain streaming down from his bald front pate. "The Ottawa and Chippewa want English blood. Pontiac will soon attack Detroit. Minavavana has gone north, back to Chippewa lands around Michilimackinac."

"What are you saying?" Sam shook his head. "The Ottawa are friendly to us," he said, remembering his time in L'Arbre Croche and its genial faces. "William has even married one!"

"The daughter of Langlade," Otayonih said evenly, showing how well informed he was.

"How do you know all this?" Sam wiped water from his brow. "Is this some Seneca sorcery?"

"I told you Hahgwehdiyu visited me. He told me of Fritz's death. He told me of the marriage."

"A well-informed fellow, he is," Sam said, not attempting the name.

"Hahgwehdiyu is the Creator," Otayonih informed.

Sam's brow went up. "Ah. I guess he would know."

A smile came to Otayonih's lips. "I also had discourse with Captain Campbell. He informed me of much that's happened in the Upper Country."

Sam nodded, understanding who the real source of Otayonih's information was. "True Seneca sorcery." he chuckled.

"Listening is no sorcery," Otayonih huffed, not understanding the humor. "If the English did more of it, I would not have to be here. I called upon your Major Gladwin with the warnings of my people. His ears were closed."

Sam held his hands open. "Along with his mind. But I am only a Corporal, Otayonih. I have no sway over gentlemen."

"I did not come for your sway," Otayonih said, looking at him as if he were simple. "I came because I heard an English soldier married the daughter of Langlade. I came to Langlade's spring trading grounds guided by Hahgwehdiyu–"

"And Captain Campbell," Sam interrupted.

"…to tell William he is in danger."

Sam winced, knowing what was coming.

"In Detroit, Kinonchamek told every Indian who would listen that the Englishman who took his woman is a dead man," Otayonih continued.

Sighing, Sam said, "We suspected as much. Fritz was killed by men in his employ, or men who sought to curry favor with him. That's why we're here."

"You cannot stay in the Upper Country. Danger is coming for all English."

Sam shook his head in irritation. "We can't just walk away. The Army will find us and have our backs for desertion."

Otayonih took another step, coming face to face with Sam. Only inches of rain-soaked air separated them. "Tell your commander to not trust the Chippewa. Your fort is in danger."

Exasperated, Sam said, "I'll do what I can, but as I said, I am only a Corporal."

"And if you will not flee Kinonchamek, you must do something else."

"What?"

"Kill him," Otayonih answered, "or watch William die. I found you. He will find you. There is no safe place for the Averys in the Upper Country."

With a long breath of trepidation, Sam begged, "Will you please just come in so we can discuss this?"

"I must go east," Otayonih said while raising his hood. "I have delivered my warnings. This is no place for a Seneca." The man hefted his musket and turned, but stopped himself, turning back a moment. "No place for Englishmen." Then he moved off into the rain. He was gone before Sam could wipe the water from his eyes.

***

Sam burst into the cabin and made for the fire. Domitilde cursed in irritation as he stumbled by and showered her with raindrops. Sam thrust his hands over the coals to warm them and shook from more than cold. William and Langlade watched in amused silence, both taking long sips of rum as they stared at Sam's shivering back.

"That was some piss," William finally broke the silence.

"You'll never believe who I just saw," Sam said.

"King George the Third?" William jested, holding up his rum in a toast.

"*Ridicule*," Domitilde said, smiling.

"King Louis?" William tried again.

"I should be so lucky," Langlade said under his breath.

"Otayonih," Sam said, not peeling his eyes from the flames.

"Iroquois!" Langlade stood and reached for his musket.

Sam stopped him. "He's gone."

William stood and went to the cabin door with an eager look. "He was here!" he gasped, opening the door to look out on the rain.

"He had a warning for us," Sam said.

"A warning?"

"We're in danger."

William shrugged. "That's why we're here."

"Not just from Kinonchamek." Sam turned from the fire. "It seems Pontiac and Minavavana are on the warpath."

Langlade stared hard at Sam. Then he reached for his mug. In one mighty gulp, he drained the rum and slammed the mug against the rough wood of the table.

***

A sharp crack of wood upon wood woke him. Sam opened his eyes to see the faintest sign of day's first light falling on the canvas overhead.

Another crack sounded, and Sam reached for the hatchet he kept always in arm's reach now that danger seemed to be following them through the wilderness. His fingers closed around the haft, and he was just about to wake the snoring privates he shared the tent with when he heard Langlade's voice, calm and betraying no danger, answered by that of his brother's.

Sam wrapped his blanket around his shoulders and drew back the tent flaps with his hatchet, poking his head into the frigid morning air. In the half-light, he saw Langlade and William some ways off in the clearing, their breaths billowing about them from exertion. William had on his shirt and britches, but was barefoot. Langlade wore only his britches, his chest bare to the cold, his lean muscles glistening with sweat.

Just then, Langlade lunged towards William. Sam saw the tomahawk and knife gripped in the man's hands. William barely parried the attack with his own hatchet, that same crack of wood-on-wood reverberating throughout the otherwise silent clearing. Sam hefted his hatchet and poised himself to rush to William's aid, but stopped when both men lowered their weapons. Langlade began explaining some technique to the attentive William that Sam couldn't hear, but it became clear that some sort of lesson was underway. Sam relaxed as he watched William nod along and mimic the movements Langlade made. The man was trying to teach his new son-in-law to fight.

Remembering his years of easily besting William in brotherly combat, Sam smirked and shook his head. Langlade might be better off showing the lad how to strap on as many loaded pistols as his gangly frame could carry, then teach him how to turn and run when all the barrels were fired.

But just then, William doffed his shirt, wiped his brow, and held up his weapons in renewed preparation. Where there was once skin and bone, Sam now saw lean muscle clinging to his brother's frame. William's spindly arms no longer looked as if they'd snap at the first blow, and his long reach gave Langlade something approaching trouble as the two rounded on each other again. Sam also noticed that his brother's movements no longer seemed hampered by the clumsiness of youth. The lad now moved his frame with the agility and speed inherent to its length. It seemed he might finally have gotten comfortable with the body several growth spurts had given him.

Sam nodded in appreciation as he watched William duck an attack from Langlade and send out a long leg in an effort to trip the man. Langlade easily avoided the attempt, but he heartily praised the effort in rapid French as he turned back to the lad.

Looking east, Sam figured there was still half an hour until he'd have to muster the others. He yawned, then dropped the flap and crawled back into the tent. He'd seen enough, and hoped he could steal a few more winks before the day started.

Ch. 11

L'Arbre Croche. May 1763

The flotilla, empty of trade goods and loaded down with furs, pulled under the great crooked tree in the last days of May. Langlade made straight for counsel with Nissowaquet, bringing the Avery brothers with him. They found the chief sitting outside his longhouse surrounded by confidants under a brilliant spring sun. Seeing their arrival, Nissowaquet stood and greeted his nephew happily. Langlade's demeanor soon turned the man's expression, and they sat in the sun while Langlade informed him of all that Otayonih had told Sam.

Nissowaquet listened intently, then asked, "Can you trust this Iroquois?"

Langlade translated Nissowaquet's words, then looked to Sam, who answered, "Otayonih is a friend of the English, and a friend to William. He would not lie."

After Langlade's translation, Nissowaquet replied, "The Iroquois and Anishinaabek are old enemies, much like the French and English. Is it not possible that they are sowing rumors to interrupt the new-found peace between the English and Anishinaabek? The Iroquois might see their place as favored sons of the English under threat."

Sam listened to Langlade, then shook his head. "I cannot speak to the delicate dance of tribal politics in the Upper Country, but the threats made by Kinonchamek against William I must take serious. Is there anything you can do to help us?"

Nissowaquet thought for a long while, then said, "I have heard nothing from our brothers the Chippewa of any ill deeds intended for our new English fathers, and Pontiac has said nothing to me of going on the warpath, so I do not believe tomahawks will fall on English heads. My people, the Anishinaabek of L'Arbre Croche, will honor their agreements with King George, and I will tell your Captain Etherington the same."

Sam listened and nodded. "But what of William? He is now a relation to you. Will you not seek to end this talk of retribution by Kinonchamek?"

After another long pause for thought, Nissowaquet said, "My pleas to Pontiac have not fallen on deaf ears. He has assured me that Kinonchamek will not seek retribution. If his word is not enough for you, and you trust this Iroquois to be truthful, I shall make a personal entreaty to Minavavana and Kinonchamek at Michilimackinac."

Sam leaned forward. "Kinonchamek has returned north?"

"Have you not heard?" Langlade translated, looking intrigued himself. "Your Captain Etherington has accepted the invitation from the Chippewa of a feast and a game of baggataway to honor King George's birthday. It is to take place on the second day of June. Minavavana and Kinonchamek, along with a host of Chippewa, are already encamped outside the palisade at Michilimackinac."

"Bloody hell," Sam groaned. Langlade wisely did not translate.

"I am departing at sunrise for Michilimackinac," Nissowaquet added, "to pay my respects to my new English father and to sit at the feast. You will join our party, and our bonds will be laid bare for all to see. If Kinonchamek does indeed have thoughts of revenge, they will disappear when he sees William with me as my kin."

Not knowing what else he could say to convince Nissowaquet of the danger ahead, Sam could only shrug in acceptance.

***

That night, while Domitilde slept, William, Sam, and Langlade met beneath the crooked tree. Sam asked the question they'd all been pondering, "Shall we flee?"

"No," William said flatly.

Sam stared hard at his brother in the weak moonlight. "Nissowaquet is naive to think this can end without blood, William. The man will kill you. And the Chippewa might kill us all if Otayonih's words ring true."

"Precisely," William answered quickly. "We cannot leave our fellows to be butchered, Sam. If we run and there really is an attack, we will have the blood of the entire garrison on our hands. We must at least warn them."

"We can send a message with the privates, or with Nissowaquet," Sam shot back.

"Etherington will not accept the message of two privates. Especially when it was given to them by two deserters. He will suspect that we're trying to cover up for our cowardice."

"And where will you flee?" Langlade asked. "Domitilde is only weeks from birth. She cannot suffer hard travel."

"And I will not leave her," William said, and straightened.

Sam rubbed his neck in irritation. "An absent father is better than a dead father," he said.

"In my experience..." William raised his chin. "Both are equally terrible."

Sam huffed. "What then? Row north and go like lambs to the slaughter?"

"We row north and warn Captain Etherington what's coming," William answered.

"And when he doesn't believe us?" Sam retorted.

"We do everything in our power to stop a slaughter."

"And your own slaughter?"

"Maybe Nissowaquet is right," William said hopefully. "Maybe Otayonih is wrong. It may be that Kinonchamek is just spouting anger with no intention of action. But if he comes for me, I will fight him."

Sam laughed hollowly. "You've had a few weeks' worth of scrapping with Charles. That may buy you a few more breaths on the day you face him."

"You forget, Sam," William said evenly, "I have faced death twice now, and yet I'm still here."

"Thanks in no small part to me," Sam added quickly.

"You have improved," Langlade interjected, looking to William, "but Kinonchamek will not be troubled much by you in a fair fight."

William sighed and looked out on the waves. "There is nothing more we can do here but worry. I am going to bed," he said.

The lad clomped off into the darkness, leaving Langlade and Sam alone beneath the tree. Sam held his own council for several minutes while Langlade pretended to examine the bountiful stars above them. Finally, Sam said, "I cannot allow my brother's death, Charles."

"*Non*," Langlade agreed.

"My father spared your life those years ago," Sam said softly. "His son, my brother, will be the father of your grandchild." Sam turned and faced him. "Will you help me protect my brother?"

"*Absolument.*"

Sam nodded in relief. "How shall we do it?"

"We must kill Kinonchamek," Langlade said easily.

"You would make us murderers?"

"Did you murder that creature, Ol' Bill? Did you murder Boucher?"

"Absolutely not. I was defending William."

"And would killing Kinonchamek not be the same?"

Sam thought for several moments, not liking the answer he kept coming to. "And I suppose we'll have many opportunities to murder the son of a Chippewa chief?" He almost laughed.

Langlade shrugged. "All we need is one *good* opportunity."

Sam shook his head. "And after this murder? Every Chippewa in the Upper Country will be after us instead of just one."

"Then it must look natural."

"The natural death of a young warrior?" Sam spat. "How does one achieve that?"

"Baggataway," Langlade said, as if it just came to him.

"Bagga-what?"

"*Lacrosse*," Langlade explained, using the French word for the game. Sam's blank stare prompted him to further explanation. "It's an Indian game. Two teams of many warriors, armed with sticks, fight to advance a deerskin ball to the opposing goal. I assure you that it can get quite violent. Many young warriors have died on the field."

"So we hope the man dies from a game?"

"A game that you will play." Langlade pointed at Sam. "Nissowaquet will allow you to play for the Ottawa of L'Arbre Croche. You will kill him then. No retribution can be sought for a death on the baggataway ground."

After several moments' thought, Sam said, "It sounds like our best chance. But what about this supposed attack?"

"We will warn Etherington," Langlade said, and shrugged. "That is all that we can do."

After another long minute's thought, Sam echoed slowly, "That is all we can do."

Ch. 12

Michilimackinac. May 1763

"Would you look at that!" William exclaimed.

From his oar bench, Sam craned his neck to look over his shoulder.

Michilimackinac had been transformed since last they saw it. The gray fort was now wreathed in the green of spring. Wildflowers of every color blossomed at the base of her palisade. Vines climbed the cracks of her old wood and reached for the blazing sun above, garnishing the fort with life. Gone was the white snow that had encased her. Thick grass now stretched around her like an emerald carpet. The old fort looked as if she had come alive out of her winter dormancy.

But that was not what drew William's exclamation. The normally sleepy outpost was as busy as a beehive during flowering season. The fields surrounding the fort were crammed with every manner of shelter, from rough wigwams to giant canvas pavilions. The sound of hundreds of people carried across the water as men and women of every Indian nation in the Upper Country went about the business of trade with the British and French merchants sitting in front of their tents. Smoke rose from a hundred fires, telling of the industry taking place on the fallow fields. It was as if a city had sprung from the ground along with the flowers.

A great host of Indians gathered along the shore to welcome the Ottawa of L'Arbre Croche. Sam made sure to stick with the middle of the flotilla as they began beaching themselves far down the shoreline from the fort, the only ground not already occupied by canoes and bateaux. Pulling in the bateau, Sam turned and scanned the mass of people.

This was a happy time for the Indians. Winter was over and summer had finally come, and along with it came the chance of seeing old friends. Ottawa mingled cheerfully with Chippewa and Sauk they'd not seen in months or years. The place had the atmosphere of Christmas time back home. But Sam was anything but happy with the teeming mass of people around him and William.

Langlade appeared from the crowd with Domitilde. He nodded to Sam as he took up position next to him. They began pushing through the crowd, politely but firmly trying to extricate themselves from the mass. Nissowaquet, harassed by well-wishers, found them and fell in on William's left. Sam, his hand in his coat and gripping the haft of his hatchet, moved his eyes constantly from person to person.

No assassin shot from the crowd. The only thing the group was assaulted with were greetings and embraces. They finally cleared most of the great host and stepped off for the fort half a mile away. The party neared the Water Gate, followed by most of the Ottawa warriors of L'Arbre Croche. It was there that they first saw Kinonchamek.

Outside the gate, standing next to his father and Etherington, the great warrior watched the approach of the Averys. The detached look on the man's face made his intentions unclear. But his stare followed William as if the lad were game at the other end of his musket barrel. Sam gripped his hatchet tighter as they closed.

Minavavana stepped forward and greeted Nissowaquet, stopping the procession only paces from the open gate. The two shared a long conversation as everyone else stood by respectfully. Sam's eyes never left Kinonchamek as he waited for the man to strike. Kinonchamek's eyes never left William, boring into the lad. William tried to stare back, but he was unable to hold the gaze for more than a few moments at a time.

The chiefs finally moved on to greeting each other's retinues. Langlade greeted Minavavana, then turned and cocked his head to Sam. Sam quickly grasped William's elbow and pulled him away from the two parties and towards the gate. William grasped Domitilde and moved with him. In only a few steps, they were past the sentries' bayonets and into the safety of the fort.

William strode away with Domitilde to greet Madem Langlade while Sam turned back to the gathering. Kinonchamek's gaze had finally left William. His brown eyes were now firmly fixed on Sam. The big warrior's face was so unreadable that Sam imagined it could be carved from wood. The Chippewa slipped unnoticed from the greetings and moved towards the gate. The knuckles of Sam's hand cracked against the haft of his hatchet as he squeezed tighter.

The glint of a bayonet fell across Kinonchamek's face. "No Indians in the fort," the private on duty drawled, blocking Kinonchamek's path with his musket.

Kinonchamek didn't protest. He only looked over the private's shoulder at Sam.

Minavavana, noticing his son's behavior, gave a sharp command in Ojibwe. Kinonchamek kept up his stare. Sam stared back with all the courage he could muster.

Finally, Kinonchamek turned and strode away. Sam's shoulders sagged and he let out a sigh of relief. They'd survived their arrival.

***

Twilight lingered in spite of the lateness of the hour. The Avery brothers stood across the parade ground outside the commandant's house, both taking satisfying pulls from tankards of ale. The brothers commented now and then on the fineness of the weather and exchanged other trivialities while they awaited the end of the party.

Sam had drained his mug and was thinking of fetching another when the door opened, spilling light over the parade ground. Langlade, Nissowaquet, and Minavavana, along with notables from the other tribes, exited the house into the warm night air. The Indians said their goodbyes to Captain Etherington and moved off with their escort of soldiers toward the Land Gate. Minavavana offered the Averys only a passing glance as he strode by, his face emotionless.

Langlade lingered with Etherington for several minutes. At the end of their conversation, the captain gave a shrug, then said his goodbyes before entering his house.

Looking after the officer for a moment, Langlade finally turned and joined the brothers.

"I'm sorry, Charles, but we're out of ale," Sam said, greeting his approach.

With a smile, Langlade removed a flask from his coat and motioned for the brothers to hold out their mugs.

"You're a godsend," Sam said with a smile as Langlade poured.

The men went about sipping their rum for several minutes before Sam finally asked, "What was said?"

"Minavavana has pledged his allegiance to King George, stating that any rumors to the contrary have been spoken by enemies who wish to see the relationship between the British and Chippewa damaged," Langlade explained.

"And Etherington accepted that?" William asked.

Langlade took a sip from his flask and shrugged. "He says he has doubled the guard already and allows no Indian into the fort unescorted. He asks what else he can do?"

"And Kinonchamek?" Sam asked. "Everyone had to have seen what happened at the gate."

"Minavavana has acknowledged that his son's blood runs hot at the sight of William, but he has pledged that no harm will come to the lad. It has been decided by all that William shall remain in the fort until the departure of the Chippewa, to avoid any unpleasantness."

"*Unpleasantness*," Sam said, and spat.

"And that is that?" William asked.

Langlade could only shrug.

***

"Your stick," Langlade said, and thrust the hooked branch into Sam's chest.

Sam caught his breath and examined the sinew pocket sewn into the hook at the stick's end. "What am I to do with this?" he asked.

Langlade sighed. "I am to teach you. The game begins tomorrow. If you are not to look like an ass that wandered in from the fields to find himself in the middle of a game, you need to learn the basics."

Irritated, Sam said, "Fine."

Domitilde and William looked on from their shaded porch as Langlade began his lesson.

"One hundred warriors on each side–" Langlade began.

"One hundred! It will be a melee," Sam interrupted.

Langlade looked at Sam with mild annoyance. "*Oui*. Now, as I was saying, one hundred warriors to each side. Tomorrow, a pair of posts will be erected a few hundred paces apart in the field outside the Land Gate. Those posts–"

"What are the boundaries?" Sam interrupted again.

Langlade closed his eyes in irritation. "There are no boundaries once the game begins, only the posts, which I am trying to explain to you if you would be so kind as to shut your mouth."

"Why is Sam playing in this...*game*? Remind me," William chimed.

"Maybe he's trying to catch the eye of an Indian maiden with his prowess on the field," Domitilde teased from her spot in the shade next to William. Her swollen belly looked ripe for bursting under her loose dress.

"Sam," Langlade huffed, "is playing at the invitation of Nissowaquet. An honor that can't be refused. Now, if everyone would shut their mouths, I will get back to making sure this lad doesn't make a fool of himself."

All parties kept their traps shut while Langlade looked to each for several long moments.

"*Bon!*" Langlade exclaimed, picking up his own stick and looking to Sam. "Two posts, a few hundred paces apart, and the goal of each team is to advance the ball to the opposite post to score."

Langlade held up a deerskin ball the size of an apple and threw it at Sam, who fumbled his stick and tried to catch the ball with his hands. He failed miserably, further annoying Langlade.

"There is only one rule," Langlade said. He held up a finger while Sam picked up the surprisingly hard orb. "Do not touch the ball with your hands."

Sam immediately dropped it, giving a sheepish grin and saying, "Sorry."

Langlade ignored him. "To score..." He trotted forward and deftly scooped the ball into the sinew pocket of his stick. "A team must strike the goalpost with the ball." Langlade spun quickly, using his momentum to launch the ball with alarming velocity at a hitching post down the lane. The ball struck the post dead center with a satisfying *thump*.

"*Tres magnifique!*" Domitilde cheered as she and William clapped from the porch.

Unable to hide his pride, Langlade gave a little bow before trotting to retrieve the ball. He again scooped it deftly and turned to Sam. "Catch it with the stick," he called out, flinging the ball.

Sam held the stick out awkwardly, and the ball bounced off it and skittered into the dirt. Domitilde whistled derisively as William hooted, "Bad show! Bad Show!"

With a grimace, Sam set off and retrieved the ball while Langlade showered him with instructions. Sam struggled to scoop the ball, then flung a poor pass to Langlade, much to the continued amusement of William and Domitilde.

After an hour of errant balls and harsh curses, a passable game of catch finally took shape. Sam became comfortable enough that he even started asking a few questions while concentrating on not looking like a fool. "You said there is only one rule?" he asked.

"*Oui*," Langlade answered, stretching to catch another deficient pass. "No rules but the one: no hands."

"So a man may take his stick and crack another man across the skull?" William called out from the porch.

"*Absolument*," Domitilde answered in morbid delight.

William looked at her sideways. She smiled sweetly back at him before he turned to Sam. "Are you sure you wish to play? Will Kinonchamek be out there?" he asked.

"He will be out there, and Sam must play," Langlade answered, catching a well-thrown pass and hurling it back. "Besides, there will be two hundred men on the field, and Sam will have the Ottawa of L'Arbre Croche at his side."

William remained unconvinced. "Do men die during these games?"

"*Oui*," Langlade answered flatly.

"This is how Indian men prepare for war," Domitilde explained. "They push and shove, bite and kick, punch and pull. It is war with no weapons, excepting the stick."

After another few moments, William asked, "This isn't some plot the two of you have hatched, is it?"

"No plot," Sam said, catching the ball and sending it back. "But no man can say what will happen during the game."

William cursed. "You're going for him."

"I'm going to play a game, William. A game where men have died. If Kinonchamek happens to die, that's what Gitchi Manitou allows, right, Charles?"

"*Oui*," Langlade answered.

William stood and moved to the railing. "He'll kill you, Sam," he said.

"Not if I get him first," Sam replied.

William strode down the porch. "I'll play!"

"*Non!*" Domitilde shrieked.

Sam caught a pass and turned to face his brother, who stepped forward and held out his hand for the stick. "I *will* do this, William."

"I will not have you murder a man," William said.

"I have no choice. Just like the night with Ol' Bill."

"Not in my name!" William ignored him. "Not in my name!"

That upset Sam mightily.

"How about in your wife's name?" Sam asked. He stepped forward, staring point-blank into William's face. "Or your unborn baby's name? The man will surely kill you and leave your wife a widow and your child fatherless."

William flinched at that.

"Who's to say he won't turn on them when you're in the ground?" Sam asked.

William stared back for several moments before he asked, "What would father say to this?"

Sam winced at the mention of their father. "I don't know, but I'm sure you can ask him soon if you keep me from doing this."

With a shake of his head and a look of sorrow, William turned and strode into the cabin. Domitilde followed behind, murmuring in French as she went.

Sam turned back to Langlade and flung the ball. Langlade caught it easily and flung it back.

***

June the 2nd dawned under a sky empty of even the smallest wisp of cloud. Birdsong filled the air around the fort as the sun climbed from the Huron Lake and cast its first rays across the straits. The temperature was warm, but a constant, pleasant breeze blew across the still frigid water of Lake Michigan and cooled the land and all who walked it.

While most of the fort still slept, several respected elders from the different tribes gathered under the palisade and debated in the field outside the Land Gate. An agreement was finally struck after much back and forth, and the first of two goalposts was dug into the ground at the determined spot. When that was done, the elders moved several hundred paces and began the debate anew. The sun had risen well over the horizon, and people were stirring about the field when, finally, the second goalpost was planted.

Sam had been awake for hours by then, unable to keep his mind from racing as he'd reclined on his pallet through the short night, his only company the light of the moon leaking through the cracks of his cabin. He soon found himself standing in the warm air outside Langlade's house, his stick held across his shoulder while he waited. The door opened and Langlade, looking as refreshed as a young pup who'd slept by the fire, stepped into the brightening morning.

The pair passed William's cabin when his door opened. Sam checked his stride and saw his brother step forward. He waited for William to slowly approach, until they faced each other. "Don't try to stop me," Sam said calmly.

William looked at him for several moments, then surprised Sam when he stepped forward and embraced him. "Do what you must," William said in his ear. "But make sure you come back to us." William stepped back and looked at him and smiled. "You're going to be an uncle soon."

With a smile of his own, Sam nodded, then reached into his shirt and brought the medal over his neck.

William took a step back and raised his hand. "No," he said.

Sam thrust the medal into his brother's outstretched hand and closed William's palm around it.

"You must keep it safe," Sam said.

"Sam–" William tried to protest.

Sam cut him off with a gesture. "It must stay in the family. You'll give it to your child someday."

Langlade put his hand on Sam's back and said, "We must go."

"Swift and bold, William" Sam said, then he turned and stepped off with Langlade.

"Swift and bold," William called out after them, the medal heavy in his hand.

***

The Ottawa camp hummed with activity, looking as if it were preparing for a war. Women huddled over cooking fires and tended to corn cakes and venison. Warriors shaved each other's pates with sharp knives and painted each other's faces in hideous designs while they scarfed the food their women gave them. Older men checked the sticks of their sons, making sure the wood was strong and the pockets were tight.

Langlade and Sam threaded their way through the camp to Nissowaquet's shelter. The chief sat at the cooking fire with one of his sons and several other painted warriors. The son, Makwa, would lead the Ottawa on the field, and last second discussions on strategy took place between the company. The Ottawa wanted to win.

Sam and Langlade waited until the conversation died before they stepped forward. Nissowaquet greeted them warmly, then spoke to his son.

Looking not at all happy, Makwa cast an appraising eye from Sam's moccasins to the top of his queued head. He spoke something quick, and several of the warriors present couldn't keep from chuckling.

Langlade said, "Makwa asks–"

"If I'm up to the job," Sam finished for him.

Langlade smirked. "*Oui.* That was the feeling behind his words."

Langlade turned to Makwa and spoke for a minute. The warriors around the fire looked thoughtful, and one by one nodded their heads in understanding. Makwa nodded last.

"What did you tell them?" Sam asked.

"I told them that your skills are shit, but you have a thick skull, and you are willing to take much punishment for the Ottawa. I explained that with a white man on the field, the Chippewa will be falling over themselves to maim you, and it should open lanes for our runners. They understood this as sound strategy," Langlade explained.

Sam smiled mirthlessly. "Glad to be of service."

Nissowaquet spoke a quick command, and Makwa stood and gestured for Sam to follow him.

Sam looked to Langlade for explanation.

"You are to play as a member of the Ottawa," Langlade said. "You must look the part."

Sam sighed. "Very well," he said, and allowed himself to be led away.

Makwa ordered Sam to strip behind a wigwam. He did so quickly and stood awkwardly while the warrior produced a loincloth and buckskin leggings. Sam already had his own moccasins. Makwa nodded in appreciation at the knife wound on Sam's thigh and the furrows the Cat had cut in his back. *Maybe the white man's not so soft*, he thought as Sam quickly put on the garments. Makwa gestured for him to kneel down. Sam obliged and felt the warrior come behind him. A knife was drawn, and Sam didn't flinch when Makwa started shearing the sides of his head. It was not a gentle process, and droplets of blood ran down his scalp with each pass of the blade. The warrior finally stepped in front of him. Makwa nodded in admiration of his own work.

Sam brought his hands to his head. His soldier's queue was still intact, but the sides of his head were smooth, save for small globs of drying blood. He could only imagine how he looked. He hoped it was more frightful than comical.

Makwa knelt in front of him with a bowl of black paint. After a few moments' thought, he slathered his hand in the bowl and pressed his palm to Sam's face. With some final touching up, the warrior smiled and declared something in Ojibwe. Sam took it as satisfaction for a job done well.

Back at the fire, they found the men now standing and bearing their sticks. Some bounced on the balls of their feet and looked like coiled springs. The warriors looked him over and none smirked or commented at his appearance. Some even nodded in greeting. He almost felt as if he'd stepped into the tribe, if only for the moment. Langlade came forward and showed his approval with a quick nod.

At an unheard command, the men began setting off. "You must go with them now," Langlade said. Sam gave the man a slap on the back and fell in with the departing warriors.

Nissowaquet led the way through camp. Silent warriors fell in with the procession as the party weaved through the shelters. All kept their eyes fixed forward on some distant thing only they could see. They ignored the goodbyes of their women and the chatter of their excited children. The occasional yelp escaped an eager warrior. Sometimes it was answered. The women of the camp began piercing the air with shrill cries, which set a fire in the men and quickened their pace. Sam kept up, feeling the blood pumping in his veins and his stomach turning in anticipation.

The band reached the field and pushed through a crowd thick with French and Indians. Sam guessed some five hundred people had gathered under the palisade in front of the Land Gate. Captain Etherington and Lieutenant Leslie stood front and center before the crowd. Red-coated soldiers stood on the sentry walk, eager for a view of the game. It looked as if the whole garrison had turned out to watch the spectacle.

Craning his neck over his fellows, Sam tried to find William in the crowd. It was no use. There were too many faces staring back at him.

A terrible cry carried from the far side the field. Three hundred paces away, there stood the opposition – the warriors of the Chippewa and Sauk.

The presence of their opponents set the Ottawas' blood to boiling. Warriors let loose great yelps and whoops at their foes. Several warriors rushed forward dozens of paces in mock charges, then checked themselves suddenly while calling out what Sam guessed to be insults. The Chippewa and Sauk answered their challenges. Mock charges and gestures of derision rippled through the hundred warriors across from them. It was as if these men were not the brothers they were said to be, and that they truly hated each other.

Caught up in it all, Sam gave a piercing a cry of his own. The fellows around him whooped at his eagerness, and they pushed him to and fro. One warrior slammed his stick into Sam's chest and screamed in his face. Sam returned the gesture, his fear replaced with a desire to charge across the ground and crack his stick against someone's skull.

The energy built to near breaking point while Sam jostled with his fellows in the Ottawa line. Nissowaquet stood in front of his warriors and said a few final words. Sam didn't know their meaning, but he erupted in screams along with the other warriors when Nissowaquet trotted off the field to join Etherington.

Minavavana, standing in front of his men, pointed across the field and uttered some unheard entreaty. His warriors raised their voices and bared their teeth as he trotted to join Etherington and Nissowaquet.

Now only empty ground stood between the two sides.

Sam felt his stick might crack from the force of his grip as he surged forward with his lads and checked himself. The line performed this dance several times, charging and checking, charging and checking. The waiting had become unbearable. It had to begin.

A ball arced through the air and landed in the middle of the field. The tension broke as the men whooped in rapture and surged forward at a dead sprint. Sam's feet carried him forward with the line, and he soon found that his adrenaline had carried him to the head of the pack.

The Chippewa and Sauk bore down.

A dozen warriors steered themselves toward the ball. The majority ignored the little ball and instead targeted the opposition. Sam could care less about the bit of deerskin. His eyes were peeled for Kinonchamek.

The hosts came together in a great crash of sticks and bodies on the field's center. Sam dropped his shoulder and upended a Sauk whose stick was poised to fall on his newly-shaved dome. The man flew over his shoulder and landed with a thud behind him. A Chippewa with his face painted red sent an elbow flying towards Sam's face. He ducked it just in time, but he was rewarded with a donkey kick from the retreating Chippewa. Pain shot through the back of Sam's thigh. Knowing it would not be the last pain he felt that day, he steeled himself.

The melee settled as the teams' focus finally fell on the ball. Gone were the elegant passes Langlade and Sam had threaded to each other the day before. Now it was entangled bodies and mad scrambles.

An Ottawa warrior finally broke from the scrum, holding the ball triumphantly in his pocket. He ran a hundred yards down field before the pursuit caught up to him. A Sauk laid him low with a stick across the shin. The scrum reformed on the crumpled man and the struggle began anew. It went back and forth like this for quite some time. A man would gain the ball and elude the brawl, maybe fling an arcing pass to a waiting straggler across the field, and the chase would be taken up again. The fight marched up and down the field with the rising and falling fortunes of each team.

It was battle, with sticks in place of blades.

Even the strongest among them could last no more than a few minutes in the melee without rest. The men worked in shifts about the ball, dropping off to regain their breath while fresh legs surged forward. Injuries began piling up. Several fellows were already limping, and a couple of warriors had already been dragged unconscious from the field.

Sam shied from the scrum, constantly scanning for Kinonchamek. He'd caught glimpses of the giant a few times. He'd seen the man strike his stick across the face of an unseeing Ottawa, sending the warrior into the dirt. By the time Sam had charged forward, the battle had moved on and Kinonchamek had disappeared. But then he caught sight of the brute.

Sam dug his heels in for a charge when the ball popped from the mass. The deerskin ball bounced a few times and came to rest against his foot. A great whoop erupted from the scrum. The whole mass changed direction and came tumbling for him like a tidal wave. With the instinct of a hare caught in the open, Sam scooped the ball and broke into a sprint.

He ran with all his energy to the opposing goalpost. A lagging Sauk made to cut him off. Sam shifted his weight one way, sending the man lunging, then shifted back. The Sauk lost his footing and sprawled helplessly in the grass. Sam heard the man's cries of pain moments later as the horde trampled him.

A hundred paces from the post, a Chippewa loomed in front of Sam. The man thought Sam would try to avoid him but, not having the energy for another move, Sam lowered his shoulder and plowed over the taller, skinnier warrior. When his stride steadied, Sam looked up to see empty grass between him and the goalpost. Looking left, he saw that a group of Chippewa would cut him off before he reached it, and he didn't trust his aim with a long throw, so he bared right, away from the goalpost.

An Ottawa in the scrum must have sensed his intention and broke off pursuit to jog toward the goalpost. Sam passed by the post fifty yards to its right. The scrum pressed down on him. After another thirty paces, with what strength he could muster, he turned and flung the ball back towards the goalpost. It arced over the heads of his pursuers, over a few defending Chippewa, and into the pocket of the waiting Ottawa who had held back.

While the scrum barreled over Sam, the Ottawa warrior strolled to the undefended goalpost with the disdain of a conquering emperor and flicked the ball against the wood for an easy score. The Ottawa erupted in whoops of triumph from all over the field. The women on the sidelines shrieked with joy. But there was one guttural yell of fury.

Kinonchamek stood over Sam with his stick poised to fall. Helpless, Sam looked up and realized his life was resting in the balance. But a tide of cheering Ottawa pushed Kinonchamek aside and scooped Sam up in celebration. As the warriors bore Sam back across the field, Kinonchamek stared after him. Sam could only smile at the man as he was swept back to the Ottawa side.

With the goal marked by a stone placed near the Ottawa post, the two teams prepared themselves for the resumption of hostilities. Sam took the time to scan the palisade. He caught William's lanky frame standing next to the diminutive Domitilde on the sentry walk. William threw him an enthusiastic wave while Domitilde blew him a kiss. Sam acknowledged the gestures by raising his stick triumphantly.

But there was still work to be done. The reason for his presence on the field was not athletic victory, no matter how sweet it tasted. He must meet Kinonchamek.

Sam took his spot in the line of warriors and looked across the field. This time, there was no missing him. Kinonchamek lined up his ample frame directly across from Sam. The big man stood placidly as his fellows whooped and hooted around him to work themselves into a frenzy, his gaze trained on Sam.

The ball rose and fell across the blue sky, landing in the middle of the green field. The line stepped off at a jog this time, the men having spent much of their energy. Sam kept his bearing on Kinonchamek. If both stayed their course, they would meet at midfield.

Sam was thinking of how to attack when, with twenty paces still separating them, Kinonchamek hurled his stick like a tomahawk at Sam's nose. Sam barely managed to duck the spinning stick. It struck an Ottawa behind him with a sickening *crack*.

Recovering, Sam brought his stick up to strike the now weaponless Kinonchamek. The hickory haft of his stick cut through the air, but it stopped cold against Kinonchamek's outstretched paws. Sam's face registered shock at the man's strength and tolerance to what must have been bone-numbing pain, then Kinonchamek upended Sam over his shoulder.

The wind left Sam when he struck the hard ground. He rolled quickly, knowing what was coming. His own stick, now hefted by Kinonchamek, slammed into the grass he'd only just occupied.

The brute let out a roar of frustration as he came forward. Sam managed to rise to his feet. By reflex, he sucked in his gut and pulled his waist back as the stick sliced the air in front of his navel. The wood just barely grazed his skin.

An Ottawa flew from the periphery and put his shoulder into Kinonchamek. The massive Chippewa barely registered the hit. Hardly looking, Kinonchamek lashed his stick at the newcomer. It stove in the man's front teeth, and he was on the ground and out of the fight that instant.

Kinonchamek turned his attention back to Sam.

Sam gave ground, realizing he was near helpless without a stick.

The ball landed a dozen paces to their right. The pair barely noticed while the scrum coalesced on the prize. In their struggle within the struggle, Sam and Kinonchamek did not see a young Chippewa warrior, lithe and shifty, dart into the pile and retrieve the deerskin ball. The warrior took half a dozen steps and stopped almost between Kinonchamek and Sam. With the melee bearing down, the young warrior gave the ball a mighty hurl.

Instinctively, Sam and Kinonchamek tore their eyes from one another and watched the ball's flight. The scrum halted as they scrutinized the ball's path and tried to deduce where it would land. It was as if the whole field had froze.

The ball arced impossibly high, then started down. It disappeared behind the wooden palisade and landed in the fort.

A tremendous war cry erupted from the lips of every Chippewa and Sauk warrior, and they swarmed towards the Land Gate as if the throw were something more than an errant pass. The Ottawa warriors stood dumbly as their opponents seemed to be abandoning the field. Sam looked back to find that Kinonchamek had joined his brethren in the headlong dash for the Land Gate.

Captain Etherington and Lieutenant Leslie stood with confused looks as Chippewa warriors rushed down on them. The sentries behind them shifted nervously, unsure of what to do.

British fears became reality when Kinonchamek used Sam's stick to stave in the befuddled Leslie's skull. What brains the lieutenant possessed splattered across Captain Etherington's shocked face.

Sam looked on in horror as the Chippewa women standing near the gate began pulling every manner of war club and tomahawk from under their skins, distributing them to the arriving warriors. Captain Etherington, frozen in place, was swarmed and restrained by two young Sauks. The sentries barely managed to level their muskets before they were both struck down and cut to pieces without having discharged their shot. The Chippewa and Sauk then streamed into the fort behind Kinonchamek, yelping like wolves on a wounded moose.

***

Looking upon the palisade, Sam made out his brother and Domitilde gaping with a few other soldiers at the bloody scene.

"William!" Sam screamed.

William's eyes tore from the carnage at the gate and found Sam in the field.

"The bastion!" Sam commanded.

Understanding quickly, his brother grasped Domitilde and pulled her down the sentry's walk, making for the southwest bastion.

Sam's feet were already churning through the grass by the time the couple began their retreat. At a sprint, he threaded through dazed Ottawa and reached the Land Gate just as it was being drawn closed. Diving, he barely managed to get his frame between the heavy cedar doors before they shut with a loud *thunk*.

Thinking him only a lagging fellow Chippewa, the warrior who closed the gate ignored him and dropped the heavy cross bar into its brackets, sealing the fort. The man turned in time to see Sam's fist coming at him. His knees buckled and all went black before he'd even hit the dirt.

Sam turned from his victim and only just managed to avoid a bayonet tip. The steel stuck into the cedar of the door, and the Sauk wielding the captured musket dropped the weapon instead of trying to withdraw it. The man raised a tomahawk and made to split Sam's skull, but Sam ducked beneath the blade and took off at a run, unwilling to get bogged down in a fight he might not win.

He sprinted down the palisade to where he last saw William, hearing the terrible sounds of a fort being sacked over his labored breaths. British screams of pain and fright echoed through the alleyways. Indians gave war cries and shouted commands. Muskets cracked from all corners as men fought desperately to save themselves, for the fort was already lost.

A group of Chippewa had already gathered under the southwest bastion, their attention fixed on the blockhouse above them. A musket poked from a firing slit and belched a cloud of smoke, causing the Indians to flinch and shirk back. Someone was making a stand in the fortification, and Sam hoped William had made it in.

Without hesitating, Sam came to the first Chippewa in his path and wrapped his arms around the unsuspecting warrior's neck, then dropped to his knees with all his weight. A sickening crunch issued as the neck gave way, and Sam was up and stepping over the lifeless body before it made its last spasm. Another warrior turned and saw him, then belted out a warning to his fellows. Sam picked up the fallen warrior's war club and made ready to defend himself, knowing he was hopelessly outnumbered.

Another shot cracked from the top floor of the blockhouse. One of the Chippewa dropped to his knees and gasped. Sam looked up to see Sergeant Kane poking another musket through the smoke in the firing loop overhead. Having no muskets to return fire, the Indians scattered for cover. The heavy door at the foot of the bastion swung open, and William excitedly beckoned for Sam to dash for it. Obliging, Sam closed the gap and fell through the door before it was shut and barred behind him.

Seeing an Indian sprawled before him, a private taking refuge made to run Sam through with his bayonet, but William knocked the man's musket away. "It's Corporal Avery, you damned fool!" he admonished.

Sam rolled to his feet and reached for his brother, pulling him in for a hug. "Thank God!" he managed, winded from the run.

"Come," William said, and pushed him back. "Domitilde's up this way."

Sam followed his brother up the ladder and through the trapdoor to the upper floor of the bastion. Just as he stood straight, a pair of arms closed around him and almost knocked him back through the hole.

"Sam!" Domitilde exclaimed. *"Dieu merci!"*

Sam returned the embrace and looked about the space. In the half-light of the fortification, he watched Kane discharge another musket through the firing loop facing into the fort. The sergeant then turned and gave him a wild grin and a nod. William exchanged a loaded musket for the sergeant's spent one, then went about priming and loading. The firing ports facing outward were closed with heavy wooden shutters, and the door to the sentry's walk was barred. Sam's eyes then fell on Domitilde's swollen belly.

"We have to get you out of here," he said, his words little more than a whisper.

"Have a look, Corporal," Kane beckoned, nodding to the loop.

Sam steered Domitilde into William's arms and took the now loaded musket. "Sergeant," Sam greeted Kane.

The Irishman stepped aside and gestured out the firing loop, his face almost jubilant from the fighting. "The boggin savages have us over the coals, Sam!"

Sam looked out on Michilimackinac. Bands of Indians moved throughout the fort. Several were armed with muskets, having already captured or received them from the outside, and warriors went methodically from building to building, forcing their entry and rounding up inhabitants. He watched as a British trader was ripped from his hiding spot under a mound of hay. The man pleaded for his life before his throat was cut and his scalp taken to cries of merriment. French residents scurried about unmolested, as if they weren't the targets of the Indians' wrath. It seemed the Sauk and Chippewa desired only British blood. On the parade ground, a Sauk warrior tore down the Union Jack and trampled it in the dirt.

"The fort's lost," Sam said flatly.

"Aye," Kane agreed.

A Chippewa poked his head from behind a small cabin to scrutinize the bastion, then ducked back quickly when he saw Sam scrutinizing him with a tracking musket.

"We must get them out," Sam said, and nodded to William and Domitilde.

"How?" Kane asked.

An excellent question. The blockhouse was itself a tiny fort within a fort. The only exits were the heavy door leading into the fort proper on the ground floor and the barred door that led to the sentry's walk. Neither would do for a well-armed band, much less a few soldiers and a woman about to drop a child.

"What about the firing ports?" Sam asked. He gestured to the square ports on the exterior face of the blockhouse. They were rather bullishly meant for cannon, but the few small artillery pieces the garrison had were always kept on the shore side of the fort, meant to protect the straits. "Drop out the cannon ports?"

"Aye," Kane agreed, "we'd take the drop, but what about the girl?" All eyes fell on Domitilde and her belly. "'Tis fifteen feet down."

"William, open that port," Sam commanded. More sunlight flooded the interior of the blockhouse as William unbarred and pulled back one of the ports. "Can you see anyone about?"

William stuck his head out the narrow opening, then popped back in. "The Ottawa are at the gate," he said.

Sam gave another quick look out the loop. Several more Chippewa heads ducked back below him, and the roving bands were beginning to organize on the parade ground at the fort's northeast corner. "We don't have much time," he grumbled. Turning back to William, he asked, "Can you rouse them?"

William stuck his head back out and yelled frantically to the Ottawa.

"Are we fleeing, Sarge?" one of the privates called up hopefully from below.

"Hold your boggin ground," Kane cursed back at him.

Sam went for another look out the loop. A shot cracked. Wood splintered against his cheek from where the ball imbedded in the frame only inches from his head. Sam stepped back quickly and wiped at his face. Blood covered his fingers.

A great crash hit the blockhouse door, shaking the very bastion itself. Another crash followed it, then another.

"Sarge, they're bringing the door down," one of the privates yelped.

Kane moved past Sam and tried to aim his musket out the firing loop. That drew several shots from below, and he had to duck back quickly.

"They'll take your head off if you try again," Sam said calmly.

Just then, the butt of a musket cracked against the door that led to the sentry's walk of the palisade.

"They'll be in before long," Kane said.

Sam looked back to William. "Any luck?"

"They can't seem to hear me with all the commotion," said William.

Cursing, Sam closed the distance between them and thrust his musket into William's hands. "Then fire over their heads. But for God's sake, don't hit any of them."

William nodded once and squeezed back through the low port. The musket discharged only a moment later. "That upset them mightily!" he called through the port, then he began yelling and flailing for the Ottawa warriors to notice. "They're coming!" he yelled triumphantly, squeezing back inside.

Sam pushed by his brother and looked down to see Makwa and a dozen Ottawa come to a halt below the bastion.

"Sam!" a familiar voice rang out. Langlade pushed through the Ottawa and looked up at him with worried eyes. "My daughter?"

Without wasting a moment, Sam called, "We'll have to drop her down."

Langlade turned to the Ottawa and barked several commands in Ojibwe. The strongest warriors came forward and looked up, their arms extended to catch the precious bundle.

Sam turned and held out his hand. "Domitilde," he said.

The girl didn't hesitate. She came forward, kissed William on the cheek, then saddled up next to Sam, turning her back to the low port. William took up her other side and the brothers bent, grasping her ankles and armpits. Her feet went out the port first, followed by the rest of her.

Sam commanded, "Now!" and the brothers released. William practically followed her out, and only just caught himself in the frame. He saw her land in the safe embrace of the Ottawa warriors below, and Langlade nodded his thanks.

William came back through the port. "She's safe," he said.

"Privates!" Kane barked through the trapdoor. "On me!"

The two men scrambled up the ladder, the sound of the door caving following behind them.

"Out you go," Kane said, and gestured to the port.

"I'll break my bleedin' neck," the first private squealed.

"Aye!" Kane bellowed, "and I'll split your boggin head!"

Needing no more encouragement, the private stuffed his frame through the port and dropped. The second private gave Sam his musket and said, "It's loaded, Corporal."

Sam gave him a nod, then the second lad was through.

A great crash echoed from the ground floor.

"They're in," Kane rasped, leveling his musket on the ladder's trapdoor.

"Out you go," Sam said. He grabbed William by the collar and manhandled him to the port.

William's feet fell through the opening, and his hand shot out and latched around Sam's neck. Their eyes met. "I'll not leave you here, brother," William swore.

Sam smiled wildly. "Right behind you." He pressed a firm hand onto William's chest and pushed, sending him out and down into the waiting arms of the Ottawa.

Just then, a Sauk poked his head through the trapdoor. Kane rewarded the man's bravery with a musket ball through the ear. Sam shouldered his musket and covered the opening. "Now for you, Sergeant!" he called.

"After you, Avery," Kane answered, reloading.

Sam was just about to slip through the cannon port when the door to the sentry's walk crashed open. Kane was quickly mobbed by rushing Chippewa and went down cursing. Sam discharged his musket and rushed to his sergeant's aid, jabbing his barrel at the swarming attackers.

A huge figure pushed through the broken door, and Sam only realized it was Kinonchamek when the big man deftly knocked his musket away with a war club. Kinonchamek then struck him square in the ribs, taking the breath from him. Sam staggered back and fell. Kinonchamek towered over him.

Thinking himself dead, Sam relaxed as the big man raised his club and swung. Everything went dark soon after.

***

A scream woke him.

It took Sam several heartbeats to realize it wasn't his own voice that had bellowed in pain. He opened his eyes to a darkness so total that he believed he might be dead. Another guttural cry cut through the blackness. *Am I in hell*, he asked himself? It wouldn't surprise him in the least if that's where he'd ended up. He'd done things the past year that would set a pastor's knees to shaking.

He could move, he realized, coming up on his elbow. The floor felt like dirt. *Is there dirt in hell*, he wondered?

Another scream of pain rang out from some poor soul, one so hideous it could only have been coaxed forth by a demon.

That was when he heard the sound of others breathing in the dark. "Is anyone there?" Sam asked the blackness.

"Aye," came Kane's Irish lilt. "You're in the magazine."

"Thank God," Sam sighed. "I thought this might be hell." He chuckled weakly.

"Don't be thanking God yet, lad. Before this night's over, you might wish he'd sent you down to Ol' Scratch."

Sam tried to ignore another shriek of pain. "Who all's here?"

"I," Kane began, "you, Captain Etherington – though he's in a bad way – and privates Cooper and Davies. Poor private Wessel is who you be hearin' outside, though I don't think he has long left. They're taking him apart slowly."

Wessel let out another scream at the unseen torture he was being subjected to.

"Lord, take him quick," Sam said.

"Keep quiet!" one of the privates whispered. "You'll bring them down on us!"

Sam ignored the man. "The rest of the garrison?"

"Dead or fled," Kane answered.

A key entering a heavy padlock rattled the magazine's door. Torchlight flooded the space, and the prisoners squinted at the brightness. Sam shielded his eyes and looked up. The flames outside the magazine indeed looked like the fires of hell.

A huge figure entered the door and blocked the light. Sam felt strong hands close around his neck and lift him from the floor. He struggled weakly against the grip, but his strength soon failed him and he submitted. Kane's curses rang out as Sam was carried from the magazine.

The heavy door closed behind him, and he was led into the torchlight and thrown to the dirt. Raising his head, Sam saw black night surrounding a ring of torches. In the center of the torchlight, bound to a pole that loomed over him, was the naked form of what was left of Private Wessel. The lifeless body was cut up and devoid of many of its most important parts. Kinonchamek stood beside the charnel, his face unreadable as he looked down on Sam.

Sam looked the man in the eye and spat.

A quiet command from Kinonchamek saw a Chippewa cut the rope that bound Wessel's remains to the pole. The slab of meat thudded to the earth with a sickening sound. Two Chippewa came from behind Sam and hooked him under the armpits. Before he could offer much struggle, he was slammed against the pole and his wrists were bound high above him.

Kinonchamek appeared in front of him holding a sharp buck knife at eye level. Sam couldn't stop himself from wincing at the sight of the steel. The Chippewa warriors around the pole laughed and jeered at his cowardice.

Kinonchamek studied Sam for several breaths, then he said something in the Ojibwe tongue. Sam shivered, though the night air was warm.

"Does English greed know no bounds?" A voice asked from the darkness.

Minavavana slowly made his way into the torchlight. The chief came to his son's side and gave Wessel's corpse a poke with his moccasin. Then his brown eyes fell on Sam.

"Kinonchamek asks if English greed knows no bounds?" Minavavana repeated.

"What?" Sam asked, shaking his head as if to clear it.

"When will your people rest?" Minavavana asked. "You tell us you're masters of the oceans, that your flag shades much of the world. You fought a war against our fathers, the French, for much the rest. And now you tell us the French have given you this land and its people in a treaty signed in Paris," Minavavana said, "yet you can spare nothing of gifts or shot and powder for those who dwell here."

A chuckle escaped Sam's lips. "I'm not the man to bring your grievances to," he said.

Minavavana ignored him and continued, "It's said that in the east you have even taken the Indians' gods from them, and that you make them worship the bleeding god on the cross. Will you do this to the Anishinaabek, Englishman?"

"I'm no Englishman," Sam huffed. "I'm Pennsylvania born. American."

"Hah!" Minavavana said. "*Pennsylvania, America.* I do not know these places. I hear only worthless words spoken by a white tongue. Those names were only conjured when your people came to our shores. They mean nothing to the Anishinaabek"

"I'm just a corporal," Sam said, trying again. "Not the man to know or care what it is you speak of."

"And now…" Minavavana leaned forward. "English greed has grown such that they even take our women."

Sam grimaced.

Minavavana's strong features broke into a smile in the torchlight. "I think, Englishman, you are the man to bring *this* grievance to."

The chief turned to his son and spoke quickly in Ojibwe. Kinonchamek nodded and responded.

Minavavana turned back to Sam and said, "My son asks for your forgiveness. He must take something from you now."

Before Sam knew what was happening, Kinonchamek reached out with his free hand and gripped Sam's right ear between his thumb and forefinger. The steel blade easily sliced through the skin, severing Sam's ear in a shower of blood. Sam screamed in blinding pain and writhed against the pole. The Chippewa warriors witnessing the scene cursed at his weakness, taunting him as he sputtered for breath and tears came to his eyes.

Sam came back from the brink of unconsciousness and his vision slowly returned. He saw Kinonchamek hand his severed ear to a Chippewa and issue a command he couldn't understand. The warrior slipped into the darkness.

Sam took a deep breath and said, "You're beasts."

"Beasts?" Minavavana asked. The chief shook his head. "We would be here until the sun rose if I were to tell you of the horrors the white man has visited upon my people. Look to each warrior here Englishman. Look!"

Slowly, Sam raised his bleeding head and looked at the faces in the torchlight. The dark eyes of the young warriors stared back at him devoid of any pity, but the unmistakable sheen of sadness could be seen in many of them.

"Each has lost someone," Minavavana continued. "Some lost wives and children to the white man's pox. Some lost brothers, sons, or fathers to your wars for dominion over all things. Many of those taken were tortured by English and Iroquois hands so monstrously that this…" He gestured to Wessel. "This is mercy."

Minavavana pointed at Sam's chest. "Look to yourselves to see the beasts in the Upper Country, Englishman. You are devourers, taking everything from us."

"Spoken by a man who could do that to another," Sam said, gesturing to Private Wessel's remains.

Minavavana looked down at the corpse and said, "I see only a dead beast that can devour no more."

"Then be done with it!" Sam yelled. "Kill me."

"Kill you?" Minavavana asked. "Are the English stupid as well as greedy? We wait for an answer."

"Answer?" Sam breathed.

"I hope an ear is all young William need see to understand our sincerity," Minavavana said. "It would be a shame to have to take more from you."

Sam recoiled. "He won't deliver himself to you."

Minavavana cocked his head. "Would you leave your brother in our care?" he asked.

The answer was plain for all.

"He'll not come!" Sam yelled.

"We will wait for William's answer," Minavavana said, looking up at the moon. "It won't be long."

Sam's mind scrambled for quite some time as he searched for a way to save his brother. The Chippewa watched the moon move across the sky and listened to the crickets chirp while Sam pondered.

Finally, Sam said, "Domitilde will not come back to Kinonchamek. Killing William will do nothing."

Minavavana shook his head, and translated Sam's words for Kinonchamek. Kinonchamek listened passively, then responded.

"My son knows this," Minavavana explained. "But this is no longer about a woman. My people need to see that our suffering of English greed ends now. Tomorrow, your people's contempt of the Anishinaabek will be answered with blood."

"You already have the fort!" Sam cried. "There's no need for more killing!"

"You're wrong," Minavavana answered. "More English will come. More English will need to die. Your brother's death will show my people that we can kill you, and give them courage for what's to come. Tomorrow, a new wind blows across the Upper Country, and it will scour the white man from our lands."

"Please!" Sam begged as tears welled in his eyes. "Just take me! Kill me!"

Kinonchamek reached out and tenderly wiped a teardrop from Sam's cheek. He spoke, and his father translated, "If your brother agrees to fight, take pride in his bravery. Kinonchamek says that he cannot make it quick, but it will be a good death."

Sam lashed out with a kick, which the chief and Kinonchamek easily sidestepped.

"*Gibichiwebinan!*" someone called from outside the torchlight.

Charles Langlade stepped into the circle.

"Charles, don't let him do it!" Sam yelled.

One of the Chippewa warriors stepped forward and delivered a punch to Sam's gut. The air in his lungs flew from him in a great rush, and he coughed and gagged for several seconds. He felt a calming hand come to his shoulder, and he looked up to see Langlade standing at his side.

"How do you fare?" Langlade asked.

Sam's white teeth were red with blood as he smiled. "No complaints, so long as William is well. Any chance you could end it now, though? Wrench my neck?"

Langlade's face soured.

"You can't let him, Charles!" Sam said, leaning into the man.

With sorrow etched across his features, Langlade said, "William means to fight Kinonchamek in exchange for your release."

"No!" Sam screamed. "End it now. Kill me, Charles! Kill me!" More tears came to Sam's face. "You can't let him, Charles. I'll not trade my life for his. He must live for the child."

Holding his hands open helplessly, Langlade said, "I've made that argument, and a dozen more. He means to do this."

"He'll be killed!"

"He's at peace with that," Langlade said, a touch of pride filling his voice. "When a man decides to give his life for another, you must let him."

"Charles!" Sam yelled. "You can't let him! You mustn't!"

Langlade ignored his cries. "William will meet Kinonchamek at dawn outside the palisade, and you will be released. No more harm shall come to you before then." With that said, Langlade turned and walked towards the boundary of the torchlight.

"Charles!" Sam screamed.

Langlade turned.

"My father let you live!" Sam cried. "You must see that William lives! That's why he left you alive, can't you see! You're meant to keep William alive, Charles!"

Langlade's face betrayed nothing more, and he turned and disappeared into the night.

"You're meant to keep my brother alive!" Sam called out again.

No answer came back from the darkness.

***

Sam opened his eyes.

He looked up to see his bonds still firmly tied overhead to the pole. Wessel, his only company throughout the long night other than the sentries, was starting to stink at his feet. The wound on his head throbbed, but the blood had stopped flowing under the makeshift bandage the Chippewa had applied. He shook his head to clear his senses. The two sentries remained at their post around the fire, their muskets across their laps as they poked at venison resting over the flames. A third paced with his musket in hand.

A cock crowed loudly from somewhere in the fort. Sam looked up to the sky and saw that dawn was not far.

He wished it would never come. Dawn meant the death of William, the only family he had left.

Too soon, Kinonchamek – looking menacing in fresh warpaint – appeared in front of the magazine with Minavavana. The sentries stood in respect as the big man drew close to Sam. Towering over him, Kinonchamek looked down into Sam's eyes with a placid look.

Kinonchamek spoke in the Ojibwe tongue. Minavavana translated, "My son says you need not fear for the safety of Domitilde or her child after your brother's death. This misfortune between our families will be over, and he promises no Chippewa will ever raise a hand against them while he draws breath."

Sam wanted to spit at the man, but the words he spoke didn't warrant such a response. He only nodded once in understanding.

Kinonchamek went on, and Minavavana translated, "Once this day is done, Englishman, you should leave the Upper Country. Go east. Do not stop until you reach the sea. This land is for the Anishinaabek."

With a gesture, Kinonchamek ordered the sentries to cut Sam down. Sam dropped to the dirt, his legs unable to support his weight. One of the sentries rolled Sam over with his heel and went about tying a rope to his wrist bindings. When Sam was secure, the sentry helped him to his feet, supporting him for several moments until he found his balance.

A shove from Kinonchamek sent Sam walking forward, his wrists tied behind his back and his tether in the hands of Kinonchamek. He looked over his shoulder at the magazine.

"God be with you, lads!" Sam called out.

"Aye, and with you, lad!" he heard Kane's muffled reply.

Detritus from the sacking lay in heaps around the three men as they passed through the fort. Many of the domesticated animals within the palisade had been killed, their corpses already bloating in the heat and adding to the stench that hung over the place. Dead soldiers lay where they'd fallen, most with their scalps removed and their bodies mutilated. British traders caught within the palisade had suffered similar fates. French citizens shuffled about the wreckage unmolested, a few of them even going through the ransacked cabins of murdered Britishers. Sam noticed that French cabins and property remained untouched by the Indians. All the Frenchmen they came upon avoided Sam's gaze, their eyes downcast in either fear, indifference, or shame. Here and there, Chippewa and Sauk who had imbibed captured rum stores lay in drunken heaps.

Reaching the Land Gate, Sam was greeted by a sight that chilled his bones. Hundreds of Chippewa warriors lined the southern palisade, their eyes boring into him as he approached. Not a sound escaped from the great host. Sam was led through the Land Gate with only the thundering of his heart filling his ears.

In the field outside the gate, he found William standing before him at the head of the Ottawa of L'Arbre Croche.

"William!" Sam said, and surged forward.

Kinonchamek gave a mighty tug on the rope attached to Sam's wrists. He fell backward and landed painfully. He rolled in time to see William coming to his aid. Minavavana held up a hand and stopped William's approach.

Minavavana turned and spoke a few words to his son. At the command, Kinonchamek unsheathed his knife and made for Sam. William let out a sharp exhalation, but the muskets of the Chippewa on the palisade kept him from moving. Kinonchamek reached Sam's prostrate form and forced him roughly onto his belly, cutting his bindings with the buck knife. Free, Sam scampered through the grass and came to his feet, moving to William as quickly as his weak legs would carry him.

The brothers threw their arms around each other, an embrace made awkward by the hatchet in William's right hand and the knife in his left.

"Don't do this," Sam begged, wasting no time.

William squeezed him tighter. "I must, brother," he said.

"Not for me."

"It's not only for you, Sam." William breathed, pushing Sam back to look down at him.

Sam didn't try to understand his meaning. "He'll kill you," he said.

"Maybe," William said lightly, as if it were a trifling thing.

Sam stood on his toes and whispered, "Turn and run with me."

"The men on the palisade would shoot us down in a heartbeat."

"Then we'll die together."

"You're not dying today, Sam."

"Let me fight him," Sam begged.

With a scoff, William looked down at the dried blood that covered Sam and the bruises on his face. "You can barely stand, brother. And besides, he wants me. You've fought my battles long enough. I'll fight this last one."

Sam pulled him close again and sobbed into his shoulder. "I'll be all alone."

"Nonsense," William soothed, again pushing Sam back to look upon his face. "If I'm to die, I want you to raise the baby as your own."

Sam could only shake his head. "It should be you."

William smiled. "Have faith, brother. I may yet win."

Sam sighed. "I don't think there's a man in the Upper Country who could take him in a fight."

William stiffened. "Then promise me you'll look after the child."

Seeing no way to stop this madness, Sam nodded in defeat. "You know I will."

Kinonchamek, standing with his war club slung over his shoulder, spoke sharply. The brothers turned to see him gesture in annoyance at Sam's continued presence on the field.

"It's time," William said.

Sam turned again and clutched at his brother. "Run with me. I won't have you die for me."

William's focus was on Kinonchamek, and with a hint of irritation in his voice, he said "As I said, it's not only for you." William turned and looked to the Ottawa.

Sam joined him and saw Domitilde supported by her father. The girl was weeping in agony for her lover.

"Take care of them both," William said, and his voice finally cracked.

Sam grasped William's collar and forced his eyes back to him. "I swear it," he said.

William nodded once, then said, "Take father's medal from my neck."

"No!" Sam gasped.

"Do it!" William commanded in a voice Sam had never heard before.

Unable to disobey, Sam quickly pulled the medal over his brother's head.

"Swift and bold, Sam," William said, then he pushed his brother away and set off to meet the waiting Kinonchamek.

"Swift and bold," Sam repeated softly, then the strength left his legs and he collapsed in a heap. Two Ottawa warriors quickly came forward and picked him up from the ground. They brought him to Domitilde, and she wrapped her arms around him as if she were drowning and only he could keep her afloat.

***

Five hundred paces away, a light that seemed to rise from the very earth itself streamed through the cracks of Charles Langlade's cellar floor.

The false floor flew open to reveal Makwa hunched with an outstretched lantern. The Ottawa warrior was still as a statue, scanning the cellar with the aid of the light, listening for any footfalls on the floor above. Satisfied the house was empty, he emerged from the tunnel and motioned for his fellows to follow. Seven handpicked warriors soon joined him in the cramped confines of the cellar. Each of them carried only clubs and knives, having decided to forgo muskets for fear of rousing the Chippewa.

Makwa whispered to his men, and their nods of understanding told him all were ready to proceed. He made his way to the stairs and lifted the cellar door an inch so he could inspect the area. Daylight flooded into the space, and he had to squint until his eyes adjusted. When they finally did, he saw no one in sight. Silently, he raised the door and stepped into the day, his men not far behind.

***

Kinonchamek spent most of the first few moments of the duel pumping up his fellows along the palisade. He made every effort to ignore William's presence on the field, and he circled and orated without hardly looking at his coiled opponent. Kinonchamek's tribesmen rewarded his speechifying with great whoops of passion.

Sam prayed the man kept at it, hoping that perhaps William would have a chance if Kinonchamek showed him no respect. They were about equal in height, so reach was not a factor, but the muscle of the Chippewa far exceeded the meat on William's bones. And Kinonchamek was a killer. William was not.

William just circled along with the Chippewa, his eyes never leaving the man. He didn't seek to strike, knowing the warrior might be trying to goad him into a foolhardy assault.

The Ottawa that formed the half-moon of the fighting area remained silent while the Chippewa howled.

Kinonchamek finally turned his attention to William, as if noticing his opponent for the first time. He slowly stepped forward, closing the gap between the two. At five paces, he stopped and bared his white teeth in a fearsome grimace. Then he turned to his people and let out a war cry that had turned the stomachs of a hundred doomed men throughout the Upper Country. The Chippewa erupted at the howl, their answering calls buffeting William like a thousand deadly arrows.

William ignored it all. Instead, he gave his hatchet a workmanlike twirl, as if his only care in the world was the weapon's balance. The disdainful move drew whoops of appreciation from the Ottawa behind him, and it set the veins in Kinonchamek's temples throbbing.

"That's it, William!" Sam yelled with pride. "Let him crow all he wants!"

***

Cheering from the Land Gate drew the eyes of the Sauk sentries posted over the Water Gate. Makwa ducked back behind the cover of the soldier's barracks and waited a few breaths for the commotion to die and the sentries to shift their attention. Slowly, he peeked an eye around the corner of the barracks. The Sauk were again scanning the beach and the straits for any treachery or approaching British vessels.

With a wave of his hand, Makwa sent his first four men across the main thoroughfare of the fort, into a small garden south of the parade ground. The warriors disappeared in the thick fauna. The sentries remained ignorant of the crossing, and Makwa led the last three warriors in a dash to the covering garden.

After another pause to see if their movement had been detected, Makwa led his men through the gardens behind a row of houses. The men moved quickly and quietly, and the only alarm they raised was from a sparrow. She flew off in a huff at the invasion of her favorite bush.

***

Kinonchamek strode forward with his war club poised. His first attack was a lazy, arcing swing of the heavy, ball-headed club. William easily dodged the contemptuous strike, taking a few steps back and raising his hatchet. The Chippewa women along the palisade gave shrieks of delight at his giving ground, and Kinonchamek held his club high at their calls.

William circled right, his hatchet up and his left hand ready to defend with the knife. Kinonchamek's gaze fell back on him and he deigned to circle along. The smile on the big warrior's face only grew with each revolution. He started talking in Ojibwe.

"He says if you're man enough to take his woman, you should be man enough to strike him," Langlade called, translating from the Ottawa gallery. "He dares you to come forward."

"Thank you, Charles," William answered steadily, his eyes never leaving Kinonchamek.

The Chippewa let out another long oath.

"Do you want me to translate?" Langlade called.

"Some words need no translation, Charles. And I think I'd rather concentrate on staying alive," William responded.

"Right. *Pardon*."

With a swiftness that stole Sam's breath and silenced the hum of the crowd, Kinonchamek pounced. William almost lost his footing as he gave ground, but he caught himself just as Kinonchamek's club came in with far greater speed than his first strike. William raised his hatchet and barely managed to deflect the club from connecting with his brow.

Kinonchamek's momentum carried him forward when the club missed, and he staggered to catch his balance. Stunned by the man's quickness, William couldn't take advantage of the missed strike and only gave more ground, causing a groan to rise from the Ottawa at the lost opportunity.

"Don't worry, William!" Sam called. "Just keep moving!"

Recovering, Kinonchamek turned to William. He knew his opponent was on the back foot. Fear was as much his ally as his strength and skill. He spun the club in his hands several times and came forward again.

***

Two Chippewa sat around a smoldering fire in front of the turf-covered mound that held the King's powder, their muskets resting near them. Behind them, the heavy door that protected the magazine was closed and barred from the outside, proof that men were being held within, just as Charles Langlade had told them. Ten paces from the sitting warriors, a pole had been hammered into the ground, and the wood was stained with dried blood. At the foot of the pole lay the naked body of a white man, or what remained of it. His sex had been removed, along with great strips of flesh from his thighs and calves. There were only empty sockets where his eyes had once been. His scalp had been yanked away to reveal the white bone of his skull. The man's mouth, grinning grotesquely from a lack of lips, lolled open to reveal a tongueless cavity. Crude designs had been dug into his chest by Chippewa and Sauk knives.

The sight elicited no emotion from Makwa, who hid behind the thick vines of a garden fence only a dozen paces away. The Englishman was a trophy fairly won. It was the right of the Sauk and Chippewa to do with their vanquished as they pleased.

Instead, Makwa only looked for opportunities. They had to do this quickly and quietly so as not to alert the Chippewa enjoying the show in front of the Land Gate. That became even more difficult with the appearance of a musket-cradling warrior striding around the side of the magazine. The warrior stopped in front of his fellows, ripped a hunk of venison from a skewer, and strode on for another orbit of the mound.

Makwa watched for two hundred steady heartbeats, hoping that the routine might change or break down. It did not.

Turning to his nimblest warrior, a youth of only seventeen, Makwa issued a quick command. The youth was off and slithering through the garden like a snake as soon as Makwa uttered his last word.

Unseen, the young warrior retreated from the magazine, crossed a small lane to get behind a storehouse, and came at the turf mound from the north. There, he took up a position behind a small fence, and had an excellent view of the rear of the magazine, with about ten feet between its back and the palisade. He watched the sentry make his round, then he waited while the man came back on the reverse course.

Silent as a fox, the young warrior slipped from cover and approached the back of the ignorant sentry. He wrapped his left elbow around the windpipe of the sentry while jamming his right thumb into the space between the hammer and pan of the man's musket.

The sentry's first reaction was to let out a cry of warning, but his attacker had closed his throat, and only a guttural sound came forth. His second reaction was to fire off his musket, but no shot cracked, and no fire belched from the barrel. The hammer fell on his attacker's thumb. Not long after, the world faded to pinpoints in his eyes, then it was gone altogether.

The young warrior, turning over in his mind Nissowaquet's order that no Indian be harmed, lay the sentry down with a gentleness that contrasted greatly with how he'd incapacitated the man only moments before.

***

Another fierce attack left William staggering away. The Chippewa outside the Land Gate eagerly pushed him back toward the oncoming Kinonchamek. William had to duck and roll beneath the heavy club's arc. Sam saw his brother's queue ruffle from the disturbance of the club passing so close.

Coming to his feet and turning, William waited as the big man bore down on him again. William dug the toe of his boot into the dirt and sprayed the oncoming Kinonchamek with debris. The man barely squinted before unleashing another swing of the club.

William wasn't quick enough this time. The ball head glanced his left shoulder. Sam winced and exhaled at the damage his brother must have incurred. William scrambled away, seeking distance and managing to keep hold of his knife. Kinonchamek did not follow. The man gestured in triumph to calls of adoration from the crowd. William used the respite to test his left arm. He swung it in a few shallow circles, and Sam saw him grimace at the pain this drew. The arm was injured, but not yet useless.

With Kinonchamek ignoring him yet again, William made to take advantage. He darted forward for a strike. Only cries of alarm from the Chippewa saved Kinonchamek from a hatchet between the shoulder blades. He turned just in time, his face registering surprise at the fight in the Englishman, and he barely deflected several lightning swings as he gave ground.

***

The roar of indignation that rose from the Chippewa crowd carried to Makwa's ears. He cocked his head and thought, *perhaps the Englishman is winning*. But the cries soon turned to cheers, showing the thought to be folly.

Makwa knew he had to act before the fight was over, and just then a whistle issued from behind the magazine. Both sentries heard it, but their reaction was more curiosity than alarm.

The time had come.

***

William was close to being overwhelmed. After another narrow escape, Sam marveled at the stamina of Kinonchamęk. The man's brow was free of sweat. His attacks hadn't faltered in the least. If anything, the Chippewa was only becoming more dangerous, his movements sharpening to a deadliness that could not be long avoided.

Knowing his time was running out, William tried something foolish. With a movement that all could see coming, he hefted the hatchet and threw it with what strength he could muster.

Sam offered a prayer that the blade would land as he watched it tumble end over end. Domitilde gasped beside him. The Ottawa drew in their breaths as they watched the weapon's flight.

A flick of Kinonchamek's club deflected the hatchet and broke Sam's spirit. With a wail, Domitilde collapsed against him. Langlade groaned along with the Ottawa as the Chippewa host erupted in triumph. William was surely dead now. The only weapon left to him was his knife, which he switched to his right hand.

***

A mighty roar rose from the Land Gate, and Makwa pounced.

He vaulted the fence and landed in full view of the Chippewa sentries. The men's eyes bulged in shock at the appearance of an Ottawa warrior deep within the fort. But they recovered quick enough to leap to their feet and fumble for their muskets.

Makwa covered the short distance by the time the first sentry managed to cock his musket. Ripping the musket from the

Chippewa's grip, Makwa used the heavy butt to club his opponent in the gut. With a great expulsion of air, the Chippewa doubled over and made an easy target for another strike. Makwa brought the butt down on the back of the man's neck with enough force to knock him into a daze but leave him alive. Three Ottawa tackled the second sentry before he could fire, and it wasn't long before he too was knocked from his senses.

***

Planting his feet, Kinonchamek used the muscles of his thick legs to brace his body and rotate his torso. He stretched and swung the club's head through the air at William's pathetically small knife. The heavy ball struck William's right forearm. Bone shattered with a sickening crack, and William's hand lost all power to grip. The knife fell to the roar of Chippewa cheers.

***

Makwa found only four Englishman in the magazine. It took several moments of gesturing and calm words to explain to the fierce-looking one that the Ottawa were the English's saviors, and soon the man relented and let himself be picked up. The other soldiers were quickly gathered, each braced by an Ottawa warrior as the group moved back through the fort. Coming to the main thoroughfare, Makwa halted the party and stole a glance at the Water Gate from behind the corner of a storehouse.

The sentries had abandoned their orders to scan the straits and had their eyes fixed on the Land Gate, straining to see anything other than the backs of the Chippewa.

Makwa hissed through his teeth. There was no avoiding detection now. They would have to make a break for Langlade's home in the open, under the sentries' guns.

***

The force of Kinonchamek's attack put William on his back foot and drove him towards the Chippewa contingent. The big man feinted left, and when William moved to dodge him, Kinonchamek recovered and swung the club from his right. The heavy head went unchecked and struck the bone of William's left hip.

Sam made to charge. Domitilde clung to him tighter, and Langlade reached out and grasped his other arm, prohibiting him from rushing to William's aid.

"*Non*," Langlade whispered. "They will cut us down." He glanced up at the armed Chippewa lining the palisade.

William's knees gave out and he tumbled into the dirt while the Chippewa women erupted in joy. The Ottawa answered with groans of dismay.

Kinonchamek stepped to the prostrate form of William and let loose a triumphal howl. The time had come for the final blow.

Sam broke from Langlade's grip and rushed forward. Kinonchamek sensed him coming and struck quickly, sending his club into Sam's ribs. The impact stole Sam's breath, and he collapsed beside William.

The brothers' eyes locked. William smiled weakly and said, "Don't worry, Sam. I have him now."

Sam reached for William as tears streamed down his cheeks. But William shrugged him off, showing Sam the knife he clutched in his left hand.

Blinking, Sam realized William must have fortuitously landed on the blade.

Kinonchamek's mass blocked out the sun. He stood over the brothers with his war club poised, his face filled with purpose. With a grunt, the man raised the heavy club to strike.

With the speed of a coiled snake, William lashed out with his left arm.

But the club still fell.

Sam gasped and shut his eyes, hearing the sound of a skull giving way.

Domitilde's sorrowful cry carried across the ground.

Sam opened his eyes to see that William was gone.

With a cry of victory, Kinonchamek hefted his club to Chippewa roars.

Sam looked up to find the giant looking down on him. But something was amiss. The life behind Kinonchamek's eyes fluttered. The man's rich skin slowly lost its color, turning to a shade of ash. A sound of bemusement escaped Kinonchamek's throat as he looked down to his thigh.

Red blood pumped from the Chippewa in great gushes with each beat of his strong heart. It came in torrents that no man or god could stop. It sprayed the ground and soaked into the earth. William's pathetic final strike had found the life-giving artery that runs through the leg, and its rupture would be the death of Kinonchamek.

The club fell to the ground, and the mighty warrior followed it. He lay quietly while his blood filled the grass around him, the Chippewa host silent with him. Sam heard the great man's last breath – a weak and ragged gasp – then nothing.

But the silence was soon broken. Muskets popped within the fort.

***

Balls hissed and whined as they passed between the group. Makwa was the last across the lane, and a ball fired from the Water Gate skipped off the ground and struck his calf. But its power had been much diminished, and it barely slowed him as he dashed to cover.

The group reached Langlade's house and made for the cellar doors. One of the soldiers, the fierce one whose voice carried authority, had to be pushed through the doors, his desire to stand and fight was so great. The Ottawa roughly handled him into the hidden tunnel and made their escape to the sound of the man's curses.

***

Sam could still feel the warmth from William's body as he cradled it. He didn't notice the excited shouts of the Chippewa, nor their mass retreat from the palisade to investigate the firing in the fort. All he could do was brush the blond, blood matted-hair from William's eyes, shooing away flies that were already congregating on the gore as he mumbled, "I see what you did, William. It wasn't just for me. You saved the others as well." He shook his head and smiled sadly. "How far you came in so little time."

Domitilde was on them soon after. She pressed her head to William's breast and wept. Sam used his bloodstained hand to gently caress the back of her neck, seeking to offer some comfort. A moan escaped the girl, and she seemed to double in on herself. The sorrow in Sam turned to concern. Domitilde gave another low moan and clutched at her stomach. Sam turned in a panic to see Langlade coming for his daughter.

"Papa," she gasped.

Langlade knelt beside her, and his hand came away wet. He looked to Sam with concern and said, "The child comes."

Sam pushed the sorrow from his soul and focused on what would remain of William. "We must help her," he said. He tried to stand, and pain shot through the ribs Kinonchamek had broken. He doubled over and coughed violently. Every breath he drew couldn't fill his lungs, and the agony was close to unbearable.

Langlade called to the Ottawa. Several warriors came forward. Two lifted Sam to his feet as others diligently raised the sobbing Domitilde. As he was being carried from the field, Sam stopped his bearers and turned to Langlade.

"Charles. My brother," Sam said.

Langlade issued another command, and Sam looked back to see several warriors reverently lift William from the ground, settle him on their shoulders, and begin carrying him from the field.

Turning back, Sam's gaze fell upon a lone Chippewa still on the field. It was Minavavana, and he was looking across the ground at the empty shell that had been his son. Sam saw tears in the chief's eyes. Just then, Minavavana turned to Sam. A long moment passed between them. Sam held no sorrow for Kinonchamek, but he was sorry for a father's loss of a son. Minavavana shed no tears for William, but he understood the pain of a brother losing a brother. The moment ended with a curt nod from the chief, which Sam returned. Both men recognized their role in the life of the other was over.

With that, Sam slumped against his supporters.

Ch. 13

L'Arbre Croche. June 1763

Charles Langlade ushered the still bandaged Captain Etherington and Sergeant Kane to Nissowaquet's longhouse. The chief sat with his retinue around the low fire at the center, bare-chested like his fellows in the heat of the day. Captain Etherington took the space offered him across from the chief. Kane grimaced in pain as he squatted down at his officer's side.

Etherington cleared his throat and said, "I want to thank you again for saving our lives. His Majesty King George will know all about your courage, and you will be rewarded for your loyalty."

Langlade translated. Nissowaquet nodded once. Langlade turned back to Etherington and said, "The chief is sorry at the betrayal the Chippewa visited upon you, and for the men you have lost. He believes you and your remaining men should make for Montreal immediately."

"Montreal?" Etherington leaned in. "I believe Detroit–"

"Detroit," Langlade interrupted, "is besieged by the war chief Pontiac as we sit here and speak. The attack on Michilimackinac was part of something much greater than we could ever have imagined."

Etherington stiffened. "Pontiac?" he asked in disbelief and worry.

"Nissowaquet will not raise his tomahawk and join him," Langlade explained, "though many Ottawa wish him to."

An audible exhalation of relief passed Etherington's lips. "That pleases me, and it will please King George. But It would please the King even more if Nissowaquet assisted us in retaking Michilimackinac. With your help, we would surely succeed in dislodging the Chippewa."

Langlade didn't even bother translating that for Nissowaquet. He said, "The Ottawa will not raise their hands against fellow Indians. The Chippewa deserve what punishment King George chooses to levy, as does Pontiac, but Nissowaquet will have no part in its discharge."

"But as a loyal subject of the King, it's his duty to help the King's representatives. We need his warriors."

"Nissowaquet would remind you," Langlade said softly, "that the King's representatives would all be in pieces if not for his intervention."

Etherington blanched. "Quite right."

"You will be escorted to Montreal," Langlade said in finality. "We hope you convey to General Amherst all that we have done for you."

"Absolutely," Etherington conceded weakly.

Langlade made to stand, but Kane stopped him with a question. "Excuse me, sir. What has happened to Sam Avery?" he asked. "We've not seen him since our arrival here, and we would like to know his condition."

Langlade looked at him with piercing eyes. "Sam died from the wounds Kinonchamek inflicted upon him," he said.

With a heavy sigh, Kane hung his head. "I should like to see his body. I'd like to say goodbye to the lad."

"*Impossible*," Langlade answered quickly. "Domitilde has charge of his body, and she plans to take him and William to our burial grounds, as is our custom. Until then, no one may lay eyes on them."

Kane cocked his head at the declaration and examined Langlade for several moments. Langlade looked back at him, his face an unreadable mask.

"Well," Etherington finally said. "That is unfortunate. First William, then Sam. I shall be sorry for their mother."

"Their mother is long dead," Langlade answered. "As is their father, who served in your regiment."

Etherington coughed uncomfortably, not remembering the man. "A shame. A whole family gone."

"Not all," Langlade said dismissively, standing and gesturing to the entryway.

Kane winced and stood, along with the captain. "Aye," he straightened to look at Langlade. "Your grandchild was born this past night."

"The loss of William pushed Domitilde into labor," Langlade acknowledged.

A concerned look crossed Kane's face. "Is the babe healthy?"

"*Oui*," Langlade couldn't hide a smile. "A healthy boy."

"What did she choose as his name?" Etherington asked.

Langlade's smile turned to one of sadness. "She's named him William."

Epilogue

"Come along, lads," Sergeant Kane encouraged. "Not far now."

The young faces looked up from their oars and nodded solemnly as they bent their backs to the work. The bateau churned through the calm water of the straits with each stroke. The sun of a new year blazed high overhead, casting its rays on a flotilla of small boats and canoes carrying the King's soldiers back to Michilimackinac.

"What was it like, Sarge, the massacre?" one of the privates asked.

Kane turned his sharp eyes on the boy. The lad, only seventeen – if that, if he'd lied to the recruiting sergeant – shrunk into himself at the intensity of his sergeant's gaze. Kane tried to soften his face as best he could and said, "Don't go worrying yourself about that, lad. Ol' Pontiac buried his tomahawk months ago."

"How many lived?" the private's bench mate couldn't resist asking.

Kane blew air through his teeth and looked up at the sun. These privates might pester him for the rest of the journey if he didn't offer them something. "Well, the savages killed all but ten of us straight away when they took the fort."

"How did they do it?" the first private asked. "Is it true the Indians will take a man's tongue as well as his scalp."

"Aye, and much more," Kane confirmed with a grim nod. "The savage will take your lips, ears, balls, and asshole if he has the pleasure of killing you."

Both privates' eyes widened and their throats bobbed as they swallowed.

Kane smiled at the effect of his words and continued, "Six of us were taken prisoner, to be used at the pleasure of the Chippewa. That first evening, while the rest of us were locked away in the magazine, most wounded something grievous, they worked on poor Private Wessel." The privates leaned in with horrified fascination. "They kept him alive most of the night, they did, which was wondrous considering the amount of flesh they took from his body. His heart still beat well past midnight, though I'd say his spirit had long since departed from that terrible place, to seek its peace somewhere else.

"But salvation soon came for us. Private Avery had made his escape outside the fort during the sacking. His brother, Corporal Avery, was locked in the magazine with us, so Private Avery challenged the champion of the savages for the life of his brother."

"He won?" the second private asked.

Kane shook his head sadly. "Private Avery was a fine lad, but he was no match for the brute he faced. Kinonchamek was the cunningest, strongest son of Satan the Upper Country ever spat from its womb. Avery knew that, and didn't think he could best such a man, so the fight was just a ruse to distract the Chippewa long enough for us to be freed by our Ottawa friends."

Kane fell into silence as he remembered that terrible day. For a few moments, the only sounds on the water were the dips of the oars and the creaks of the planks. The privates looked to each other, each seeming to dare the other to get the sergeant back on track.

With a sigh, Kane looked back to them and said, "Saved our lives, Avery did. Lost his in the bargain." Then a smile fell over his lips. "But he took the brute with him. Stuck his knife deep in Kinonchamek's leg before he died. William hadn't lost after all."

"And his brother?" the first private asked.

"Died of his wounds," Kane said quickly.

"A shame."

Just then, the boat rounded a bend and Michilimackinac came into view. Kane turned in his seat to get a good look at the place. No smoke rose from its walls. No Indians walked along the sentry walks. The Water Gate stood open, its heavy doors pulled from their hinges by the Chippewa. The palisade had creeping vines crawling up its face, and the shore was becoming overgrown with all manner of weeds. The place was clearly abandoned, the Chippewa having fled for the safety of the vast interior when word came that Pontiac's rebellion had faltered and the fighting had stopped. Only the Lord knew where the French residents had gone.

It would take the lads some time to get her back into shape. But soon her gates would be up, and her walls made strong again.

Kane turned back, and his gaze fell on a low dune along the shore. A lone figure caught his eye. Shielding the sun, he focused on the form, which he soon saw was a man, a man leaning against a musket.

At first, Kane thought the man to be an Indian – perhaps just a curious Ottawa who had come to witness the return of the King's soldiers after their yearlong absence. But then he noticed that the leggings the man wore were in fact buckskin breeches, and a fine homespun shirt stretched over the man's barrel chest. A tricorn sat cocked at a jaunty angle on the man's head, and dark hair hung down to his shoulders. This was certainly no Indian, but the man didn't look like one of the rough French trappers that infested the woods in these parts. Even though he'd thought the Chippewa had chased them all from the Upper Country at the start of Pontiac's rebellion, Kane decided it must be an Englishman he looked upon.

Coming level with the man, at a distance of only three hundred paces, Kane saw the stranger's right hand rise in a greeting. Kane stood as carefully as he could in the unsteady boat, and he squinted his eyes in scrutiny. He could only just distinguish the pale complexion and rosy cheeks under the stranger's hat. If he'd been closer, Kane would have seen a silver medal dangling from the man's neck.

"By Jove!" Kane exhaled.

"Who's that, Sergeant?" one of the privates asked.

Kane looked down at the private in disbelief, then back to the beach. It was empty, not a trace of anything except seagulls and beachgrass.

"Sergeant?" the private asked again.

Though he knew he'd seen all he would, Kane kept his eyes on the beach for another few breaths. Smiling, he finally turned and sat back on his bench. "Never you mind, Private," he answered with a chuckle. "Never you mind."

Historical Notes

On a near-flawless June the 2nd, 1763, a deerskin ball was hurled over the palisade of Fort Michilimackinac during a ceremonial game of Baggataway, Lacrosse's forefather. Hundreds of men of the Chippewa and Sauk nations, under leadership of the great Chippewa chief Minavavana, followed the ball, easily sacking the fort from the stunned garrison commanded by Captain Etherington. Many British soldiers and traders were killed outright, but Etherington and a few others were taken captive.

Ottawa chief Nissowaquet, either horrified by the attack or upset at the lack of an invitation to join in, took control of the surviving prisoners from Minavavana. He eventually sent them on to Montreal under Ottawa protection, and he was rewarded handsomely for his loyalty to the crown.

The Avery brothers did not witness this explosion of hostility because they didn't exist. Their story is a fictitious one, but I feel it's representative of the journey taken by many young, poverty-stricken boys through the ages, which is to enlist and go where told, experience what the world may bring, and maybe fall in love along the way.

Domitilde, Kinonchamek, Makwa, Otayonih, Corporal Kane, and jovial Fritz are also fictional characters, though some of their traits may have been lifted from those who really existed.

Charles Langlade, a fascinating individual if ever there was one, did witness the violence that day. The son of a French father and Ottawa mother, he had served the fleur-de-lis by fighting the British at Fort Duquesne, Fort William Henry, and Quebec before changing his allegiance when he saw that France was going to lose the continent. After a bit of questionable behavior during the capture of Michilimackinac, he remained a loyal subject of the British for the remainder of his life.

The 60th Regiment of Foot, trained in forest warfare, served with distinction in America during the French and Indian War and Pontiac's War. Lieutenant Colonel Bouquet, Major Henry Gladwin, and Captain Campbell were real officers within her ranks. The brainless Lieutenant Leslie was not. CELER ET AUDAX.

Minavavana's speech to Major Gladwin in Detroit, if it actually occurred as documented, was really given to a British trader in the Mackinac Straits area, and it was a warning of what was to come. Pontiac did start a war against the British for the grievances contained in that address. After initial successes, like the fall of Michilimackinac and the siege of Detroit, the war simmered for several years along the colonial frontier, with many atrocities committed by both sides. The fighting eventually petered out after British reinforcements flooded the area and Pontiac's allies started negotiating their own peace with the crown.

I took several liberties with Fort Michilimackinac's characteristics and dimensions for the sake of this story. There never was a smuggler's tunnel in the sandy soil under her palisade. Today, you can visit a lovely recreation of the fort on its original site overlooking the Mackinac Straits.

Printed in Great Britain
by Amazon